The stainless steel floor was slippery, covered with a thick pad of ice and frost. Racks lined the walls, most of them empty, but several held stainless steel canisters of different sizes.

Picking one up, Wilson pressed the button on the side. A viewscreen opened, leaving the bulletproof glass in place. Electronic data contained in the canister's nano-chip information display juiced the circuitry. He read it at a glance: CONTENTS: HUMAN HEART. DONOR, 22-YEAR-OLD FEMALE ALCOHOLIC. NO DISEASES, NO INFARCTIONS, SLIGHT AB-NORMALITY IN LEFT VENTRICAL THAT CAN BE . . . A chill touched his own heart as he thought of the husked bodies that had been left in Miami.

Wilson looked up, saw Newkirk coming for him, one hand out to slam against his chest.

"The place is wired," Newkirk said.

Wilson went backward, propelled by Newkirk's charge. He grabbed the man's jacket and yanked him toward the door, scrambling to get out.

They'd almost reached the hallway when the freezer exploded.

MEL ODOM

OMEGA BLUE

📚 HarperPaperbacks
A Division of HarperCollins*Publishers*

This is a work of fiction. The characters, incidents, and dialogues are products of the author's imagination and are not to be construed as real. Any resemblance to actual events or persons, living or dead, is entirely coincidental.

HarperPaperbacks *A Division of* HarperCollins*Publishers*
10 East 53rd Street, New York, N.Y. 10022

Copyright © 1993 by Mel Odom
All rights reserved. No part of this book may be used or reproduced in any manner whatsoever without written permission of the publisher, except in the case of brief quotations embodied in critical articles and reviews. For information address HarperCollins*Publishers*,
10 East 53rd Street, New York, N.Y. 10022.

Cover illustration by Danilo Ducak

First printing: October 1993

Printed in the United States of America

HarperPaperbacks and colophon are trademarks of HarperCollins*Publishers*

10 9 8 7 6 5 4 3 2 1

For Robert Lynn MacDonald—

When you're fighting for survival in the Ring of Life,
there's not a better cut-man to have in your corner.
Thanks for being there, Bob.

For Danielle Lynn Odom—

You weren't with us for long, baby,
but know that you were loved.
Uncle Mel.

ACKNOWLEDGMENTS:

Learning to live alone again—especially when you've got four children between the ages of nine and two—is hard. If it hadn't been for the help of family and friends, neither I nor this book would be here. You people know who you are, and the list is long. Know too that I love you for being there.

And special thanks go out to Jessica Lichtenstein and Ethan Ellenberg, my editor and agent, who both believed in me during some rough times. I couldn't have done this without you.

CHAPTER 1

Slade Wilson loosened the Colt 10mm Delta Elite strapped to his left thigh and peered through the pouring sheets of rain slamming against the windshield. The wipers barely compensated for the deluge, and traffic was slowed down to less than the posted sixty-five miles per. The ruby taillights of the eighteen-wheeler ahead of them were hazy, but he locked onto his target, and pretended the pursuit hadn't taken almost fourteen hours and that the headache wasn't finally getting the better of him.

Atlanta, Georgia, slid behind them as they made the turn off I-95 north onto I-20 west. The city's lights became a glowing bubble trapped by the night and the thunderstorm blowing in from the coast with hurricane force. The storm had been brewing for days in the Atlantic, deciding to strike only hours before Wilson had tracked his prey up from Miami to Atlanta.

"Coffee?" Emmett Newkirk sat in the passenger seat. In his late fifties and nearing retirement, the man looked like a bloodhound. The fatigue of the last three days of sitting in a car on surveillance and eating take-out food made the bags under his eyes even more pronounced. His jacket was unbuttoned and his tie was lost somewhere in the backseat with the accumulated litter they hadn't had time to jettison before leaving Miami. Once the eighteen-wheeler had taken to the interstates, it had rolled relentlessly. Newkirk's dark hair was parted neatly on the left, and despite his age he was less than ten pounds overweight by Bureau standards.

"No, thanks." Wilson kept his eyes on the truck and massaged his leg to attempt once again to alleviate the cramped muscle. When the operation came to a head, he needed to be in top shape. The people who owned the truck wouldn't be taking any prisoners. Too much money was at stake.

He was a contrast to the other agent. He was thirty-five, his reddish blond hair styled in a street cut, short on the sides and long enough to touch his shoulders in back. At six two, he had the rangy build of a fastball pitcher. With both men in the front seat, the midsize sedan was a tight fit.

Newkirk poured himself a cup from the one-gallon aluminum thermos between his feet on the floorboard. "It's going to happen soon. These guys wouldn't leave the interstate if they didn't have a destination in mind."

"I know." Wilson scanned the rearview mirror, ignoring the burning redness in his hazel-brown eyes. He caught sight of the abandoned Six Flags over Georgia amusement park off the highway. The twisted threads of the roller coasters and skeletal outlines of other rides were suddenly brought into sharp relief against the dark sky by a searing bolt of jagged lightning.

"The storm's going to make it harder."

"Yeah." Wilson turned his attention back to the truck. "But it'll work for us too."

"We could take them down here," Newkirk suggested. "Maybe bust these drivers hard enough to put the fear of God into them. Sweat them a little, they may give it up anyway."

"No." Wilson knew Newkirk was only playing the devil's advocate. They'd worked together since the beginning four years ago. Wherever he chose to lead the team, Wilson knew Newkirk would follow without complaint. "The guys waiting on this delivery will close up shop and move on if the truck doesn't show. By the time we're able to move on whatever—if any—information we get, they'll be gone. By tomorrow, there'll be another truck rolling from somewhere else like Miami. If we put these guys out of business, they'll stay out for awhile till their bosses can neutralize the fallout."

The truck slowed.

Wilson registered the fact a moment late. The intervening-distance indicator warning light flared on the windshield's idiot lights, and he had to tap the brake to drop the necessary speed.

The eighteen-wheeler's signal came on, a heartbeat of racing yellow that pointed to the right. The truck slowed as it took the off-ramp.

Wilson squinted through the rain as a cannon burst of thunder rattled the inside of the sedan. He pulled onto the off-ramp as well, and closed the distance between his vehicle and the truck. The cramp in his leg faded. He spotted an exit sign and called the numbers and street names out to Newkirk.

The man opened the glove compartment and popped the small computer out. The rectangular screen glowed as it came on instantly. Newkirk recapped the thermos and stowed it under the seat, then hooked up the sedan's mobile phone to the modem and stroked the keyboard.

Reaching for the handset clipped to the rearview mirror, Wilson juiced the frequency. "Redball One to Redball teams, do you copy?"

"Three copies." Maggie Scuderi's voice was alert, showing no sign of the long drive.

"Six copies." As usual, Lee Rawley's voice revealed nothing.

"It's going down," Wilson said, and gave them the exit number. "Close up ranks." He cleared the channel.

"I got a couple maybes," Newkirk said. The gray monitor screen wavered, reflecting the electric war raging overhead.

Wilson mentally reviewed the information he'd read in the Fodor's travel book during the first leg of their journey, while Newkirk drove. He'd worked at a few street maps of the major cities in the southeastern sea coast afterward, and learned there were a number of places the jackals could hole up while their grisly business was transacted. Atlanta had remained a flourishing manufacturing and commercial region in inland Georgia, despite the international economic depression that had landed the United States just short of bankruptcy in 2016. Now, seven years later, residential areas that had held promise even after the fall were ghost towns housing the uncounted homeless and diseased. The Six Flags over Georgia amusement park was one of the more colorful memorials to an extravagant way of life many Americans were beginning to doubt had ever existed.

The truck paused briefly at the stop sign before the overpass, then took a left and headed over the interstate.

Wilson glided to a halt and checked the rear and side mirrors.

Scuderi pulled her sedan in behind him. On the passenger side, Bob MacDonald was busy pulling armament from the rear seat. Lee Rawley halted his Ford minivan behind Scuderi's vehicle. When lightning snaked across the wine-dark sky again, Wilson noticed Rawley's cowboy hat and sunglasses. Darnell January sat beside him, a massive black hulk.

"Spread it out," Wilson said as he put his foot on the accelerator and took off in pursuit. "Rawley."

"Go."

"Take point position in the van, see if you can find out where our guy is headed before he gets there."

"On my way." The van accelerated and shot past Wilson and the eighteen-wheeler as the driver struggled to rebuild his speed despite the truck's load and the rain-slick streets.

"Access the computer as Newkirk provides voice-overs," Wilson went on. "If you shoot past their destination, you can double back without losing too much time."

"Right."

"I have four warehouses on the screen," Newkirk said. "All of them show to be nonoperational."

"What were they?" Lightning cut through the sky again. Past the interstate and the off-ramps, the countryside turned hilly and forested with scrub brush and stunted pine trees interspersed with white and red oak, hickory trees, and maples. Indian summer had colored the leaves, but the drenching rain and the night leached out all color.

"Cancemi, Incorporated. They were a textile plant until four years ago, then the money petered out. Opare Industries, a chemical plant. Cashed in five years ago when local law enforcement teams found out the management was turning out blue angel as a sideline investment. Boatright Mills. They handled paper but weren't outfitted to handle the recycling required by law. They closed this plant down, opened up a new one on the east side of Atlanta."

"They're still in business?"

"Yeah."

The eighteen-wheeler was back up to speed at fifty miles per hour. Wilson trailed along in its wake, partially shielded by the truck from the storm's buffeting winds. "What's the last one?"

Newkirk smiled. "I saved this one for you. Walkoviack Packing."

"Meat packers?" Wilson remembered from the Fodor's that cattle and pigs were still big business in Georgia.

"Yeah."

"Bingo." Wilson felt triumphant for a moment.

"I checked," Newkirk said. "Georgia Gas & Electric has been providing them power for the last fourteen months. That coincides with the information the SAC at the Miami bureau turned up. According to courthouse records in Atlanta, Walkoviack Packing went bust a couple years ago. No new licenses have been issued for commercial purposes regarding that property."

"And Georgia G & E doesn't check the paperwork that flows across their desk?"

"Yeah."

"How far away are we?"

Newkirk pointed. "There it is."

Wilson strained his eyes to make out the low building hugging the gently falling hillside a half-mile away. A flash of lightning ignited the countryside, sparked from the fenceline running around the property. There were no lights visible. He reached for the handset, then keyed it to life. "Redball One to Redball teams."

"Go," Scuderi said.

"Go," Rawley answered.

"We're on top of the operation now, and we're going in with the truck."

"I've got a satellite lock," Newkirk said.

Wilson glanced at the monitor and ignored the truck's turn signal when it came on. The picture was black and white, revealing the rectangular building shown from above. The fenceline was highlighted through Newkirk's own programming. He tried to estimate how many men would be working inside. Jackals liked to keep the numbers low. The more people that knew about a meat dump, the greater the chances of someone finding out about it. If law-enforcement people didn't show up on their doorstep soon, other jackals would. As a guess, Wilson figured thirty or forty men on site. It was a lucrative sideline, with parts going for hundreds of thousands of dollars.

"There's a guardhouse," Rawley said. "It's built into the fenceline. With the night and the storm, it's really hard to see. But you can bet that gate is strong enough to keep that truck out unless they're ready to allow it in."

"Can you take the gate out?"

"Yes, but they're sure as hell going to know something's up when I do."

"Take it out," Wilson said, "just ahead of us."

"You got it."

Ahead of the truck, Wilson saw the van pulled over at the side of the road, its lights extinguished. He couldn't see January or Rawley, but that was fine because it was their job to be unseen.

Newkirk shoved the computer back into the glove compartment as the sedan gained speed, reached under the seat, and pulled out the sliding rack that held an Armalite AR-18 and an Atchisson Assault 12 combat .12-guage shotgun. He slipped the Atchisson into the clips mounted on the dash for quick release, and held the Armalite in his lap.

"Are you belted in?" Wilson asked as he put the accelerator on the floor. The power plant screamed with high-pressure performance.

"Oh yeah." Newkirk held the support mounted on the inside of the roof over his head.

"Redball Two," Wilson called out, "you stay with the truck until the drivers are down."

"Roger."

Wilson knew Scuderi wasn't happy with the call, but he also knew she wouldn't question him during a play. He went out wide around the eighteen-wheeler, felt the tires hydroplane for just an instant, and backed off on the accelerator till the silicon and ceramic tread grabbed traction again. He cut the wheel hard as he passed the truck. The sedan skidded for a few feet, barely ahead of the eighteen-wheeler's blunted nose, the headlights glaring through the side windows, then the back one as he got the car straightened out.

The side road dipped as it exited off the highway,

and the sedan's undercarriage slammed against the pavement. A brief flurry of sparks flared in Wilson's rearview mirror, then the eighteen-wheeler turned in behind him, the big rig's lights washing the sparks out of existence.

The gate was thirty feet away and closing fast. Wilson watched it swell into view, then saw the triple strands of barbwire curling across the top of the fence become jagged daggers of light as another bolt of lightning seared the sky. A rolling crackle of thunder sounded almost immediately. The intervening-distance indicator warning light went nova on the windshield, and the audio kicked in with high-pitched squeaks. He ignored the system as he kept his course straight on the gate.

"Where the hell is Rawley?" Newkirk asked.

Wilson hung onto the steering wheel and didn't reply. There were a number of things Quantico didn't know about Lee Rawley during the years preceding the two that he'd been with the Omega Blue unit. Rumor had it that the man was a CIA operative who'd gotten too hot to operate outside the continental United States and was buried in Quantico to cool off. Rumor also had it that Rawley was an ex-Organization hit man who'd turned state's evidence and was in the FBI on a Witness Protection Program deal.

Personally, Wilson didn't care. Rawley had established himself as one of the best snipers in the FBI, and had a string of successful takedowns to testify to his skill. Wilson had found out about the man and had gone to Earl Vache, Omega Blue's liaison with the rest of the Bureau, to recruit him. Rawley had listened to the pitch, then said "Sure" in the laconic voice that was his trademark. There was a lot more to Lee Rawley than met the eye, and Wilson was convinced of two things: Rawley wasn't Rawley's real name, and Rawley would never let the team down as long as it didn't conflict with his personal agenda—whatever that was.

"Fire in the hole," Rawley said.

The fence was close enough now for Wilson to see the mesh clearly in spite of the rain. His peripheral vision caught the movement of at least two people in the cleverly hidden guardhouse on the right side of the gate. Then a sheet of fire flowed from the center of the gate. The flames snapped and licked like anxious hounds, rolling over the sedan's windshield in a molten wave. Skeletal outlines in the middle of the explosion showed the two gates separating under the impact of the LAW's 94mm warhead.

The sedan caught the gates as they swung, and added enough force to rip them from their hinges. Metal screeched and ripped, and *gong*ing noises sounded as the spinning gates slammed into the car.

Wilson powered through the opening with a pool of fire sitting on top of the car's hood. The truck was barreling down on him, the horn wailing louder than the thunder. He juked right, then cut back left. As the truck passed, unable to keep up with his maneuvering, it clipped the rear of the sedan and spun it around. With a final shriek, the intervening-distance indicator warning system registered the impact in a curtain of scarlet light across the windshield, then went dead.

Wilson hit the brake and shrilled to a rocking stop twenty feet from the guardhouse. Opening the door, he grabbed the Atchisson from the clips and stepped out. He was dressed for the night in black jeans, black low-cut British Knights, and a navy short-sleeved sweatshirt under the Kevlar-lined black motorcycle jacket with matte-finish zippers. The Colt 10mm Delta Elite, which was the pistol chosen by Bureau standards, rode in a drop holster counterterrorist fashion along his thigh. He kept a 9mm Heckler & Koch VP70Z in an ankle holster as backup, with a specially silenced Walther model TPH .22LR in a paddle holster at the base of his spine. A Crain combat dagger was housed in a spring-loaded sheath under his right forearm. Other devices equally deadly and incendiary were in concealed pockets inside the motorcycle jacket, along with extra magazines for the pistols.

A man ran from the guardhouse, an assault rifle clutched in his hands and spitting autofire.

Being left-handed, Wilson took a step in the opposite direction from the one the jackal expected as he lined up the Atchisson. The big .12-guage roared and blossomed a muzzle flash almost a foot long.

The one-ounce rifled slug caught the jackal in the shoulder and spun him around, dropped him to the pavement. He went down rolling, came up on his elbows with a pistol clutched in his good hand.

Wilson dodged to his left and felt the lightweight Kevlar weave lining his jacket stop at least two rounds. He fired again, aiming at the center of the man's head, and watched the corpse roll away like a leaf caught in the swirling wind. He shouted at the other man struggling to free himself from the debris inside the guardhouse. "FBI! Throw down your weapons and come out with your hands in the air!"

A burst of autofire cut a swath through a pool of water in an uneven spot of the pavement only inches from Wilson's foot and drenched his pants legs.

Newkirk's assault rifle barked once and the second jackal went down.

Mercury-vapor lights flared into life around the perimeters of the plant with audible clangs, then splashed white fire against the falling rain. Five delivery vans painted red and gold were parked at a loading dock near the rear of the building. Two of the dock doors opened with the rush of chains running through electric hoists. A half-dozen armed jackals spilled out into the night, their shadows long and edged against the white of the building.

Reaching into his pocket, Wilson took out his T-jack. He touched the chrome elbow of the miniaturized walkie-talkie to his right jawline and triggered the electromagnetic field that adhered it to his flesh. Slightly larger than a finger's width, the T-jack's transmitter curled up like a question mark next to Wilson's lips, while the receiver was tucked just inside his outer ear without interfering with his normal hearing. He switched it on, then blew on the mike to activate it. "Count off," he said softly.

Newkirk reported in first, followed in swift succession by MacDonald, January, Scuderi, and Rawley.

The eighteen-wheeler had jackknifed across the open parking area. The driver was working frantically to free the rig while Scuderi and MacDonald closed in. Scuderi hit the brakes and sent the sedan into a skid that left them covered from the fire of the advancing line of jackals. The sedan spun, slammed its ass end into the eighteen-wheeler's rear tires, then rebounded. Before it came to a halt, Scuderi and MacDonald were in motion.

Scuderi's golden blond hair was cut short and spiky, shot through with strands of platinum. In street clothes she could break a man's heart. Tonight she looked like a wraith cut from the shadows, dressed all in black. She was lean and trim and moved with the grace of an athlete. She kept the 10mm pistol in both hands as she ran toward the truck's cab.

Bob MacDonald flanked her, ducking under the belly of the big truck and coming up on the other side. Mac was no taller than Scuderi and might have weighed twenty pounds more. At fifty-one, he was the second most senior member of the team, but Wilson had yet to find a man better able to operate on sheer cussedness and determination when the chips were down and the odds were stacked against them. Mac's silver hair reflected the light from the mercury-vapor lamps. A CAR-15 hung upside down at his side from a shoulder strap. He carried his pistol at his other side.

Wilson climbed into the sedan again. The hood was smoldering now with a cloud of white smoke clinging to it. He slipped the transmission into drive and waited for Newkirk to drop into the passenger seat. Wilson had the car in motion before Newkirk had settled, then stretched out a hand for the bandolier of extra twenty-round drums for the Atchisson.

Autofire ripped into the truck's cab as the jackals either decided on their own to sacrifice the drivers in an attempt to get to the FBI strike force, or were given orders to do so. The eighteen-wheeler jerked, then the engine died. The glaring lights carved tunnels that trapped the line of jackals in them.

Newkirk opened fire at once, and emptied a forty-round clip that sent some of the jackals searching for cover while others dropped in their tracks.

"You can scratch the truck," Mac radioed. Though years and miles from the hills in southern Oklahoma where he'd grown up, the man's words reflected the Western twang of his roots.

"Affirmative," Wilson said.

Newkirk slammed a fresh magazine into the Armalite.

Movement in the rearview mirror caught Wilson's attention for just a moment, and he saw the Ford minivan speed into the parking lot. He blew on the mike and accessed the frequency. "Rawley."

"Go."

"You and Darnell have the front door."

"Roger." The minivan altered course, then streaked for the front doors of the building.

"Maggie."

"Go."

"You and Mac have the outside cleanup. Once we're inside, you're to maintain a support position in case we have to pull back. In no circumstance are you to allow that load of evidence to leave our possession."

"Understood."

"And get on the air. Let the locals know we're in town and what's going down."

Scuderi cleared the channel.

Assault rifles opened up on the sedan, ripped jagged lines down the sides. The windshield spider-webbed with bullet holes, and the rearview mirror disappeared. Wilson had a brief impression of the twisted hunk of steel and glass sailing over his shoulder.

He twisted the steering wheel hard, using the sedan as a blunt instrument to track down two of the jackals. If possible, he'd wanted to take them alive and let the courts decide their fates. But he couldn't leave them loose to possibly injure his people. He remembered the pictures and video footage he'd seen about what had happened in Miami: the trail of eviscerated bodies. He hardened himself and put his foot down more firmly on the accelerator.

The two men tried to break and run, but it was too late. Wilson didn't fall for their feints, and crunched into them before they could get away. One man went down, disappearing under the wheels as the sedan rolled over his body. The second man was thrown into the air and battered against the windshield before bouncing over the sedan and landing behind it.

Turning the wheel, Wilson yanked the sedan back on track and headed for the docks. "This isn't going to be gentle," he warned.

"And it probably won't be pretty either," Newkirk said. His feet were braced against the floorboard.

The surviving jackals had already targeted the back of the sedan and were chewing holes in it with their assault rifles.

A hundred feet from the concrete-and-steel posts fronting the docks, Wilson hit the brakes. It helped slow the speeding sedan a little, but the forward momentum still slammed them hard against the loading docks. The front end crumpled, sent the hood winging up, and the car came to a sudden rest between two of the delivery vans.

Wilson tried the door, heard the lock pop, but it didn't open. He rammed his shoulder against it twice, then it grated open with a painful metallic howl. Stepping out, flanked a moment later as Newkirk pushed himself out on his side, Wilson pushed himself up on the rear of the car, ran across the car top, and jumped onto the loading dock.

The sound of running feet slapping against concrete reached him just before the jackal did. The guy saw Wilson and tried to stop, backpedaling furiously and trying to bring his machine pistol to bear.

Letting the movements come naturally, Wilson pivoted into a roundhouse kick that had all of his weight behind it. His boot caught the man in the face. Something broke. The jackal stumbled backward, his eyes rolling up in his head before he hit the metal warehouse door behind him. By the time he slid bonelessly into a sitting position, Wilson had a pair of disposable handcuffs out. The FBI man cuffed the jackal to a length of chain leading from the hoist.

Newkirk gained the high ground as Wilson stood and kicked the jackal's guns away. The older agent was bleeding from a cut over one eyebrow, but he looked alert.

"You okay?" Wilson asked.

"I'm fine. Let's drift."

Wilson took the lead, the Atchisson hard in his hands. Inside the warehouse, he slipped a pair of night-vision bubble goggles from a pocket of his jacket and put them on. The night and the shadows went away and left a world painted in black and white and grays. With the wraparound design of the goggles, his peripheral vision remained intact.

He shoved the ball of his thumb against the small button mounted under the skin along his jawbone on the opposite side of the T-jack and activated the SeekNFire circuitry wired into the neural network along his spine. His palm closed more securely over the shotgun to pull his flesh up against the identification plate that was built into the stock, so the circuitry constructed under the skin of his palm could meld with the weapon. It didn't make him symbiotic with the weapon, but it read off the specs from the stock and keyed his eye-hand reflexes to get optimum usage from the shotgun. SeekNFire wasn't available on the open market. The system was extremely expensive and still in its testing phase. The Omega Blue team members had the work done as a matter of course before hitting the bricks. Anyone who couldn't successfully undergo the operation was bounced from the Sensitive Operations Group unit, despite his or her qualifications. With the unit limited to six people, they needed every edge available.

A staccato burst of thunder echoed inside the empty warehouse. Broken and vacant wooden skids lay haphazardly around the room and were propped against the walls. Two forklifts sat silently near the doors, in preparation for off-loading the cargo aboard the eighteen-wheeler.

Wilson sprinted for the door in the corner of the warehouse, trying to recall a blueprint of the building. They had a map of sorts—if the warehouse hadn't undergone construction in the last seventeen years. He focused on the freezer area.

Going through the door at almost a dead run, aware that time was running out, Wilson used his free hand to push himself off the wall ahead of him and cut left. A shadow took form in front of him, becoming clearer as the night-vision goggles amplified the existing light. He felt the familiar thrum of the SeekNFire circuitry locking into his reflexes, and followed its guidance as he swung the Atchisson up.

The jackal fired from a Weaver stance, appearing almost calm.

Bullets whipped by Wilson's head. He squeezed the Atchisson's trigger, loosed three rounds that caught the jackal above his belt buckle and tracked up to his sternum. The smell of cordite stung Wilson's nostrils as he brushed the still-falling corpse out of his way and ran on.

Gunfire from the other end of the building echoed through the maze of hallways.

Wilson blew on the mike to access the T-jack. "Rawley. Check."

"Check. We're still standing." Machine-pistol fire that sounded up close and personal stopped as the channel cleared.

"Here," Newkirk called out.

Wilson turned, saw Newkirk opening a stainless steel door that let a rectangle of harsh yellow light spill out onto the tiled floor. Dark patterns that Wilson recognized as blood were worn into the tiles in front of the door, then trailed down the hallway in a series of thin streams.

The chill wind turned gray in the hallway, blasting Wilson as he stepped inside the meat locker. The cold made his wet clothes and hair cling to his body and seem to gain weight. The stainless steel floor was slippery, covered with a thick pad of ice and frost. Maintenance hadn't been a big priority since the jackals had moved in. Racks lined the walls. Most of them were empty, but several held stainless steel cannisters of different sizes.

Picking one up, Wilson glanced at its sealed mouth. He pressed the button on the side, and the cap hissed as it released and moved over. A viewscreen opened, leaving the bulletproof glass in place. Electronic data contained in the canister's nanochip information display juiced the circuitry. He read it at a glance. CONTENTS: HUMAN HEART. DONOR, TWENTY-TWO-YEAR-OLD FEMALE ALCO-

HOLIC. NO DISEASES, NO INFARCTIONS, SLIGHT ABNORMALITY IN LEFT VENTRICLE THAT CAN BE . . .

He pressed the button again, stopping the flow of information that trickled across the glass. An interior light came on and a purplish red organ, slightly smaller than his fist, was displayed: perfectly suspended in the saline solution. A chill touched his own heart as he automatically thought of the husked bodies that had been left in Miami. He flicked the light off and returned the canister to the rack. On the black market, the jackals could turn more than a quarter of a million dollars on a quick sale—more if the buyer was desperate.

The Bureau preferred any interception of organ jackal cargo to be handled quietly. But Wilson didn't care that this operation had turned ballistic. The public needed to know what kind of monsters were waiting for them in the shadows.

"Oh, shit."

Wilson looked up, saw Newkirk coming for him, one hand out to slam against his chest.

"The place is wired," Newkirk said.

Wilson went backward, propelled by Newkirk's charge. He grabbed the man's jacket and yanked him toward the door, scrambling to get out.

They'd almost reached the hallway when the freezer exploded.

CHAPTER 2

Standing in the shelter offered by the nose of the eighteen-wheeler, Maggie Scuderi saw the orange-and-black explosion rip the roof off the meat processing plant and throw it fifty feet into the air. Flaming debris sailed across the sky like confetti scattered by partygoers from hell.

Scuderi blew on the mike and activated the T-jack. "Slade!"

Another string of explosions ripped through the building. Metal and mortar slammed against the pavement and the body of the truck.

"Goddamnit, Slade, answer me!" Scuderi held the Delta Elite tightly in her fist. The four other members of the team were scattered throughout that maelstrom.

A handful of jackals ran from a side exit and started for the truck, then Mac's sniping skill with the CAR-15 brought two of them down. The survivors pulled up short and sprinted for the fenceline.

"That was the meat locker area," Mac said grimly.

"I know," Scuderi replied in frustration. Wilson's orders were not open to question. Once given, they were forever. "Unless you're dead, damn you," she whispered to herself.

The three jackals disappeared into the night outside the reach of the perimeter lights. The whole building was going up as prearranged incendiary packages continued to erupt.

Scuderi blew on the mike again. "Rawley."

"Standing."

"Darnell."

"Here, Maggie." January's voice was a pleasant bass.

"Are you all right?"

"Yeah," January said. "The main explosion was at the other end of the building. But we're blocked here."

"Did you find the records?"

"Affirmative," Rawley replied. "And I saw them go up in hellfire a heartbeat later. I put down three guys in there. The fireblast took out the rest of them. I didn't have time to retrieve a damn thing."

"Can you get to Slade and Emmett?"

"Negative. I'm blocked too. Most of those charges were set to implode the building. If these guys had been any better, the walls would have fallen in on us."

"Get out of there and stand ready to greet the locals. They should be here in minutes. Mac and I will be able to reach Slade and Emmett before you guys can get clear."

Mac gazed at her around the nose of the eighteen-wheeler. "You plan on leaving the truck? We lose the cargo, we don't have a case."

"We're not leaving the truck." Scuderi pulled herself onto the running board, opened the door, and shoved herself behind the wheel. The Delta Elite slid uncomfortably between her thigh and the seat, but it was ready at a second's notice. "Hell, it's the best door opener we've got." She keyed the ignition as Mac crawled up into the passenger seat and strapped himself in. The big diesel engines rumbled with power and made the entire chassis shiver.

Mac patted the pockets of his brown bomber jacket down in a characteristic habit Scuderi recognized.

"You feel like smoking?" she asked.

His blue eyes never left the flaming building on the other side of the bug-splattered windshield. "Hell no. Just wanted to make sure I hadn't lost 'em so I'll have 'em for after."

Scuderi fastened her seatbelt and engaged the transmission. The tractor's rear wheels dug into the pavement with enough force to buck the cab. "That sounds pretty damn optimistic."

"If you're going to do what I think you're going to do," Mac said with real feeling, "I'm going to need a cigarette when we're finished."

The eighteen-wheeler rolled forward with increasing speed, came around in a semicircle as Scuderi pulled on the wheel with both hands. Her thoughts were on Wilson and Newkirk. Ever since Wilson had taken over as chief of the Omega Blue unit, the three of them had been together. Five other people had died over their three-and-a-half-year history. The faces of the dead floated through her mind's eye. She breathed a silent prayer and made the sign of the cross as she held the blunt nose of the truck on course.

Her hands never left the wheel when the eighteen-wheeler smashed through the side of the building, and she didn't allow her eyes to close. The seatbelt closed over her breasts with enough force to leave bruises that would be there for days. Her head snapped at the end of her neck when the big rig came to a sudden halt against a reinforced support pillar twenty feet into the structure.

Lightning flared behind her, poured into the hole the truck had made, and electric-white light robbed the shadows for an instant. Bricks, timber, and mortar thudded against the cab and trailer, then cascaded off as things settled down.

Fisting the 10mm from under her leg, Scuderi shoved her door open and jumped down lithely, avoiding the bulk of the litter. Her night-vision goggles easily penetrated the darkness.

"We're on the killing floor," Mac said quietly.

Scuderi scanned the large room, saw the rails that permitted single-file movement only. Chain hoists with meat hooks at the end hung overhead, and coiled water hoses connected to spigots in the walls testified to the grim efficiency of the processing plant. Red-eyed rats hugged the shadows in the corners.

"This way." She jogged along the length of the trailer and checked it for any compromises in the metal. There weren't any. Even if there had been, she was sure the organ canisters inside would have survived the impact. The jackals spared no expense when it came to packing their wares. The product was hard to get, even harder to keep till a sale could be negotiated.

Voices sounded out in the hallway.

She paused at the tear in the wall, signaled to Mac to let him know what was going on, and pressed the SeekNFire button on her jaw. Her nerves tingled as the programming took hold and made the connection through her palm. She nodded to Mac, received a quick nod in return, then wheeled around the corner into the hallway.

Her gun settled comfortably into a two-handed grip as she faced the pair of jackals trotting toward the hole in the wall left by the truck. They saw her at the same time, and turned with their guns blazing from fifteen feet away.

Without hesitation, Scuderi put a pair of 10mm rounds through one man's knee. As he toppled, she threw herself forward, under the burst of submachinegun fire that rapped out a vicious tattoo on the wall behind her. She slid her hands forward like a baseball player stealing second, then rolled on her side. As she came over, she kicked out in a front snap-kick that caught the second man in the groin. She swung the pistol in a short arc that caught the man's Uzi along the barrel and knocked it out of his hands.

The jackal stumbled backward, one hand going to his crotch while the other grabbed for the pistol holstered on his hip.

Pushing herself up with her free hand, she set herself as the jackal's gun cleared leather. Out of the corner of her eye, she saw Mac taking control of the first jackal.

"You goddamn bitch," the jackal snarled in pain and anger. "You're gonna die now."

Scuderi launched a side kick that caught the man in the face and popped his head backward. His pistol crashed and sent a round into the ceiling. She spun, threw her hip against him as she took hold of his shirt, butted his bleeding face with the top of her head, then pulled him over her hip. He lost his gun as he came crashing down on his face. Scuderi kneeled and put a knee between his shoulder blades to hold him down. Fisting her pistol tightly, she screwed the barrel into his neck. "Try one other smart move, asshole, and you won't get to say hello to your buddies in the federal pen after the trial. I'm FBI. Now assume the goddamn position."

The man spread his feet, groaned, and placed his hands behind his back.

Scuderi cuffed her man's hands and feet as Mac finished up with his. She peered into the shifting dust clouds and shadows, then tried the T-jack again, wondering if Newkirk and Wilson were even still alive. She went forward, shocked at how much damage the explosions had done on the inside of the building.

Flames painted the insides of Slade Wilson's eyelids, and heat seared his face. It wasn't till he started to move that he realized Newkirk was lying on top of him and they were both covered with blood. He also realized he wasn't breathing. Calming the sudden anxiety that triggered the fight-or-flight reaction, he leaned his head back and willed his lungs to take in air. When they did, the pain felt like a half-dozen steel fence posts had been driven through his back and chest.

He groaned with the effort, then carefully rolled Newkirk to one side. He'd lost the Atchisson somewhere in the confusion. When he looked at the rubble covering the floor and the huge smoking hole where the meat-locker door had been, he realized how lucky he'd been.

The same couldn't be said for Newkirk. A handful of irregularly shaped shards of stainless steel jutted from the man's back. His breathing was raspy and strained. Perspiration covered his face despite the chill air blowing from the meat locker, and knowledge of what was coming dawned dark and flat in his eyes.

"Emmett," Wilson said as he eased his body out from under the other man's, "just hang on. You're going to be all right."

Newkirk reached up and grabbed a fistful of Wilson's jacket. A trickle of blood ran from the corner of Newkirk's mouth. "Leave me here, kid. There isn't anything you can do for me."

A hard lump settled under Wilson's breastbone. He kept his face impassive as he held Newkirk's head in his hands on his thigh. "Can't."

More bloody spittle streaked the side of the man's face. "You have to." He coughed weakly and struggled for another breath. "Rawley and January are somewhere in this mess. If they need help, you have to be there to give it to them."

"I can't leave you like this."

Newkirk's grip slipped and he made an effort to re-tighten it, but Wilson could tell the man's strength was going fast. Newkirk had trouble focusing his eyes, and his head lay more heavily in Wilson's hands. "I'm not afraid of being alone, kid. I've been alone most of my life. That's the nature of this kind of work. You know that. Your daddy told you that too. Now you get your ass out there and do your goddamn job."

Wilson remained silent, drawn into Newkirk's fading world.

"You can't come with me," Newkirk said. "Not this time. You take care of your people."

A helpless feeling surged over Wilson, followed by anger at the men ultimately responsible for the meat dump. He nodded and started to move away.

"Hold it, cop!"

The voice was less than ten feet away. Wilson turned his head slowly until he could see the jackal standing on a mound of rubble. The wicked snout of an Uzi was brandished in his hands.

"Don't you fucking move unless I tell you that you can, asshole." The jackal shifted the machine pistol in a warning gesture. He was disheveled and looked as though he hadn't weathered either the raid or the explosions well. "You're my ticket out of here. You blow it, and you're a dead man. If I kill you, that doesn't make the years I'm looking at in prison any longer." He grinned ferally, his long hair hanging down over red-rimmed eyes.

"Sure," Wilson said. "Just let me help my buddy."

Newkirk tried to pull his pistol but had lost too much control over his body.

"Get up," the jackal ordered.

"Give me a minute." Wilson twisted his right hand and triggered the release on the Crain dagger. The hilt dropped into his palm.

"Now, douche bag, or you're going to be dying with him."

Reaching forward, Wilson acted like he was pulling Newkirk's jacket tighter. The Crain dagger came free of the unzipped sleeve of the motorcycle jacket. He kept it concealed from the jackal.

The shrill of approaching sirens cut through the thick, dusty air flooding the processing plant.

The jackal took a step forward. "You're out of time, asshole."

Whipping his arm backward in a powerful sideways motion, Wilson threw the dagger at the man's face. It became a glittering steel dart, winked once as it covered the distance, then buried itself to the hilt in the jackal's eye socket.

A muffled groan escaped the man's lips as he crumpled to his knees, then fell forward. Bone crunched when the knife was driven deeper. A quiver ran through his body as life left him.

More sirens were outside now, and Wilson knew he had no choice. The unit was in Atlanta without local sanction. If he didn't run interference, some of his people might get injured. He turned to face Newkirk and gave him a grim smile. "There's help here, Emmett. You just hang on till I get some of it your way."

Newkirk nodded. "Go."

Wilson pushed himself to his feet reluctantly. He drew the Delta Elite from the drop holster. Pausing at the jackal's corpse, he put his foot on the dead man's face and yanked the dagger free.

He took a final look at Newkirk, then plunged into the whirling confusion filling the wrecked hallways of the building. Taking a firmer grip on the 10mm, he felt the SeekNFire circuitry acknowledge the pistol and tune his body to it. He jogged across broken rubble, almost lost his balance twice, and cut left around a corner.

Three jackals were scrambling toward him. The beams of their flashlights were small, uncertain cones in the smoky haze, darting quickly over the walls and ceiling.

Wilson stepped around the corner and let them see him.

They came to a stop and raised their weapons.

"FBI!" Wilson shouted.

A moment of indecision held the three in thrall, then the man on the right cut loose with his pistol.

Autofire chased Wilson around the hallway corner. He took a two-handed grip on the Delta Elite as he made his neural connection with the SeekNFire programming even more complete. Listening to the gunfire die away as the weapons ran empty, he placed the three men firmly in his mind, then wheeled around the corner.

They were more spread out than they had been, but the SeekNFire system had no problem picking them up. Wilson became a living gun sight as his pistol dropped into target acquisition. His shots came in groups of two. All of them took their targets above the neck where body armor wasn't worn. He was moving again before the last dead man hit the ground.

"Slade." It was Scuderi's voice.

Blowing into the mike, he accessed the T-jack. "Go." He jogged forward, pausing only to slam a fresh clip into the 10mm.

"Where are you?"

"Making my way forward from the meat lockers. Have you heard from Rawley or Darnell?"

"Yes. They're clear and doing the liaison work with the state police and sheriff's department."

Wilson considered that and knew that Scuderi was somewhere inside the building. "Where are you?"

"Just ahead of you. Mac and I are making our way from the killing floor."

"Where's the truck?"

"We brought it with us. It's okay."

Wilson decided to drop the issue. Scuderi had stayed within the parameters of his orders even though she knew she was straying past what he'd intended.

The Omega Blue unit wasn't made up of hard-liners who lived for the rule books. To do their jobs effectively, they had to be just as creative and ruthless as the enemies they hunted down.

"Where's Emmett?" Scuderi became visible around the next corner. Mac was a half-step behind her.

"He's down near the meat lockers."

January broke into the frequency. "There's an EMT team out here."

"Can you get them inside?"

"For one of ours, sure. I found an old running buddy of mine in the Staties. We're okay here. The sheriff's pissed, but he'll have to get over it." Before joining the FBI, January had spent seven years with the Savannah Police Department.

Wilson gave them directions to Newkirk, then turned and went back toward the meat lockers. "Did we get any of the files?"

Scuderi was at his side while Mac returned to keep the truck sealed from any other prying agencies. The case was the Bureau's, and Wilson wasn't going to let anyone screw it up. With Newkirk on the ground, it had cost too much to chance letting anyone foul the evidence. "Rawley couldn't get to the admin room," Scuderi replied. "A firebomb took the place out and destroyed everything inside."

"Prisoners?"

"Some. We got the driving team, a few more along the way. Darnell and Rawley found five of the doctors waiting to handle the merchandise and make sure it was properly stored."

Wilson rounded the final corner and saw the four white-jacketed EMTs already at work on Newkirk. The Bureau man accessed the T-jack. "Rawley."

"Go."

"Anything you can tell me about the meat-dump medtechs?"

"They had a buy set up." The man's voice was flat and uninflected as always. "There was a road locker already fueled up and ready to fly behind the admin offices. My guess is they had a special order waiting somewhere."

"We'll check into that." Wilson cleared the frequency and stood back out of the way as the EMTs worked quickly, talking to each other in the abbreviated code words he understood well enough to know that things weren't hopeful. He blew into the mike. "Darnell."

"Go."

"See if you can arrange us some working space at the Staties' county office."

"Sheriff's already offered."

"What kind of working relationship can we expect from them?"

"My friend tells me Sheriff Dawes is a hands-on kind of guy."

"He'd be underfoot."

"Yeah, to put it bluntly."

"If you have to, put it bluntly. What can we expect from the Staties?"

"Cooperation. They'd want to observe. And they'd want a share in the limelight."

"They can have the limelight. We don't need it. Vache isn't going to be happy when he finds out about this." Wilson holstered his Delta Elite and crossed his arms over his chest. Newkirk's face looked more pale than a full moon. "Get us the space. Access to computer hardware. Cells to hold these guys in. And two interrogation rooms."

"Can do." January cleared the frequency.

One of the EMTs stood up with Newkirk's blood staining his blouse. His face looked grim and frustrated. "I'm sorry." Behind him, two of the group unfurled a white latex sheet and spread it over the dead agent.

Wilson listened to the silence of the room that underscored the small movements of the EMT men as they finished up. His throat felt tight and he didn't trust himself to speak. He went forward and dropped on his knees beside Newkirk as the EMT unit spread out to make room for him.

"Give us a few minutes," Scuderi said brusquely.

"Sure. Just let us know when you want us back."

Wilson uncovered Newkirk's face and worked at sealing the emotions away so they wouldn't influence the job he still had to do with the jackals. Scuderi sat silently at his side. Her hand moved in the sign of the cross. With a hand that trembled only slightly, Wilson reached up and gently closed his friend's eyelids.

"Goddamnit, Slade! Do you know what the hell you're doing?"

Wilson looked up from pouring a stale cup of coffee as Earl Vache slammed the office door shut behind him. He finished filling his Styrofoam cup, then reached for another from the short stack beside the microwave that was used to heat the instant coffee. It was two A.M. It had only taken Vache three hours to shake free from Quantico and jet down. He handed the cup over and Vache took it.

"Yeah, I know what I'm doing," Wilson replied.

"Tonight my team took down a jackal team that left thirty-one husked corpses in Miami, Florida, a couple days ago. And I lost a member of my team that was one of the few close friends I have these days. That pretty much sum it up in your book?"

The Omega Blue liaison to the FBI was a heavyset man with thinning hair streaked with gray. He had a gruff voice that went with a physique that showed a lot of hard usage. He wore a pressed suit and an olive-colored trench coat, allowing him to blend in whenever it suited him. He stabbed a blunt finger in Wilson's direction. "You were told to lay off the jackal operations."

"Somebody forgot to tell them they were supposed to lay off too."

"You're supposed to clear operations through me."

"You wouldn't have cleared this one."

"You're damn right I wouldn't have. We're dealing with political hot potatoes here."

"Wrong, Earl," Wilson replied. "I'm dealing with whatever heat comes down the pike on this one. Just like every other one the Omega unit has handled. You're liaison for the unit, not the director. And Omega clears whatever it damn well wants to clear. You know that. Even the Bureau isn't above having people on the payroll that tip off the various organizations we target. Our autonomy is what makes us dangerous to those people."

"That autonomy is also what's drawing fire from the House subcommittee that holds the purse strings on you people."

Wilson walked behind his borrowed desk and rummaged through the stack of files that was piled up there. Finding the CD-ROM he was searching for, he inserted it into the feed slot on the office Ringo++ and stroked the keyboard. He bypassed the monitor mounted on the desk and put the display up on the thirty-inch screen built into the wall behind the desk. As it came on, he flicked off the office lights and dropped the room into darkness except for the glow given off by the microwave's ready light and the wall monitor.

Videotape footage stored on the CD-ROM played across the big screen. The setting was an alley. Miami PD patrol cars were in clear evidence surrounding a site marked off by yellow POLICE—DO NOT CROSS tape affixed to the walls of the abandoned buildings circling the alley. A uniformed policeman intercepted whoever was carrying the minicam and shoved the photographer back. For a moment half of the uniform's arm covered the lens, then a whirl of sky and low buildings filled the screen. A moment later, the photographer was stationary, obviously standing atop a parked car. The zoom lens moved in with dizzying speed.

Wilson's stomach tightened as he sipped the foul-tasting coffee and drank it down. The contents of that alley were a nightmare that wouldn't leave him for a long time.

Blood covered the alley floor in puddles. Uniformed officers moved gingerly through the passageway, and clotted blood stuck to their shoes and clothing. They wore protective suits over their clothes, with latex gloves and surgical masks and goggles as defense against possible AIDS infection. Ambulance workers joined them seconds later.

"Thirty-one people," Wilson said quietly. "All of them dead."

"I know," Vache said. "I saw the reports. I can empathize with those people, but—"

"Can you?" Wilson demanded. "I told you about

the new jackal network three weeks ago. Even then it had been operating for almost two months that we know of. You advised me against pursuing it."

"There are underlying political factors regarding jackal networks."

"You're damn right there are." Wilson tapped the keyboard and froze the images on the wall monitor. "For one, most of the victims are homeless, who many politicians don't even want to admit exist in this nation. Maybe it's more convenient to think of those people as recyclable. Since those people don't vote and don't have recourse to legal protection, they're write-offs. And, some of those congressmen on the Hill are involved in the jackal network for a profit interest."

"Goddamnit, Slade, you can't go around saying that." Vache's face colored. "You don't know if that's even true."

"The rumors are there," Wilson said. "We've confirmed them in Florida, Mississippi, Alabama, and Louisiana. Every place that we suspect these people of operating in."

"You can't say that until you have proof."

"I'll get it. It's too widespread, too prevalent not to have some kind of truth in there."

"If you don't step lightly, you won't be around much longer to find out what kind of truth is there."

"Is that the cop talking," Wilson asked in a soft voice, "or is it the politician?" Before Vache could answer, he tapped the keyboard and started up the alley scene again.

The minicam view faded and was replaced by the cool, calloused movement of a police-lab technician. Each body was photographed in sequence and became a collage of horror.

"You lose a lot with videotape," Wilson said. "I was there in that alley. You could smell the death lingering in the air. VapoRub didn't cut it much. And then there's the suction of the blood on your shoes. After a couple minutes, everywhere you walked, you squeaked." He paused. "They killed them all, Earl. Eighteen men, six women, and seven kids between the ages of four and twelve."

The procession of dead faces with empty eye sockets stared blankly at the unwinking eye of the camera.

"They killed them just like the ones in the other states. A pair of twenty-two LRs through the ear so the optic nerves could be harvested. Then they husked them."

The camera pulled back to show the naked bodies with loose flaps of bloody flesh where their stomachs and chests used to be.

"The butcher work was thorough," Wilson said, "but it wasn't neat. They were in a hurry. This was the largest number of people they'd ever husked. Not all of them were opened with sternal saws or knives. Some of them, especially the children, were opened with what the lab techs think were heavy scissors. They took the hearts, livers, eyes, kidneys, pancreases, and lungs, all in a matter of hours. We missed them by minutes, and it seemed damned convenient at the time that we were looking in all the wrong places."

"That sounds like an accusation."

"It will be when I find the proof." Wilson cut the programming and turned the lights back on. "This jackal network is big, and they're fast. If we don't shut them down soon, there are going to be more dead people turning up somewhere. They had a road locker ready to roll at the meat dump. Somebody is expecting a new lease on life somewhere at this very minute. The supplier won't wait long before going out again. There's too much money to be made in this business."

Vache drank his coffee, then reached into his pocket for a stick of gum. He took his hat off and flipped it unerringly onto the coatrack standing in the corner. "The House subcommittee is going to string us up by our peckers, you know."

Wilson smiled. "Only if they get the chance. I'm working on some angles."

"Like what?"

"It's better that you don't know."

"Terrific. Hell, I feel relieved already. You can't keep playing cowboy out here, Slade. You were put in as SAC over Omega because you got so much press over the Hubatka investigation. The press loved talking about the hero FBI agent who took on the Organization almost single-handedly and won."

"You and I both know that wasn't true. There were a lot of other people involved in that."

"No, but it made a hell of a good read. The Omega Blue unit was put into play during an election year and received a lot of popular support."

"We're in an election year again."

"Yeah, but the popularity of cowboy cops is in decline. The bureaucrats might not be willing to stick their necks out quite as far this term."

"If we can give them a big win in the next couple of months before the election rolls around again, maybe that feeling will change."

"Yeah, well until then let me remind you the subcommittee controlling Omega Blue funding is looking for ways to shoot down our current president's hopes for reelection. Since your unit was a pet project of his, and has had a lot of notoriety in the media, making us look bad could be a big step for them. Just giving them the blue-collared stiffs working the jackal network isn't going to be enough."

"Then we're going to have to give them the people behind it, aren't we?"

"What have you got to work with?"

"Two interrogation rooms. Rawley and Mac are working the prisoners in one of them now. So was I until I was told you were in the building. Maggie and Darnell are following up leads on the street. A lot of the talent at the meat dump was local. That means there was a lot of money coming into this area. Somebody had to have been brokering it. With luck, and the fact that Darnell used to work the Georgia turf, maybe they'll turn something up."

"Anything so far?"

"Not yet. Whoever's pulling the strings on this operation is clever. Either these people don't know anything about who they were working for, or they're scared shitless of him."

"Probably a combination of both." Vache took his trench coat and jacket off, loosened his tie, and rolled up his sleeves. "Can you use an old war-horse who used to be a good field agent?"

Wilson nodded. "Yeah. I figured you and I would double-team the guys in the other room. Between us, we've got six guys to go."

"Is the coffee down there any better?"

"No."

"Maybe we should think about sending out for some, while we're still on an expense account."

Shifting his attention back to the desk, Wilson picked up the yellow legal pad he'd used to jot some questions down. He handed Vache a thin manila file. "Give that a look on the way down. It's pretty straight-forward and will give you something to play off of."

Vache accepted the folder, then put a hand on Wilson's shoulder and squeezed in a fatherly way. "I'm sorry about Emmett. I know that was tough. He was a good man."

"Thanks." Wilson led the way out of the office. He pushed the dark thoughts away; he needed to concentrate on the interrogations.

CHAPTER 3

Maggie Scuderi watched the wild gyrations of the nude dancer on the fog-bound stage, her body speared by an assortment of neon lights. Scuderi leaned toward Darnell January and said, "You aren't going to tell me that you used to hang around these kinds of places when you were working in Georgia."

January seemed uncomfortable. "Strictly in the line of duty."

"Right." Scuderi sipped her wine and scanned the faces of the men, whose attention was solely on the nude woman. The dancer was actually pretty good, Scuderi knew. She'd spent five years working sex crimes in Washington, D.C., before moving on to the Bureau. Her working knowledge of places like the Veined Crayon was extensive, and in her opinion the bar's decor was scraping bottom, especially the penis-shaped swizzle sticks provided in the drinks. But she had to admit that the dancers were good.

The two state policemen escorting them had tried to embarrass her first in the way that nearly every male vice cop that she'd ever worked with had tried to do. It hadn't worked. She hadn't figured January for any of the ribbing, but she hadn't expected his reticence either.

Darnell January was six feet six inches tall, a rich, dark ebony, and built like a good football linebacker. Scuderi had acquired an appreciation for the sport during eight years of marriage. Johnny had been an avid Redskins fan. She'd stopped going to the games last year after he'd been shot and killed while working a burglary on his beat. Johnny's murderer still hadn't been found. Emmett Newkirk's death had just brought all those old memories back, a cauldron of pain she had to shut out.

"You okay?" January asked.

She glanced up at him and made herself smile. "Yeah. Just lost in thought for a moment."

January was probably the most intuitive member of Omega Blue, she realized. Although he looked big and ponderous, he moved with a catlike grace. He'd graduated from Georgia State Tech with an engineering degree but hadn't found a job in his chosen field. After two years of looking, he got a job with the Savannah Police Department. Three years ago he'd moved into the FBI, and two years later he became Omega Blue's demolitions expert. There had been a lot of other applicants for the position, but selection for the special anticrime task force didn't go by seniority or political privilege. Slade Wilson had picked January because the man was good at what he did, and because January worked well within the group's framework. With three brothers and three sisters, January was used to crowds and emotional crises.

"There's your guy," Hennesse, one of the Staties, said. He was young and lean, already hard around the edges.

"What's his name?" January asked.

"Osterbach. Terry Osterbach."

Scuderi studied the man as he threaded his way through the crowd to the four-sided bar in the center of the room. "How good is he?"

"Whatever he gives you," Hennesse said, "you can take to the bank. He's a good stoolie, but his contacts are sometimes less than what you'd hope for. He doesn't get involved in the heavy dirt."

Osterbach was three or four inches over six feet in height, but he lost a lot of that in his stoop-shouldered posture. He wore black-rimmed glasses, an oxford shirt with the tails hanging out, patched jeans, and work boots. After taking a seat at the bar, the man ran his fingers through his greasy blond hair to push it back out of his eyes, and opened a paperback book that was dog-eared and taped.

Scuderi was impressed. Reading was a skill most street people didn't have. "What's his story?"

"Twelve years ago he was a teacher," Hennesse said. "Taught grade school somewhere. Then the federal cutbacks caught up with him and he was unemployed. He tried making it on the state dole, but he had three kids and a wife with big eyes for material assets. A few years later, Osterbach was busted for moving blue angel and cocaine across the state. Not actually dealing, but doing mule work from the coast. He took a five-year fall. He did forty-two months, got out, found out he'd been divorced and that his wife had taken the kids to California with a young exec she'd vamped while he was away. It's no secret. Guy still tells the story if you ask."

"And since then?"

"He does whatever he can get his hands on. As long as it doesn't involve carrying a gun. I heard he killed a guy in the pen with a homemade shank, but that was never proved. Could be Osterbach started the rumor himself to buy some breathing room out on the street. Still, he doesn't know you people so you'd want to be careful about closing up on him."

"That's why you guys are here to do the intros," January said with a broad smile.

Scuderi envied her partner's ability to seem cheerful. Now that Newkirk's death had brought Johnny's murder to the forefront of her mind again, she knew it would be more than a week before she got another good night's sleep.

"Let's go do that." Hennesse pushed himself up out of his chair.

January followed.

Grabbing her purse and smoothing the midthigh black spandex dress she'd changed into for the bar trolling, Scuderi trailed along behind. Her Delta Elite 10mm was in her purse. There was no place for it under the leather half-jacket she was wearing.

The music was louder down near the bar pit area. Bass thumps rebounded off the walls, and the dancer onstage threw her hips to the beat as she held onto the brass rail that ran from floor to ceiling. Cigarette smoke hung in coils around the dim bulbs mounted on the unmarked walls.

Scuderi felt a hand wander out of the crowd just

behind her and start to skate down her hip. Reaching
out, she caught the offending appendage, then nerve-
pinched the little finger in a move her sensi had taught
her to perform almost imperceptibly. She walked on as
the man dropped to his knees, yelling in pain.

A pair of burly bouncers wearing polo shirts with
the club's name embroidered on them pushed through
the crowd and yanked the man up before he could get
off his knees. As he started to verbally defend himself,
one of the bouncers put a hand over the guy's mouth.
They escorted him quickly to an exit and threw him
out.

"You'll have to show me that one," Carris, the
other Statie, said.

"Get molested like that a few times," Scuderi said,
"and you'll pick it up quick."

Hennesse elbowed his way through the cluster of
people at the bar on one side of Osterbach, while January eased into place on the other side.

Scuderi stayed back with Carris to cover the floor.
During earlier sessions when they'd pumped known
stoolies for information, January had mentioned that he
had the impression that someone knew they were out
looking for leads. There was nothing solid that he could
point to, but when the big man had hunches, Scuderi
had learned to listen.

Osterbach looked up at Hennesse when the Statie
spoke to him, then gently closed his book and held his
place with a forefinger.

The music died away for a moment. The DJ,
sounding as excited as a carnival-show barker on speed,
announced the next dancer as the previous one gathered up her abandoned clothing and the dollar bills lit-
tering the stage floor. The new dancer was Asian, as

sleek and dainty as a Dresden doll, but Scuderi could tell that her breasts had been surgically augmented. She wore a sapphire gossamer gown that revealed the black teddy underneath. Hoots and whistles greeted her as she started dancing to an old ZZ Top tune, "She's Got Legs."

Hennesse nodded to January, and Osterbach looked at the FBI agent. A moment later they left the bar together and headed for the back door.

Her purse open for easy access to the pistol, Scuderi pushed her way through the crowd after them.

The door opened into a narrow alley filled with the smell of garlic, onions, pine disinfectant, rotting vegetables, and urine. Puddles from the earlier storm still gleamed wetly along the uneven pavement. Three of the bar's patrons were facing the brick wall of the building and relieving themselves by the Dumpster under the metal fire-escape stairs. They zipped up and moved off quickly, obviously reading the cop taint in the Staties' body language despite the street clothes. They went back inside the bar. Closing time was still two hours away.

A half-dozen feline shapes were clustered in the low windows of basement apartments and on the trash cans lining the alley. Jaundice yellow eyes tracked the movement of the five humans in the passageway.

January flipped open his badge case and gave his name. If Osterbach recognized what the cobalt blue shield really meant, he gave no indication. The shield didn't cut much ice with the local law enforcement wherever the team was, but it worked miracles with Justice Department personnel.

Osterbach bummed a cigarette from Hennesse,

then borrowed a lighter. Smoke curled into the dark, oppressive air.

"You know what we're here for, Terry," Hennesse said as he leaned against the wall.

Osterbach nodded. The coal of his cigarette glowed orange as he took a drag. "The meat dump."

"Yeah. What can you tell me about it?"

"The way I hear it, the FBI blew the shit out of it."

Scuderi knew from the way Hennesse moved that the Statie was about to get physical. Some of it might have stemmed from aggravation, but some of it she knew was because she was a woman and she was there watching him do his job. Law enforcement drew out the macho complex in most men, and she regretted the fact that sometimes her sex only complicated those feelings.

Moving smoothly, January inserted himself between Osterbach and Hennesse. An easy smile came to his face. "Actually, they blew the shit out of themselves when they found out we were there."

"Tried to get rid of the evidence."

"Yeah."

Osterbach squinted up at January. "That dump was a heavily protected piece of property. The people behind it put a lot of grease out on the street to make sure nobody wised up about it. Some of that grease funneled its way into the pockets of the local gendarmes."

"Don't give me that fucking shit," Hennesse said.

Osterbach held his hands up in front of his face as if expecting a blow. When it didn't come, he said, "Hey, Brian, if you can't handle the heat, stay out of the kitchen. You came banging on my door. I didn't come to you."

"Chill," January told the Statie. He turned his attention back to the stoolie. "I'm not here after the protection money. That flows in all directions once an operation like this has set down roots. I'm after the guy who put the thing together."

His jaw forming a stubborn line, Osterbach said, "What I'm telling you is that the meat dump had protection. I tell you anything I know, it's going to cost. If it's tracked back to me, and it will be, I'd better be long gone for awhile. You catch my drift?"

"If you give me something good," January said, "I'll arrange for a little vacation."

"Someplace south. The Caribbean's good this time of year."

January glanced at Scuderi as if asking permission.

Scuderi knew it was part of the act the big man was selling Osterbach. Wilson had empowered any of the team to make whatever deals were reasonable and necessary, without checking with him and possibly blowing a lead or losing time. That January had checked with her as though she were a superior lent a thin veneer of credibility to the offer. She gave him a tight nod and stepped forward. "But if you dick us around, I'll see to it that you go back inside prison for obstructing a federal officer in the performance of his duty."

Osterbach smiled. "Lady, some days I wish I was back inside because the rules in the joint are a lot easier to learn. And they're actually rules, not behaviors of convenience the way these assholes out here play. If I make a deal with you, it'll be a good one."

"How does Jamaica sound?" January asked.

Osterbach shook his head. "Something further south. Jamaica's only a short plane flight away. I want Trinidad."

"Done," Scuderi said.

Cars whipped by on the streets at both ends of the alley. Their lights sprayed out over the few people walking the sidewalks and illuminated the boarded-over windows of the abandoned buildings in the neighborhood.

"Who owns the meat dump?" January asked.

"That," Osterbach said, "I don't know. But I can tell you where some of the money's been flowing on the streets."

Scuderi nodded. Wilson had already pointed out that the probability of turning up a quick lead would be in the area of financing the site. From what they'd learned in state police files and NCIC (National Crime Information Center) records, a lot of the grunt work at the meat dump was done by local talent. "Who?"

Brakes screeched out on the street.

Turning toward the sound, Scuderi saw a black van with the lights off fishtail out of control for a moment, then line up and speed into the alley. As it roared into the mouth of the passageway, the driver flicked on fog lights mounted under the front bumper and on the roof. The alley flared to a painful incandescence. There was no more than six feet of space on either side of the vehicle.

A muzzle flash sparked outside the passenger window as the van bore down on them. Hennesse went down, driven back by two or three rounds.

"Stay clear!" January yelled as he grabbed Osterbach's shirtfront in both hands. The stoolie was frozen in place. January shoved Osterbach out into the middle of the alley and held him in place as the van rushed forward. The snitch tried to break and run, but the FBI agent held him fast.

Reaching into her purse, Scuderi freed her 10mm

and flicked off the safety. January was taking a big risk, but she knew it was the only chance they had. She brought the Delta Elite up and touched the button behind her jawline to activate the SeekNFire system wired into her reflexes. Her adrenaline level pushed the circuitry into operation in a heartbeat. She controlled her fear, becoming a gun sight as her palm read the pistol's familiar specs. She fired three rounds with pinpoint accuracy through the van's windshield on the passenger side and into the shadow just beyond.

Glass shattered and broke, opening up a black hole. The muzzle flashes died away.

Carris had his heavier Magnum out now, and the detonations sounded like cannon fire trapped between the buildings.

January waited till the last minute, almost lifting Osterbach off his feet, feinted right, then pivoted left as the van's driver reacted. He uncoiled, throwing both of them into a sprawling tumble that took them hard up against the alley wall.

As the van rushed by her, Scuderi moved out into the clear.

The double doors in back opened and a man stepped into view wearing an Uzi on a combat sling.

Going with the flow of the SeekNFire programming, Scuderi put two rounds into the elbow of the man's gun arm, then another round through both knees.

The gunner fell forward and landed off balance on the pavement. The van didn't hesitate as the driver roared around the corner of the alley into the flow of traffic. Horns blew in anger and fear as it fishtailed across the two oncoming lanes and raced toward Peachtree Street.

Scuderi dumped the empty magazine and slipped

a fresh one into the butt of the 10mm. She tripped the slide release and the first round was automatically loaded. Taking a two-handed grip on her weapon, she moved on the downed man.

The gunner shifted feebly, then reached for the Uzi lying only inches away.

Scuderi fired twice, and the 170-grain jacketed hollowpoints kicked the machine pistol away. "Darnell." She never took her eyes from the gunner on the pavement.

"We're here, Maggie," January called. "We're in good shape."

The man glared up at Scuderi with hate in his dark eyes. For the first time she noticed that he was Asian. Then his hand slipped behind his neck and his body convulsed.

"Oh, shit," Carris said beside Scuderi. "The son of a bitch is wired with an endo-skel."

Scuderi glanced at the gunner's knees and saw the wire-thin tensile steel rods in the flesh and blood and bone ruin of his knees.

With a harsh yell of pain and rage, the Asian flipped himself to a standing position and remained standing on legs that shouldn't have held his weight.

Scuderi knew about endo-skels. For a time they'd been considered for Omega Blue members. Once wired for an endo-skel, a person could be mobile despite grievous wounds that would normally be crippling. The system also took over the central nervous system and fed the body adrenaline and pain-killing endorphins as deemed necessary by the on-board biocomputer.

The drawbacks were numerous, however. If used, endo-skels drew mercilessly on a body's resources and required a huge payback later, sometimes lasting days while the user lapsed into a lethargy that could only be countered with more drugs. The user never knew when he or she would cross that thin line and accidentally overdose. The system also allowed the user to tear cartilage and joints past the point of anything less than bionic repair, which ruined their effectiveness. Too many security systems would register the bionic repair work. And the bionics themselves were never much more than self-powered prostheses; there simply wasn't a biomedical replacement for human tissue yet. Jackal networks made fortunes because of that truth. A conservative investigation had demonstrated that endoskel users cut at least fifteen years off their life expectancy.

The Asian reached up under his windbreaker and pulled out a pair of matte-finish nunchuks. He started whirling them in vicious arcs with his uninjured arm as he threw himself at Scuderi.

She didn't hesitate. Her finger tightened on the trigger and she put three rounds through the man's chest, rupturing his heart and ripping through his spinal cord.

With the adrenaline pump gone and the endoskel's messages no longer being received, the gunner collapsed in a loose-jointed heap that didn't move again. He was three feet from Scuderi's smoking gun.

Placing her pistol on the ground beside her, Scuderi started going through the dead man's pockets for ID. She glanced up at Carris, said, "Get on the phone and call this in," then went back to work. She took a pair of disposable surgical gloves from her purse and handled everything gingerly.

"Hennesse didn't make it," January said.

Scuderi nodded. She'd guessed that from the way

the state policeman had gone down. She looked at the empty pockets in disgust. "Nothing here that's going to let us move immediately."

January turned to Osterbach. He still had the man's shirtfront wound up in one big fist. "It's deal time, guy. These people saw you tonight. If we leave you here on your own, I don't figure you'll live to see the dawn break."

Osterbach swallowed hard and wiped his hair out of his face. "Guy's name is Nelson Aikman. He's an accountant, does a little money laundering for the local mob. When the meat dump went in, he took over the payroll for the staff and brokered some deals."

"You know that for a fact?"

"I recruited some of the security people for him."

January's face remained impassive. "Where do we find Aikman?"

Osterbach gave an address.

Scuderi memorized the address and asked, "Where do the Asians fit in?"

Looking at the corpse, Osterbach shook his head. "I don't know anything about them."

Scuderi grabbed the dead man's shoulder and rolled him over on his back with effort. The exploded chest cavity gleamed wetly. "They damn sure fit in somewhere."

"Oh, Christ," Osterbach said as he put a hand over his mouth and doubled over. "I think I'm going to be sick."

January yanked the snitch back. "Not there, you're not."

The paperback book tumbled free of his pocket and splatted down on the pavement near the pooled blood.

Scuderi retrieved it and glanced at the front cover. It was a science-fiction novel by Isaac Asimov called *The Caves of Steel*. Her older brother had been a fan when they were both teenagers. She handed the novel to Osterbach, who nodded his thanks. "The future didn't exactly turn out to be robots and rocketships the way they thought it would, did it?"

CHAPTER 4

"In case they didn't tell you," Slade Wilson said in a hard voice designed to bounce off the walls of the interrogation room and intimidate the man sitting across the folding table from him, "a federal cop was killed at that site last night. That means you can count on not doing your bit in your hometown. You'll be under federal lockup, and parole's not so damn lenient."

"I didn't kill nobody." The prisoner was Dewayne Ogburn. NCIC had confirmed that he'd served a four-year stretch in the Georgia state penitentiary for jackal work, and had gotten out less than eighteen months ago. "I didn't even have a gun. You guys came in, I gave myself up."

It might have been true. In the confusion, Wilson didn't know and the Atlanta PD and state units hadn't kept track. He hadn't expected much from Ogburn. The man was obviously a career criminal. Prison didn't scare him, and outside of harvesting stolen organs for a jackal network, employment prospects looked grim. He was thin, sallow, and fair haired, early thirties. For awhile he'd worked in a state-sponsored hospital, then discovered the fast money that could be made in jackal work.

"Who does the meat dump belong to?" Earl Vache asked. He sat quietly in a chair next to Wilson with his hands folded on the tabletop.

"I don't know."

"Who did you work for?"

"Eddie Roth. He was my immediate supervisor. I know you already interviewed him. Whatever he told you, that's more than I know."

Wilson surged up out of his seat and kicked it aside. The folding metal chair slammed up against the wall and made the prisoner flinch. Roth hadn't told them anything. The Bureau agent crossed the room to the manila folder sitting on a chair in the corner. "What do you know about the Miami end of things?" he demanded.

"Nothing. I stay away from the media. It can make my job complicated if I know too much."

"You knew the latest shipment was coming up from Florida?"

"Somebody mentioned it, but I didn't check into it."

Wilson grabbed the color stills he wanted and walked back to the table on Ogburn's side. The jackal tightened up on himself but didn't move away from the implied physical threat. "A jackal team husked thirty-one people in Miami." He scattered the pictures across the tabletop. "Eight of them were just kids. Look at them."

Ogburn seemed frozen.

Wilson grabbed the collar of the man's orange county-jail jumpsuit and shoved his face within inches of the pictures. "Look at them," he repeated. Wilson put his face so close to the jackal that he could feel the man's breath on his cheek.

Ogburn closed his eyes. "Man, I swear to you, I had nothing to do with that."

"You were waiting on them," Wilson accused. "You were waiting on the pieces that remained of these kids. They say that jackals are grave robbers before the earth even gets turned, that jackals don't have hearts because if they did they'd find a way to cut them out and sell them."

Ogburn's fingers trembled when he reached out and touched one of the pictures. "Fuck it, man. I don't kill them. If I didn't do what I do, somebody else would."

"Give us the guy behind it," Vache coaxed.

"I can't. I don't know him."

Releasing the man's collar, Wilson stepped back and took the pair of handcuffs he'd removed from Ogburn earlier. "Stand up."

Not facing Wilson, Ogburn pushed himself out of the chair and put his hands behind his back.

Wilson clicked the cuffs into place, then propelled the man toward the door. Ogburn slammed up against it, not hard, but with enough force to make him close his eyes. Wilson rapped on the door.

Vache turned in his chair, his face placid. "Ogburn."

The jackal looked at the Omega Blue liaison.

"Good cop/bad cop aside, guy, a federal pen is no place to spend your bit. You keep that in mind. A lot of other guys on your team are going to be in there with you. It could be one of them will opt out before you do. And we only need the information once."

Ogburn shook his head. "I tell you anything, I'm a dead man. Even if I knew for sure. The juice on this operation is pure platinum. You might keep that in mind."

The door opened and Wilson shoved the man through to the waiting uniformed policeman. Closing the door, he ran his fingers through his hair in exasperation and let his anger hiss out between his teeth along with his breath. He thought about Newkirk lying cold and alone on a morgue slab downtown.

Vache took out a fresh stick of gum, unwrapped it, and shoved it into his mouth. He rolled the paper between his palms, then dropped it into the unused ashtray in the middle of the table. "Getting nowhere fast with this thing."

"Yeah." Wilson crossed the room and took his coffee from its place on the windowsill, between the steel bars crosshatched over the glass. It was cold, but he sipped it anyway. Cold or hot, the taste didn't really matter. All his body wanted was the caffeine.

"So where do you go from here?"

"Something will break. This was a big network."

Vache shifted in his chair, and it squeaked under his weight. "It might be better to leave it alone for awhile. You've made some headway here. Maybe you should just be glad of that."

"Jackal work is getting to be like fighting jungle growth. What we chop away today will be regrown tomorrow unless we shut down the whole operation.

They can have another team on the streets by morning." Giving in to the headache pounding at his temples, he shook two analgesics into his palm and swallowed them with his coffee.

"You're going to be drawing a lot of political heat after tonight."

"That's fine. It means the media will be keeping up with this thing too. At least, the media groups that aren't owned by people wanting to keep it swept under the nearest carpet."

"You're turning into a cynic."

Wilson gave him a mirthless smile. "Earl, that's something you warned me would happen the day I took this job. I didn't believe you then."

"All I'm saying here is that it might be in the best interests of the team to let this thing settle before the House subcommittee chooses to make an issue out of it. If you stir up a hornet's nest, the least sensible thing to do would be to take a whack at it with a stick."

"If I let it go, I lose whatever ground Emmett Newkirk gave his life to help us gain." Wilson shook his head. "I'm not about to do that."

"You think getting the Omega Blue unit shut down is going to help?"

Wilson looked away from the man and tried to believe his own words. "That won't happen."

"What makes you so sure?"

"Because after almost four years I know how the political game is played. We have a certain autonomy within the Omega Blue charter, but we also cover special interests for the politicians. Remember when we were assigned to the armored-car hijackers in Wisconsin in February? Senator Kiernan was up for reelection, and a firm stance on law and order was a big part of his platform. We went into the state because they wanted to get Kiernan more media coverage. The state police took the hijackers down through leads they developed themselves. We were only there to assist. No one in the unit ever fired a shot. And Wisconsin isn't the only example I can cite. They won't get rid of me as long as the job still needs doing and I can get it done."

"I was wrong. You're not cynical. You're still optimistic as hell."

"This country needs us," Wilson said. "Somebody has to cut out the rot and decay before there's nothing left to save. If regular law-enforcement people could get it done, they would. But there are too many criminals out there now, with big organizations of their own. As long as we keep the unit small, we can keep it clean. That's why we've resisted expanding."

"You can stand there and say that, not knowing any more about Rawley than you do?"

Wilson sipped his coffee and locked eyes with Vache. "I know everything about Lee Rawley that I need to know. For now."

The phone mounted on the wall rang.

Wilson crossed the room and picked it up. "Wilson."

"Me," Mac said. "Lee and I are about to do our pigeon now. I checked in on him through the cell security vid. Guy looks like he's just about done in. Thought you might want to catch the show."

"Bring him in." Wilson hung up the phone, then turned out the interrogation room's lights and switched on the special one-way glass filling up the adjoining wall. On the other side of the viewing area, the glass was camouflaged to look like the remaining walls.

The programming juiced through the glass and

faded in patches, clearing for a view of the adjoining room. Lee Rawley stood in one corner, lean and hard, his dark hair spilling down his neck under his chocolate brown Stetson. The mirror sunglasses hid his thoughts. His wore faded jeans and a belt with a large buckle that concealed at least two deadly weapons. The sleeves of his chambray work shirt were rolled to midforearm, and a silver-and-turqoise arrowhead gleamed from the neck-lace at his throat. He was clean shaven and Wilson knew he would smell of sandalwood cologne.

By contrast, Bob MacDonald looked like he'd been through the trenches. His blue eyes were bloodshot and his dress shirt was open to midchest with his tie at half-mast. His corduroy jacket was draped haphazardly over one of the three chairs in the room. He took the jackal's cuffs off and waved the man to a chair.

The jackal sat. Worry lines showed in his hand-some, youthful face. His hair was cut in a punk style prevalent on the streets, and he was slender.

Wilson adjusted the audio part of the wall.

Mac picked up a clipboard from the table and quickly leafed through it, pretending that he hadn't really taken the time to study it before. "Well now, it looks like you've been a busy guy these last five years, Mr. Wiar. In addition to the charges you're facing this morning, you're wanted for arrest in South Carolina for forging government checks while working as a grounds-keeper in a senior citizens home. Add to that a history of burglary, assault with a deadly weapon, theft, and sev-eral counts of public intoxication, and I'd say you're fac-ing time. Maybe a lot of it."

A nerve ticked high on Wiar's forehead.

"They play him right," Vache whispered, "they can break this guy and hope he knows something."

Wilson nodded. He'd already gone over Wiar's arrest record and knew the man had never been in trouble like the kind he was presently facing, but had had enough of a taste of prison to know he wouldn't like it. Of the prisoners that had been taken, he and Mac had agreed that Wiar would be the one most likely to break.

Mac tossed the clipboard back on the table.

Wiar jumped and broke eye contact.

Taking a cigarette from his pocket, Mac cupped his palms and took his time lighting up. "First thing I want to tell you, Jimmy," he said in a soft voice, "is how much trouble you're in."

Wilson listened as Mac unrolled the spiel. The man was good. Before joining the Bureau, Mac had spent some time working out of the district attorney's office in Oklahoma City. He'd developed a good presentation style and knew the law intimately.

"Slade."

Wilson noticed the change in Vache's tone at once.

The big man looked uncomfortable. He exhaled with real feeling. "Goddamnit, there's not going to be a better time to deal with this, or a better way to bring it up."

"I know." Wilson turned back to watch the interrogation process. He tried to think of the team, and not Emmett Newkirk.

"I've got four people who could qualify for Omega Blue. However this thing goes, you people can't operate one member short."

"Yeah." Wilson's throat felt tight. He watched as the color drained from Jimmy Wiar's face.

"Emmett's specialty was computers. Maggie could probably see you guys through in a pinch, but you need somebody who knows how to hack their way around systems."

"Who were you thinking of?"

"Garry Drennan."

"He's been in VICAP too long. He's almost a burnout. He has a good feel for serial killers, but he lacks the ability to change stride in midstream anymore. Our investigations don't hold up to set patterns."

"Grace Patana."

"No. She's good at the file-and-sort stuff. I've seen some of her work. But she can't move in the hacking circles. Those people are almost from another planet. Emmett understood them, and he understood the free thinking behind computer work."

"Henry Spradlin specializes in creative thinking with computers."

"And with his fists. The guy may know how to outfinesse a cybernetic system, but he doesn't know anything about conducting himself around other people."

In the other room, Mac's voice soothingly hammered home every charge that would be brought against the jackal network, patiently took away every chance Wiar might have thought he had at escape.

"Keith Bentz is the last qualified person I have for possible promotion."

Wilson studied the jackal's posture through the glass and knew the guy was beginning to crumble. "Bentz is too married for Omega Blue."

"You thought Maggie was too."

"I was wrong. I didn't see that she believed in the program as much as I did. Still, it hurt her when Johnny was killed last year. She went through a lot of guilt for not being there more. She's still going through some of it."

"Maybe you're wrong about Bentz."

"No. The guy wants to start a family. It isn't fair for him to have to choose between that and his career."

"Are we talking about Keith Bentz here, or Slade Wilson?"

"Fuck you, Earl."

"Sorry. I was out of line. Maybe we should wait and discuss this another time."

Ignoring the memory of past hurt that had suddenly swirled up around him, Wilson said, "No. The team needs that slot filled. Wherever this thing goes, we're going to need someone skilled in computers. These people don't do cash-and-carry with the big deals."

"Then you're going to have to pick one of those four."

"No. You're leaving someone out."

"Who?"

"Quinn Valentine."

Vache hesitated before replying.

In the interrogation room, Wiar was hiding his face in his hands and struggling to maintain self-control. Mac was relentless, still talking in that soft voice.

"Valentine has a chip on his shoulder," Vache said. "You know that as much as I do. You know his background. He's young and green and feels like he has to prove himself to the whole world."

"Not the whole world," Wilson said. "Just the House subcommittee."

"Slade, in maybe three or four years, Valentine will make a hell of a field agent. He might even qualify for your team. But not now."

"I can't wait three or four years. I need the guy now. We can work with him, fast track his training. I've seen him. I've had my eye on him since he joined the Academy eight months ago. He's got a fire this team needs. Those other people don't."

"Maybe you need time to think about this."

"I don't have time. Can you get Valentine for me?"

"Yes."

"Then do it. We should be in Quantico by morning. Fix it so he's there when we arrive."

"Okay." Vache was clearly unhappy.

Wilson could sympathize with the man, but they were looking at the job from two different perspectives. Vache knew it, too.

"I want something from you in exchange," Vache said.

"What?"

"The House subcommittee meets the day after tomorrow. I want you there with me when they review the program."

"Politics aren't my game."

"I'll give you pointers."

"Why do you want me there?"

"Not as punishment," Vache replied. "I just want you to get a good look at how thin the ice is that you're skating on."

"We've been on thin ice since this unit was formed," Wilson said.

"It's gotten thinner."

"Name the time. I'll be there."

"Fair enough. Valentine will be waiting on us at Quantico. Let me make a couple calls." Vache left the window and crossed the room to the phone.

Inside the interrogation room, Mac tapped a cigarette against the back of his palm, then lit it. A blue haze swirled slowly around the room. "Do you understand everything I've explained to you, Jimmy?"

Wiar nodded. Tears, angry and unshed, gleamed in his eyes. "It's not fair. I didn't even know what was in that truck. I was just hired to unload it, that's all."

"I believe you," Mac said.

Wilson knew Mac didn't. He was too seasoned to think for a moment that the young man was an innocent. Wiar had just never been down for anything this serious before, and he'd never been in a position to deal himself out of it. That part had to be looking pretty good to Wiar now.

"The problem is," Mac continued, "the district attorney's office isn't going to believe you. And a jury probably won't either. If I was you, I'd think about copping a lesser plea if it was offered. Maybe you can cut a few years off your sentence."

"Oh, Christ," Wiar groaned.

"Sorry, kid."

Lee Rawley moved into fluid motion at once. A predatory smile gleamed below the mirror shades as he closed in on Wiar. "Shit, I'm not sorry for the sniveling son of a bitch. A cop was killed tonight. A damn good cop. He was a friend of mine, asshole. Did you know that? Or do you even care?"

Wiar turned away from Rawley.

Dropping into a crouch beside Wiar, Rawley reached out and seized the jackal's face in his hand. He yanked on it roughly until Wiar was facing him. "Look at me, you snot-nosed little punk."

Wiar's eyes widened in fright, and he had to force his hands back into his lap to keep from grabbing Rawley's arm.

A crooked-toothed grin filled Rawley's lower face.

He maintained his hold on Wiar. "You've never been to a federal lockup, have you? Only done county time. Things are a lot different in a federal prison. Bet you're still a virgin, aren't you?"

"I've had women," Wiar said with more spunk than Wilson would have thought possible.

Rawley released Wiar's face, still smiling. He rubbed the back of his fingers along the jackal's cheek in a familiar caress. "That's not what I'm talking about. Have you ever been a woman for a man? Have you ever gotten down on your knees in front of a guy who's on death row? You'll do what he tells you to, and be damned glad you're still alive when he lets you go."

Wiar turned his head away. "Ain't no son of a bitch gonna make me do something like that and live."

Rawley's hard laugh filled the room. "Boy, that kind of attitude is going to make you even more in demand. You get inside, they're going to love breaking your spirit. Pretty soon you'll get so you'll drop to your knees for a cigarette or a library pass. And they won't stop there, either. They'll take your cherry, too. It won't be like your first time with a girl. You won't think you're in love, and it won't be in the back of some car or a borrowed apartment or motel room. And you won't be alone. First-timers, they usually get a train pulled on them. You know what a train is?"

"Make him leave me alone!" Wiar yelled at Mac. "He can't talk to me like that!"

"The hell I can't," Rawley said. "You get to prison, you're going to get this same speech from the warden. Have to get you acclimated to your new environment as soon as possible so they don't find you dead some morning because you didn't know your place."

"I want out of here," Wiar said. "I want a lawyer.

Before I talk to you guys any more, I want a lawyer present. I know my rights." The whites of his eyes showed; beads of perspiration trickled down his face.

"A train," Rawley repeated. "That means five, maybe six big guys who haven't seen a woman in months or years are going to take first crack at you before the rest of the inmates move in on you. When they finish with you, you won't be able to walk for days, and you'll be bleeding out your ass for a week. If you're too shy to report to the infirmary, you could get an infection or gangrene, maybe die of the injuries. And pray that one of them isn't carrying AIDS. If they are, you're screwed for the rest of the short life you've got to enjoy."

"Nobody's going to fuck my ass!" Wiar shut his eyes as if that could make Rawley's words go away.

"If you're lucky, somebody will want you for a wife. As good looking as you are, I can see that happening. Might even have a cushy life for awhile after that. Of course, you're going to have to work hard to make sure your man doesn't lose interest in you."

Tears slid down Wiar's face now. He stared desperately at Mac. "You got to do something."

"I can't."

"You can't let them do that to me."

"Kid, I'm sorry."

Rawley stood up. "Hell, kid, I got a few hours to kill. Maybe I'll find a nice, quiet out-of-the-way cell and turn you out all by myself. Until somebody makes bond for you, you're the property of the FBI." He rubbed his hand beside his crotch suggestively.

"God, that's one cold bastard," Vache said.

"I know," Wilson said, crossing the room to the phone. "He can be persuasive in an interrogation room." He dialed and heard the phone ring in the other room.

Mac picked it up and said hello.

"You got him," Wilson said. "Bring him in." He broke the connection and hung up.

Mac pretended to listen for awhile longer, then cradled the receiver. Rawley continued to taunt Wiar, breaking him even further.

Wilson didn't like interrogations done this way, but at times there was no other way to get the job done. He watched Wiar carefully. It was important to get a feel for the answers the man would offer. If Wiar was scared enough, he'd make up anything the FBI team wanted to hear. They needed the truth.

"Look," Mac said as he sat back on the table and flicked the ashes off a fresh cigarette, "I got permission to make a deal, but only if you can provide something we want. A couple of the other guys talked first, but if you can add something to what we already know, we might be able to get your sentence reduced to probation."

"Sure," Wiar said, brushing the tears from his eyes with his forearm. "What do you want to know?"

Mac took Wiar through the whole run, beginning with Wiar's employment at the Miami end. Nothing special came up, and it was pretty much as the team had put it together. Then Mac went for the payoff while pretending to be finishing up his notes on a legal pad. "Who was running the jackal network?"

"I don't know for sure," Wiar said. "The guys over us weren't supposed to talk about it. I guess they figured the less we knew, the less we could hurt them if things went wrong. . . ."

Wilson curled his hand into a fist against the glass.

"C'mon, kid. You had to have heard somebody's name."

". . . Kramer, one of the drivers, he'd been around the jackal network for awhile. He mentioned a guy's name once when we went out for a few drinks. Kramer talked a lot after a couple six-packs."

"Who?"

"Prio. Harry Prio. Kramer called him Balls, but said that nobody called Prio that to his face and lived. There was supposed to be somebody over Prio, but Prio was the cut-out man ramrodding the operation."

"Bingo," Wilson said. He glanced at Vache. "Harry Prio belongs to Sebastian DiVarco. Boston Mafia."

"I've heard the name," Vache said. "Giuseppe DiVarco used to a big mover in Boston's North End back in the 1980s. But what the hell is DiVarco doing this far down the coast? The Boston families have been pretty much cut up these days and haven't moved anything outside of the state."

"Something's changed," Wilson said. "That's just one of the things we have to find out now."

Mac and Rawley finished up with Wiar in the other room and guided him toward the door as the phone began to ring behind Wilson. He picked it up. Maggie Scuderi identified herself and gave a quick rundown of the events that had just unfolded outside the Veined Crayon. Wilson unfolded a city map of Atlanta and marked the addresses she gave him.

"Move in on Aikman's residence," Wilson said. "That's closer to your present twenty. We'll cover his business and see about getting a court order to let us go inside. Call me when you get there."

"Right," Scuderi said, and hung up.

"We got another break," Wilson said as he headed

for the door. "Maggie may have turned up the bank on the jackal network. You want to come along or wait here?"

"We'll take my car," Vache said.

CHAPTER 5

"We aren't alone," Lee Rawley said. His voice carried in a whisper over the T-jack.

Slade Wilson didn't slacken his pace when he received the transmission. He maneuvered in the shadows around the Gresham office building in an older part of the downtown sector along Virginia Avenue NE. The Delta Elite rode in a shoulder holster under his right arm. He kept the motorcycle jacket zipped at the waist, so he could quickly seal the Kevlar body armor once he'd freed his weapon. "How many do you have?"

Rawley was on top of a three-story building across the street with a Barrett M-82 Light Fifty sniper rifle with thermal-imaging sights. "I've got four outside. At least three inside confirmed visually. And there's another guy I haven't got figured out yet. He's being marched between two of the perps and doesn't look happy about it at all."

Wilson turned the corner and went into the alley. Taking a pair of night goggles from his pocket, he slipped them on and activated the chipped circuitry. The shadows and the night went away, and the alley looked as hard and as bright as a moonscape. A skeletal fire-escape ladder wormed its way up the side of the building, reaching the top five stories. "Maggie," Wilson spoke into the T-jack's mike.

"I'm with you," Scuderi replied. She and January were en route from Aikman's home. The accountant hadn't been there, and his wife didn't know when he'd left. She did remember that he had received a phone call, but she had an early morning shift at the railway and hadn't gotten up to ask him about it. "What does the guy look like?"

"Anemic. Five ten. Maybe one sixty. Glasses. Thirty, thirty-five. Brown hair in a conservative cut, and a mustache."

"That could be Aikman," Scuderi said.

Wilson trotted to the fire escape and gazed up at the brick surface of the wall. None of the windows above were lighted. He listened, but could only hear the static hum made by the building's life-support systems.

"Where's this guy's office?" Earl Vache whispered. He stood beside Wilson, moving more quietly than a man of his size had any right to. The T-jack looked like a hard, metal scar along his jawline.

"Fifth floor," Wilson replied as he estimated the distance to the second-story platform.

"Shit."

"Can you make that fire escape?"

"Without pulling the ladder down?"

"Yeah. That would make too much noise."

"No. In my best days I couldn't have made a leap like that."

"How about if I give you a boost up?"

"Maybe."

Wilson knelt and laced his fingers together to make a stirrup. "Let's give it a shot."

Warily, Vache stepped into Wilson's hands and said, "Ready."

"Go." Wilson leaned into the effort as Vache jumped upward.

Omega Blue's liaison grabbed the lower edge of the platform, then began the laborious task of pulling himself up the side.

Stepping back a few paces, Wilson took three big strides and went airborne. His hand cleared the lip of the platform by almost a foot. He tugged and quickly hauled himself up. As he threw himself over the railing and came to a standing position, the 10mm came away in his fist and he zipped the jacket. Inside the second-story window nothing moved. He glanced at the living room furniture, blank television, and the VCR with 3:49 glaring in red numbers from the face. He leaned back over the railing, caught Vache under the arm, and helped the man up.

"Thanks."

"No prob." Wilson went upward, keeping his feet to the outside edges of the metal steps. "Stay out of the middle. You'll make less noise."

"Give me a break here," Vache said. "I was a field agent a lot of years before they gave me the desk." But he kept his feet away from the center of the steps.

Wilson kept his back toward the building as he made his way up to the third-story landing. The 10mm felt hard and reassuring in his fist. The rain had stopped now, but the air still felt doughy and oppressive. Pools of collected rainwater dotted the pavement of the alley below and looked like black ice-skating rinks. He gazed into every window he passed. There was no movement inside. He blew into the T-jack's mike and accessed the frequency. "Rawley."

"Go."

"Can you track them?"

"It's a little uncertain with the thermal imaging, but I'm getting readings on the fourth floor. Looks like the total inside has been bumped up to six."

"Stand by."

"You call it," Rawley replied, "I'll be there."

Wilson was counting on that. Aikman's office was on the side of the building facing Rawley. Even if the perps weren't visible through the windows, the thermal-imaging scope on the Barrett would allow Rawley to pick them up. The big .50-cal rounds could punch through the old brick and mortar if necessary.

"Slade."

"Go," Wilson said as he made the fourth-floor landing. Vache had fallen a half-dozen steps behind him.

"I found three cars in the parking area behind the building," Mac said. "All of their engines are hot, so I know they were just parked." He read off the license-plate numbers.

Scuderi broke in. "The first car belongs to Aikman. His wife confirmed that it was missing from the garage."

"Fifth floor," Rawley called out, "and moving toward the northeast corner of the building."

"They're going for the files in Aikman's office,"

January commented. "It's going to be strictly crash and burn for a total evidence scrub on the jackal network."

"Clear," Wilson ordered. "We move on my go."

The team cleared.

Flicking the auxillary channel selector toggle on the T-jack, Wilson moved over to the tach frequency being used in conjunction with the state police, who'd rolled on the call with them. "Falcon, this is Redball."

"Go, Redball."

"We're confirmed here. The count stands at ten perps and one hostage, but that's not a final tally."

"Roger. We've targeted at least one spotter a block from you people, but he's not moving. There's no reason to think he's made us."

"Affirmative. When I give you the signal, shut down the neighborhood. Nobody goes in or out unless they're checked through by your people or mine."

"Understood, Redball."

Wilson gained the final landing. The office building was the tallest structure in the immediate vicinity. The nearest building was across twenty feet of space and two floors down. A dome-shaped greenhouse made out of plastic tarp and pine slats sat on the roof below. Pigeons cooed and moved restlessly on the greenhouse and on the building's eaves.

Vache was on the last step of the metal stairway when the window shattered. The muffled whir of a silencer on a fully automatic weapon chased away the street sounds of passing cars and humming streetlights. Spinning glass fragments and slivers dropped to the metal landing or shot against the railing and broke in high-pitched crunches.

A hail of bullets caught Vache in midstride and drove him back down the steps.

The wicked snout of an Ingram MAC-11 pushed through the broken window. A harsh voice shouted a warning.

Moving quickly, uncertain whether Vache's Kevlar-lined trench coat had absorbed the rounds, Wilson twisted at the side of the window and reached inside. He followed the line of the gun, saw it coming around to face him when his fingers caught the material of the gunner's clothing. Closing his fist, he yanked with all his strength, pulled the man kicking and screaming across the shards of glass remaining in the window frame. Working with the impetus the initial yank had created, he kept the gunner at a headlong pace that ended in a sudden plunge over the side of the railing.

The ululating scream that followed ended suddenly, made even more jarring by the sound of collapsing metal and breaking boards.

"Vache!" Wilson whirled in time to see the FBI liaison pulling himself back up the railing.

"I'm okay. Body armor stopped the bullets." Vache's face was pasty white and his mouth was set in a line of grim determination.

Wilson nodded and blew on the mike. "Rawley."

"Go. I copied the action."

Wilson clambered through the shattered window. The Delta Elite was a compass needle before him, wavering as it sought out threats. "How many inside now?"

"Still reading six perps and possibly Aikman."

The room was a small office containing stuffed bats, owls, and snakes. Maps and star charts adorned the badly painted walls. A bookcase full of books on the occult covered the adjoining wall of the office at the side. The desk near the bookcase held a stuffed raven perched on a branch and a crystal ball at least eight inches in diameter that rested in a pewter collar.

Wilson oriented himself using the memorized blueprint Scuderi had retrieved from public records. They were in Madame Julka's office. The glass pane in the center of the door advertised palm reading, channeling, compatibility reports, personalized horoscopes, and counseling by appointment only.

"We're blown," Wilson said as he tried the door. It was locked. "Close it in and let's see what we can salvage."

The team checked off and moved into their positions. January and Scuderi had just made their debarkation point behind the office building and were scrambling.

Wilson aimed the 10mm at the lock and changed channels on the T-jack. "Falcon, this is Redball. Shut 'em down. The integrity of the covert operation has just gone bust."

"Roger, Redball." The state police commander faded out of the linkup.

Wilson pulled the trigger twice and the lock became a confused twist of battered parts as sparks sailed like miniature comets.

Bullets slammed into the glass pane from outside and dissolved it into a collection of jigsaw pieces that rattled against the bottom of the door.

Dodging against the wall, Wilson reached up and pressed the SeekNFire actuation switch. His synapses thrummed with the adrenaline rush as his palm read the stats on the Delta Elite and fed them into his reflexes.

Vache went to ground behind the cheap desk. The second burst smacked the side of the crystal ball and sent it rolling. Before it dropped over the edge of the desk, at least two rounds caught it and splintered it into dozens of gleaming pieces. The raven disappeared in a small cloud of black feathers and the stink of cordite filled the small office.

Holding the 10mm in both hands, Wilson came off the wall in a Weaver stance, pointing through the open area the pane of glass had occupied only a heartbeat before. His night-vision goggles illuminated the outside corridor.

The gunner finished loading a fresh magazine and brought the MAC-11 back up.

Wilson squeezed off two rounds that caught the man in the face and neck. The hollowpoints kicked the man back against the wall, then he slumped forward onto his face.

Twisting the knob, ignoring the heat of the metal caused by his earlier bullets, Wilson yanked the door open and went through. He secured the corridor for a moment as Vache came through on his heels. Movement caught his eye.

Unbelievably, the man he'd put down was in motion. Most of his lower face was gone, and he was bleeding profusely. Blood formed a slick covering over his dark clothes and splotched the hands that worked to pull the pistol from the belly holster. The reflexes were dulled and jerky, but they were getting the job done. The pistol came up in short arcs of movement.

Dropping his Delta Elite into target acquisition, Wilson put the remaining three rounds of the clip into the man, aiming for the vertebrae joining the skull to the neck. A final shiver coursed through the body.

"Jesus Christ," Vache breathed hoarsely. "I figured that son of a bitch was dead."

"Not dead," Wilson said as he crossed the corridor

to examine the perp. He fed a new magazine into the 10mm. "But he should have been down."

"Was he on PCP or blue angel?"

"No." Wilson pointed at the gleaming bits of metal fused to the patches of spine showing through the wounds. "Endo-skel."

"I've heard about them, but I've never seen one in action before."

"This is only the third time I have," Wilson said. "Maggie ran into a guy wired for one earlier. And he was Asian, just like this guy." He pushed himself up and went down the hall, following the map he had inside his head.

"I thought we were tracking Boston Mafia," Vache said.

"Prio is Boston Mafia, but that guy is Asian. Not the domestic variety. You don't find much endo-skel work being done in the States. In the Far East, the Triad, Yakuza, and opium warlords specialize in it."

"Doesn't that stuff shorten your life span? Isn't that why the Bureau decided against it?"

"Yeah. It may make them harder to kill, but they're thrown into the breech a lot sooner and a lot more often. Dead is still dead." Wilson jogged around the next corner and cut right, choosing the shortest route to Aikman's office.

"The Asians do jackal work too, don't they?"

"Most of them. But usually their clientele go to their hospitals. They don't operate stateside much because there're too many laws here."

"Maybe they're looking to open a local branch with DiVarco."

"Doesn't figure. DiVarco doesn't have a history of playing second-banana for anyone."

"Could be they were here to put him out of business."

"He's not that big."

"You didn't think he was big enough to be fronting a jackal network that ran all the way down the east coast either," Vache pointed out.

"True." Wilson paused at the next corridor intersection when voices reached his ears. He waved Vache back against the wall behind him, then blew into the mike to access the T-jack. "Rawley."

"Go."

"At least some of the perps are equipped with endo-skels."

"Understood. Anytime I fire, I'll be keeping that in mind."

Wilson glanced around the corner and saw two men standing guard at either side of an office door at the end of the hallway thirty feet away. They carried machine pistols like the first perp's. "Maggie."

"Copied," Scuderi replied.

Mac and January copied as well.

Wilson doubled back to the last office they'd passed. He fired two rounds into the locking mechanism, then lifted a booted foot and drove it hard against the doorjamb.

The door exploded inward and partially came off its hinges. It hung askew with the glass pane advertising Atlanta Sports Promotions, Inc., spiderwebbed in cracks.

"Depending on their time frames, they may come to investigate that," Wilson warned. He grabbed hold of the desk in the outer office and pulled it under the makeup air duct set in the ceiling. "Can you hold this room?"

"Sure." Vache took up a position beside the doorway and held his pistol in both hands.

Leathering the 10mm, Wilson clambered on top of the desk. Papers and the phone went shooting in all directions. He shoved his fingers through the duct work, secured a hold, and yanked downward.

The duct work pulled free with a screech. A cloud of dust and fiber particles followed it down, then mushroomed out again when it banged off the desk and clattered to the tiled floor.

Wilson took a miniature oxygen mask from an inside pocket of his jacket and twisted the T-jack's mike out of the way. He pressed the mask against his lower face and activated the electromagnetic seal. It pulsed and adhered itself to his flesh. The compressed air cylinders along his cheeks gave him a twenty-minute supply, more than enough time for what he had planned.

With a slight flex of his legs, he leaped up and pulled himself into the yawning mouth of the airshaft. He elbowed his way into the heating duct and crawled toward Aikman's office. Dust and debris billowed up around him, and he knew if he wasn't wearing the oxygen mask he wouldn't have been able to breathe without it filling his lungs.

The building was old, and the duct work provided enough space for him to move through at a constant pace. Gunshots sounded behind him as Vache engaged the perps.

Less than forty seconds later, Wilson was peering down through the duct in the ceiling over Aikman's desk. He drew the Delta Elite and tested the screws holding the duct in place. He guessed that he could easily knock it loose when it was time.

Aikman was inside the room with three Asians. No

one spoke. While Aikman went through hard-copy files
and tossed them onto a pile in the center of the open
floor, one man stood guard over him. Another man covered the door, and the remaining man was at the computer workstation in the corner. Screen after screen of
information bytes flashed on and disappeared as the
man stroked the keyboard.

Wilson peeled the oxygen mask away for a moment
and swiveled the T-jack mike down to his mouth.
"Rawley."

"Go."

"What kind of reading do you have on Aikman's
office?"

"I show four people, plus yourself." A special iden-
tify-friend-or-foe program was wedded to the thermal-
imaging scope. The IFF keyed off the Omega shields to
let anyone using sniper weapons know friendlies were
in the immediate area.

"Can you see the man on the door?"

"Affirmative."

"When I give you the word, drop him. We'll scramble on the others." He identified Aikman's position for
Rawley, knowing the FBI man would have the hardest
time keeping the accountant clear in the confusion.

"I'll be waiting on you."

Moving forward to position his weight in the best
place, Wilson slipped a smoke grenade free of his jacket
and armed it. "Now!" he said. His elbow came down
hard on the duct and sent it tumbling free.

The office window exploded inward, mirrored by
the guard's body slamming against the door as the big
.50-cal round impacted in the center of his neck at the
third vertebra. The sound of the shot took a beat to
catch up.

The heavy metal duct dropped into the floor. Wilson slid over the edge and followed it down. The smoke grenade left his fingers before his feet hit the carpet. He dropped and rolled, coming up in a semiprone position with the 10mm extended toward the man beside Aikman. Melded with the SeekNFire technology wired into his reflexes, Wilson squeezed off three rounds.

The first bullet caught the man's gun arm and snapped his pistol away just before an orange tongue of flame reached for the cowering accountant. The next two bullets drove the Asian into the cracked office window. Off balance and dying, he tried to right himself. The smoke grenade went off with a loud pop and unleashed a cloud of oily black smoke that filled the room in less than two seconds.

Raising the Delta Elite again, Wilson put two more rounds through the Asian's face. The man's head whipped back and he began the long fall to the pavement five stories below.

Aikman was screaming in terror, hunkering down beside filing cabinets and covering his head with his arms.

The night goggles were programmed to adjust to the special smoke and Wilson had no problem seeing. He sealed the oxygen mask back in place to save his lungs from the acrid smoke.

The fourth man came from the computer workstation and reached under his jacket for a weapon.

Wanting to take the man alive if he could, Wilson pushed himself to his feet. He could tell from the Asian man's reflexes that he could see through the smoke as well. Wilson launched a spinning side kick at the man's head. Bone-crushing force stopped him short as the man seized his foot in midkick, then yanked.

Wilson's shoulders hit the carpet. He twisted to look up as the man raised his pistol and pointed it at his face. Wrenching himself violently to the side, Wilson stamped out with his free foot and caught the man in the crotch.

The man groaned and slumped forward.

Twisting again, Wilson landed two rapid heel kicks that opened cuts on the man's face. His foot came free. Rocking back, he flipped himself to his feet, then ducked under his opponent's weapon and felt the heat of the muzzle flash burn his neck. Lashing out with his gun hand, he smashed the Delta Elite's barrel against the man's wrist. Bone broke in harsh snaps.

The pistol dropped. The perp screamed in pain and frustration.

Sidestepping the man's sudden rush, Wilson hammered out three quick blows to his face. The last one lost most of its force as it slid away over the film of blood coating the man's features. Turning after his opponent, Wilson seized the man by the neck and slammed him down to the ground. Wilson followed, landing with his knee in the man's back. Air hissed out of the man's lungs in a painful scream.

Leathering the 10mm, Wilson took out his handcuffs and tried securing the man's uninjured wrist. Sudden explosions scattered around the room knocked him off balance. Before he could move, the enormous strength granted by the endo-skel system allowed the man to surge up even though Wilson was on his back.

Fires blossomed into existence in four different places around the office. One of the explosions blew a file cabinet drawer across the room to imbed in the wall under a Norman Rockwell–print calendar. Another fire blazed from the computer workstation.

The man grabbed Wilson's wrist and pulled him from his back.

Wilson rolled with the throw and came to his feet facing the man. As he took his stance, he blocked a punch, grabbed the man's shirtfront, and fired a rapid series of bone-rattling knee kicks into the man's stomach. Once he was unconscious, it didn't matter if the perp had an endo-skel or not.

Feeling the burn of taxed muscles, grimly aware that the evidence he so desperately needed was probably being lost to flames, Wilson dragged the man's face down to meet his upcoming knee.

The impact was dulled, meaty. The man slid downward and didn't move again as Wilson cuffed his hands behind his back. The sound of approaching sirens came through the broken window.

"Slade." Maggie Scuderi stood in the doorway of the office, silhouetted by the flames racing up the walls in liquid pools. She had her pistol in front of her and was scanning the room.

"Get Aikman out of here," Wilson said, pointing. "He's in the corner."

Scuderi didn't waste words. She crossed the room, grabbed Aikman in a riot-control hold, and marched the accountant through the door.

Sprinting across the room, Wilson dragged the hard-drive system from the desk. Components scattered and bounced across the floor. Sparks shot out, bright and hard in the collected smoke. Triggering the spring holding the concealed Crain dagger, Wilson slashed the blade through the wiring connecting the hard drive to the rest of the system. It came free in his hand. Carbon had already blackened the surface, and the metal was hot to the touch. He wasn't sure if it could be salvaged at all.

The monitor blew with a popping hiss, and flying glass twinkled from the escaping sparks pouring from the unit's electronic guts.

"I'm activating the Kidde system now," Darnell January called out over the T-jack. A heartbeat later, white, puffy foam from the fire-suppression system filled the room. It was like being in a child's water-filled snow globe.

The foam left streaks across Wilson's goggles. He reached down and grabbed the unconscious man by his shirt collar, then dragged him from the room as flames rose higher and higher. The heat was searing. He doubted if the Kidde system would be able to save much.

"Slade," Rawley called out. "Hit the deck. Now!"

Wilson went down immediately. A blur of movement dropped from the ceiling above him. He released the hard drive and his prisoner as he went for his pistol. The Delta Elite came up automatically, but he knew it was going to be close as the Asian man raised his own machine pistol from a distance of less than ten feet. Whatever the outcome, he knew he was going to take some damage.

Then the wall exploded inward, scattering brick and mortar splinters. The Asian man jerked to one side as if he'd been hit by an invisible truck. As the body tumbled to the floor, Wilson saw there was almost no head left.

"Nearly missed the son of a bitch," Rawley transmitted. "Lost him in the confusion."

Wilson glanced at the grapefruit-sized hole the Barrett's 750-grain round had left in the wall. He shoved the oxygen mask out of his way and moved the mike forward. "I'm just glad you found him when you did."

Mac waded through the smoke and debris, followed by January. "We're clear here," Mac said. "Maggie's waiting by the elevator. It's still operational." He took the hard drive from Wilson's hand.

January easily picked up the unconscious prisoner and draped him over one broad shoulder. "We need to get a move on, people. The top of this structure is about to be swept by a firestorm. The fire department won't have much time to save the rest of the building."

Flaming timbers dropped in Aikman's office behind them.

Wilson nodded. "What about Vache?"

"He's with Maggie," January replied.

"Intact?"

"Standing. He looked okay."

Wilson kept his weapon in his hand as he jogged through the maze of hallways. Mac and January were close behind when he reached the elevator bank. Scuderi and Aikman stood inside; Scuderi had the doors blocked with a foot.

As soon as they were in, Scuderi withdrew her foot and thumbed the ground-level button. The cage dropped instantly while the fire-warning Klaxons shrilled overhead.

When the elevator doors opened again, they were on the ground floor, and yellow-slickered firemen were running in all directions. One of them came to a halt in front of the elevator holding a fire ax. His face was a dim shadow behind the glass plate of his oxygen mask. He waved a gloved hand. "You people get the hell out of here before the gas lines blow. Move!"

Wilson took control of Aikman and dragged the

accountant toward the door while the rest of the team followed him. Fire hoses as thick as Amazon pythons writhed across the floor as hose teams worked to set up a base in the lobby.

The air outside was instantly cooler.

Switching off the electromagnetic seal on the oxygen mask, Wilson dropped it into his pocket and swiveled the T-jack's mike forward. He blew to access the frequency, then switched it to the tach channel they'd set up with the state police. "Falcon, this is Redball."

"Go, Redball."

"How's your end of things?"

"Secure. We've got three people in custody, but one of them might not make it. Two more are dead. Once we found out they were wired with endo-skels, we didn't take any chances."

"Understood." Wilson cleared the channel and focused his attention on Aikman.

The accountant glared back at him nervously. "I want to thank you for saving my life up there. I think those guys were going to kill me."

Wilson stripped away his night goggles and let the man see his eyes. He reached into his pocket and flashed his ID. "Wilson. FBI. You're under arrest." He quickly read off the man's rights as a third fire truck joined the two in place in front of the Gresham building. A hook-and-ladder team was being elevated to the fifth floor. Splashing water rained out over the street, and steam clouds rose above the curling flames reaching for the night sky.

Aikman's face closed up. "I'm not talking till I see my attorney."

"We know about the jackal network," Wilson said. "And we know that you were laundering the money for the operation. We have a lead on Harry Prio, and that puts us that much closer to Sebastian DiVarco. Right now we're in a position to make a deal. If you wait too long, we'll make the deal somewhere else and you'll go down on accessory to murder charges."

A fire chief's red car came scrambling around a corner, lost traction for a moment, and skidded to a stop with one wheel up on the curb in front of the office building.

Aikman rubbed his chin and glanced at the hard drive Mac was holding. "To convict me of anything, you're going to need what's in that hard drive."

"We'll get it," Scuderi said, moving in to occupy the accountant's personal space.

Aikman took a step back. An uneasy sneer twisted his lips. "I'll take my chances in court and with your computer experts. Personally, I don't think you can retrieve anything from that unit. I could be wrong. If so, I'll go to jail. One thing I'm not going to do is cross somebody like DiVarco. Assuming you're right about me being involved and DiVarco ultimately being behind something like this. You saw the guys that came after me tonight. I can't say that I know what they were after—personally I think they just wanted the cash I keep in my office safe—but I can damn sure tell you I don't want anyone like them coming after me again. You understand? You feds aren't really noted for being able to keep witnesses alive these days."

Wilson turned away from the man. "Get him out of here."

Scuderi nodded and shoved the accountant toward one of the state police cars that was parked outside the cordoned-off area set up by the fire department.

Media vans and four-wheel drives drove up to the

edge of the crime-scene perimeter being enforced by the yellow-slickered firemen and the uniformed Atlanta police department. A hundred people in various stages of night dress had turned out from the nearby residential sector to see what was going on. Mac, January, and Rawley left quickly.

"Let's blow this pop stand." Vache turned to Wilson. "You're not going to get anything further here."

"Hey," a feminine voice shouted. "Over here."

Wilson glanced up and saw a trim brunette with striking features leading a camcorder crew to intercept him.

"Agent Wilson," the woman called out, dodging a red-and-white-striped sawhorse and ducking under the yellow tape put up by the Atlanta PD. "I'm Wrenne Phillips, Station Eight Action Headlines. Could I have a few words with you?" She was dressed in a red skirt-and-blouse ensemble designed to capture viewer interest even if the audio portion of the telecast was suddenly lost. Her silver filigree earrings dangled past her short-cropped hair.

"No comment," Wilson replied, making his way to the car Mac had waiting.

"To what degree was the FBI's Omega Blue unit involved in the outbreak of violence that shook this neighborhood only moments ago?"

"No comment." A uniformed cop moved out of Wilson's way. Before he could pass through, Phillips grabbed his arm.

The newscaster dropped the hand mike to her side. "Give me a break here, tough guy. I'm just a girl trying to do her job."

"Then give me the same courtesy," Wilson replied in a level voice.

"Give me the story."

"Your story's with Captain Frank Burleson of the state police."

"Damnit, Wilson, Omega Blue has a higher interest quotient than the local cop shop. If you give me the interview, there could be audio and video bytes of you and me across the whole country by morning." Over her shoulder, the camcorder operator was zooming in for close-ups.

The spray of harsh light stung Wilson's eyes as he gently disengaged the woman's fist from his jacket. "No comment," he said evenly. He showed her his back and walked away.

"You son of a bitch." Phillips said. She paused only a moment. Then a cry went out that a body had been found in the alley. Her voice was strident as she ordered her camera crew into action before the police and fire department could seal the alley.

"You should have given her the story," Vache said as he fell into step beside Wilson.

"What story?" Wilson asked. "We don't have proof of anything I could have told her."

"You could have worked around that."

"Look, Earl, I'm a federal agent, not a goddamn politician. I earn my keep by bringing people like Sebastian DiVarco down, not by pandering to the public."

"Yeah, but the public puts the pressure on the politicians who can make your job harder or easier. You need to keep that in mind."

"When I get something she and I can both use, then I'll give her the story. If I have time. Until then, if I start dodging the issues she'll bring up, DiVarco is going to know we don't have zip. I want him on his toes so

he'll be more apt to make a mistake. I want him listening for footsteps." Wilson moved away before Vache
could bring up any further arguments. He considered
what his next steps were going to be, but most of that
depended on what Sebastian DiVarco chose to do in retaliation.

CHAPTER 6

Sebastian DiVarco reached across the curvaceous redhead seated beside him in the back of the stretch limousine and punched in the code that unsealed the armored door. It rose, gull-fashion, with a pneumatic hiss. "Here you are, babe," he said. "Curb-to-curb service just like I promised." His right hand was never far from the Detonics Janus Scoremaster .45 ACP holstered on his hip.

Two bodyguards who had been trailing the luxury car in another vehicle trotted into place on either side of the open door. Before them, the charcoal gray awning ran the length of the red carpet leading into the glittering lobby of the Boston Ritz-Carlton.

Alyssa LaRocca leaned forward and put her hands on either side of his face. She gave him a champagne-stained kiss that raised his blood level. "You sure you won't come up for awhile, lover?"

"Can't." DiVarco gently pulled the woman's hands from his face, then delicately kissed her fingers. "Got some business to take care of before morning. Maybe afterward I could come by, wake you up, and show you a whole new day."

"I'd like that."

"Me too. Now scram. I'm on a tight schedule here." It was true. He'd already cut into the safety margin he'd figured for the trip from the Back Bay area to the North End by five minutes. Traveling across Boston was only slightly easier in the predawn hours than during business hours. The Massachusetts Bay Transportation Authority rapid transit lines shut down at one A.M., leaving only private traffic and cabs on the streets. It was during those hours that DiVarco scheduled a lot of his financial dealings.

She made a show of getting out of the car, as if she were trying to make sure the black spandex minidress covered her modestly. It made the flash of white bikini panties and garters underneath even more tantalizing. Once outside the luxury vehicle, she smoothed everything back into place. Her breasts were high, white, and firm. At twenty-one, she was almost ten years DiVarco's junior. She had good thighs, too. He'd decided most women didn't take care of their thighs these days. It was worth the wait to find one who did.

"Just make sure you come see me," she said. "I'll make it worth your while."

DiVarco couldn't keep the smile from his face. It was the same one his mother used to be so proud of, and the one that Aunt Rosina said was full of devilment just before she pinched his cheek. "Carmichael," DiVarco said.

"Yes, Mr. DiVarco."

"We're burning gasoline here."

"Yes, sir." The chauffeur tucked his hat under his arm and raced for the driver's seat.

Keying the security panel again, DiVarco closed the door and listened to the seal hiss as it became gas-proof. He picked up the remote control from the magnetic plate on the wet bar and aimed it at the blank section in front. A beveled panel slid away to reveal a television screen. He flicked another switch and the screen came on. He saw a picture of himself sitting in the rear seat as the image was relayed through the closed-circuit system carefully artificed into the limo's opulence. He leaned forward to see himself more clearly.

Tonight he wore black leather pants, an aqua silk pullover, and a black leather jacket with fringes hanging off the back, waist, and arms. Black-on-black Air Jordans covered his feet. His dark hair was pulled back in a tight ponytail that emphasized the severe widow's peak on his forehead. He'd gotten his beak of a nose from his father, but his cobalt blue eyes were a legacy from his mother's Irish ancestry. At six four, two hundred and twenty pounds, he stood straight and tall and worked at carrying around an air of defiance. Scars covered his knuckles, bits of the past that proved he'd worked his way up through his own resources and intelligence.

"Mr. DiVarco, Mr. Magaddino would like to come aboard."

DiVarco grinned. The chauffeur always talked about the limo like it was some kind of ship. "Let him."

The limousine stopped on Tremont Street across from the Old Granary Burial Ground.

Deliberately not looking over his shoulder at the car that had parked behind him, DiVarco studied the rolling hill of the cemetery. No one in there was buried later than the eighteenth century. He remembered summers spent there in his teen years, breaking into the mausoleums and slipping through the low, narrow tunnels smugglers had built during the years before the American Revolution. Once, he and his buddies had surprised a group of college students swapping ghost stories and sent them screaming into the alleys. He smiled at the memory. It hadn't been until years later that he realized the H. P. Lovecraft they'd been talking about had actually lived in Boston.

Sal Magaddino's robust shadow fell across the bulletproof glass of the window. DiVarco leaned over and keyed the door's security and the door rose out of the way. Seating himself with a sigh of relief, Magaddino offered his hand.

DiVarco took it reverently and kissed the black stone of the man's ring. "Don Magaddino, friend of my father, how may I help you?"

"I came to talk, Sebastian." The old man was fat; flesh hung from his jowls in loose folds. He wore a long coat and a snap-brim hat that had been his trademark.

"I always enjoy talking with you, but I am engaged in some business now."

"With Jimmy Gioia?"

The winning smile on DiVarco's face almost collapsed but he saved it. "It seems too much of my business is leaking out onto the streets. I'll have to take care of that."

"I've heard this from no one." Magaddino tapped his temple. "You forget, before life dealt me this aged body, I was once a young man of vision myself. I've been watching you. I knew it was only a matter of time before you dealt with Gioia."

"Will you ride with me? I'm pressed for time."

"Of course." Magaddino waved to his bodyguards and they dropped back to their own vehicle.

DiVarco pressed the intercom button. "Roll it, Carmichael."

The limo cruised back out into the street.

"What did you want to talk about?" DiVarco asked.

"Your great expectations."

DiVarco looked at the older man in perplexity.

"It's from a book," Magaddino explained. "A very old book by Charles Dickens that deals with a young man on the threshold of a very promising life. It reminds me of you these days."

"This book does? Maybe I should pay more attention to novels. The last one I read was *The Horny Librarian's Feather Duster*."

"Don't try to con me, Sebastian. I knew your father. I knew you when you were a little boy. You were never satisfied with your lot in life. That's why you were the source of your father's pride, and the answer to your mother's broken dreams. You've studied. Maybe not at college, but I know you've hired tutors over the years. You may not have a college degree, but you've had the training. This act you trot out for the other people, it don't work for me. You want them to think you're only street smart. But I know better."

"All my life," DiVarco said, "the people in this city have told me I was a punk, that I was going to die in the gutter like my old man. In the next couple of weeks, I'm going to show them they were wrong."

The limo came to a brief stop at the intersection. When the light changed, it took a right and headed west toward State Street, passing the Old State House, where the Declaration of Independence was read from a balcony to the citizens of Boston in 1776.

"Is that what this is all about?" Magaddino asked. "Showing these people that they were wrong about you?"

"It's about power, Don Magaddino." DiVarco clenched his hand into a fist. "I'm taking it away from the weak and giving it to the strong. I'm giving it to me."

"And Jimmy Gioia? Does he know you are coming to kill him?"

DiVarco smiled. "My old friend, Jimmy? No. He thinks I am coming to make him a part of this thing."

"But you aren't?"

"Hell no. He's a crackhead, addicted to his own product. He's of no use to anyone. Tonight I'm going to deal him out."

"When you were boys, on your way up in the families, Jimmy would have died for you."

"I'm going to let him tonight."

"And you feel no remorse?"

"No. When I was a boy, my father told it to me straight. So did you. When it comes time for a man to take action, there can be no second thoughts, no weakness. I've made myself strong. Even though the families won't recognize it, I'm a capo in this city, a man to be dealt with. I intend to be crown prince before I'm through."

"The families won't stand for it."

"Did they send you here to tell me that?" DiVarco demanded.

"No. I came of my own accord, because of the small boy I used to know. And because of a promise I made to your father to look out for you."

"I don't need anyone to look out for me."

"Then look out better for yourself, Sebastian. The moves you are making, they have made the families nervous. Soon, I'm afraid, there will be talk of retribution against you."

"Take a message back to those old men, Don Magaddino. Tell them that any man who makes a move against Sebastian DiVarco is a dead man, and the day they do it, they can carve the date on their gravestone themselves. Tell them that for me."

"Those are harsh words."

"Fuck it! I've been fighting those old men all my life. I had to carve out every piece of territory I have from the black gangs and the Jamaicans, people those old men were too terrified to take on. I bled for what I have. They won't take it away from me, or get me to be satisfied with anything less than what I want."

"And will you fight me too?"

DiVarco tried to read the older man but couldn't. He answered honestly. "I would never raise a hand to you, Don Magaddino. Nor to your family."

The old man nodded.

"They are keeping up with you more these days," Magaddino said. "An hour after the jackal network in Atlanta was busted by the FBI, people knew about it."

DiVarco turned his palms up. "That's nothing. It'll never be traced back to me. Steps have already been taken to prevent that."

"This man Wilson who is the SAC of Omega Blue is known as a fighter. He plays just as rough as his opponents do."

"He's never come up against someone like me. If he does, I'll have him buried under one of the wharves.

When they count noses later, they'll come up one FBI guy short."

Magaddino looked at DiVarco. "There is another thing I must ask you."

"What?"

"Rumor has it that you are working with foreigners. A group of Asians, and that they have helped you in your rise. This has never been our way."

"I've learned to do things my way."

"Sebastian, you should know you can't trust these people. Only blood can truly trust blood."

"My blood turned away from me. I was Drago DiVarco's only son. But you, friend of my father, did not turn from me. He was the man so many of you turned to in times of trouble. When Don Accardo's daughter ran away with that Iranian and pretended to be kidnapped to blackmail her father for money for them, who did they call? When the Rizzuto family was killed by those three black hijackers in the restaurant they'd managed for years for Don Vendemini, who did they call? My father. He died for them."

"And they respected him for that. That is a high thing in this life."

"Respect didn't put bread and meat on the table for my mother and me. She took in laundry and made her own way, became an old woman overnight."

"Your mother, God rest her soul, was a proud woman. She never approved of your father's trade. She refused offers from the families to help her out. Still, we did what we could."

"They ignored me when I became a man."

"You were headstrong, irresponsible. There were many things the families felt you still had to learn."

Anger made DiVarco's voice tight. "I've learned

those things now. And I've learned that I no longer need the families. Let them hang onto whatever they can for as long as they can. Perhaps I will feel generous."

"Sebastian, you may be writing your own death warrant."

"That was written the day I was born." DiVarco pressed the intercom button. "Carmichael, stop the car."

The limo slid to a stop at the corner of Richmond Street and North Street.

"You'll have to excuse me," DiVarco said. "I have business to attend to."

The old man allowed one of his bodyguards to assist him in getting out of the car. He didn't turn around to say good-bye, just squared his shoulders and walked to his waiting car.

The limo moved back into the line of traffic.

Jimmy Gioia's crack house was masked in shadows that were as much a part of the waterfront district as the stink of fish, diesel engines, and the throb of forklifts trundling around on the wooden and concrete wharves. Four stories tall, it hunkered between the taller warehouses like a glass-and-mortar dwarf. The cracked facade hid the steel armor underneath, and a steel mesh hurricane fence ran around the outer perimeter, providing a small parking lot in front. The lot was empty. Even though the security lights weren't working, DiVarco knew he was being observed. He could feel the eyes on him, and he was aware that Gioia maintained infrared security cameras.

Business was conducted strictly on a cash-and-carry basis from the north and south sides of the building. Gioia's cover was thin. A video rental club occupied the north side of the lower floor, and a beep-and-buy convenience store operated on the south side. Transactions were made through the windows, and both businesses were always open. During the day they had only a trickle of customers, but at night, between the hours of one A.M. and five A.M., those businesses flourished.

DiVarco had assigned accountants and information brokers to Gioia's enterprise after finding that his own drug suppliers were undergoing stiff competition. Little Jimmy Gioia, the thick slab of muscle whose only claim to fame as a teenager had been the ability to slam his big-knuckled fists through door panels without injury, had become very shrewd in his drug dealings. The crack house netted three million dollars during a decent month. The only drawback that DiVarco had discovered was Gioia's love for his own product.

He checked his watchband and made sure the transmitter was on. "Everybody out there ready to rock and roll?"

The watch pulsed against the underside of his wrist.

"All right," he said as he keyed the door open, "it's show time." He got out of the car in the middle of the parking lot with his hands spread to his sides. A glance at the north and south streets showed business booming as buyers moved through in cars, on bicycles and skateboards, and on their own two feet.

Armed men were visible at different points along the fire escape and windows. Two vans, their tires bulging under the weight of the armor plating, occupied key positions along the street.

"Okay, Carmichael, show them the lights."

The limo's lights flashed on and off three times in quick succession. In response, four men came from a side door and approached DiVarco. Two of them held Mossberg riot guns.

"Mr. DiVarco?" one of the men said. He was young and hard, and had a Snoopy tattoo on the side of his neck that drew even more attention to the old knife scar showing there.

DiVarco nodded.

"Mr. Gioia said to bring you on up."

"Let's do it."

"I got to take your piece."

"Go for it." DiVarco raised his hands and put them on his head.

The bodyguard reached under the leather jacket and took the Detonics Scoremaster away. "Anything else?"

"No." DiVarco followed the man into the crack house. Steel doors slammed shut behind him. They took a flight of stairs up to the second floor and were checked through by a group of security techs manning state-of-the-art equipment.

The head bodyguard laid his palms on panels on either side of the door. There was a hum, then a click, and the door slid away.

The room DiVarco was led into was eighty feet square. A conference table took up one third of the space at the far end. A pool table complete with swag lamps took up the middle half, along with a wet bar sporting operational pull taps against one wall. A neon light declaring BAR'S OPEN hung over the mirror behind the bar. The leftover space in the nearest corner had been used for a built-in recreation center. A large-screen television was surrounded by a stereo and two other televisions. Two pit groups with matching color schemes in indigo and violet were arranged in front of the entertainment wall.

Jimmy Gioia lounged on the pit group facing the entrance. He wore a red satin smoking jacket that hung awkwardly on his barrel chest. Light sparkled from the diamond chip earrings that ran up his left ear from lobe to tip. His blond hair was trimmed close, with razor-styled hash marks at his temples. Another ten pounds and he'd have been well on his way to going to seed. "Sebastian, come into the house, my man." He got up off the plush furnishings with more effort than would have been required less than two years ago.

"Jimmy G.," DiVarco said with a smile. "I see you haven't let success go to your head."

"You were always the one who understood elegant. Me, I prefer something that I can live with and be comfortable." Gioia picked the remote control up from an end table and muted the baseball game on the big screen. "Hey, Vincenzo, get my pal a brewski."

One of the bodyguards crossed the room to the bar. The one with the Snoopy tattoo stayed put with his hands clasped at waist level.

DiVarco surveyed the head bodyguard again and saw emptiness in the man's eyes. It was a good trait for a guy in his position to have.

"Don't mind him." Gioia dismissed the bodyguard with a wave. "That's Myron, my head bodycock. Guy has nerves of steel but worries like my grandma. C'mere and let me show you this."

DiVarco followed the drug lord to the bar.

Gioia touched the brass-plated spigots while Vincenzo took down two mugs. "Reminds you of old man Piromalli, don't it? Well, that's where I got 'em. When he went bust a few years back his old lady put 'em in storage. I found out about it and bought 'em. Helps me remember all those good times we used to have hanging out there and figuring out where we were going to steal our next dollar." His eyes glittered. "I remember those times like they was yesterday. You planning stuff and me covering your back while we pulled it off. We never should of split up, you know."

"I know." DiVarco glanced at his watch. Three minutes remained.

"I understand why you ditched me," Gioia said. "I spent some years cussing you out and bitching about it, but I understand. Not many guys can handle the drugs I do and still handle their business too."

"That's true."

"But I showed 'em. I showed 'em all. Made it to the top of one of the toughest rackets in the city. Had to chase out the Japs and the blacks and the Rastafarians to do it, but I got it done. And I'm enlarging the operation. It'll be doubled by this time next year." Gioia reached out and tapped DiVarco on the chest with his palm. "But look at you. God, you come in here looking like a million bucks. Tan. Bet you ain't put on five pounds."

"Jimmy G., this isn't all a social call," DiVarco reminded the bigger man.

Gioia waved him back to the pit groups. "I want you to know I was really sorry about that action in Haymarket Square. I didn't know that was you."

"I didn't advertise."

Gioia sat. "I knew you had the young exec action sewed up in the financial district, but I didn't know you'd moved into Haymarket Square. When I sent my boys in there to rough up the movers and the shakers, I had no idea they belonged to you."

"It's okay. That's old business. We're here to talk about new business."

"Sure, sure. I'm willing to give you a fair price for the area, but you're gonna have to work out payments with me."

"We can work it out." DiVarco watched the security cameras scanning the video and convenience stores. If the police department could have tapped into the electronic feed lines, they could have made the biggest bust the city had ever known in a single night. Whether by luck or design, Gioia had turned the drug action into one of the biggest cash cows in Boston. And it was all in liquid assets that only needed a little laundering before they could be invested in something else.

"You don't want the dope action anyway," Gioia said. "A guy like you, starting to move in the socially elite part of this city, you don't need to get your hands dirty with something like this."

DiVarco nodded.

"The day my guys busted up your action in Haymarket Square, I was doing you a favor."

DiVarco's watch pulsed against his wrist. He smiled broadly. "Yeah. A favor."

"Want to watch the ball game for awhile? The Tokyo Tigers are wailing the hell out of the Seahawks. Only the bottom of the third, and—" Gioia sat bolt upright and stared at the security monitors. "What the hell?"

On-screen, black-clad Asian men worked behind the scenes taking out the armed guards in the video rental and convenience stores. Silenced pistols bucked in black-gloved fists as they moved through in precision order. The buyers still weren't allowed to view the carnage; a maze of walls shutting the businesses off from one another was used as cover. Men stripped uniforms from dead bodies and took the places of the clerks working the windows. Before the original clerks could say or do anything, they were taken out of the rooms at gunpoint and executed.

"You son of a bitch!" Gioia roared. "You set me up!" He surged to a standing position, his body swaying dangerously. "You're working with the gooks!"

"Sit down, Jimmy G.," DiVarco said. "And maybe you'll live."

"You're a fucking dead man. I don't listen to corpses." Gioia glanced at his bodyguards. The action on the security monitors was slowing down. "Myron, waste this fucker."

Calmly, Myron reached under his jacket and pulled a Glock-17. He spun with the pistol in his hand and shot the other two guards before they had a chance to defend themselves.

"Myron," DiVarco said coolly, "doesn't work for you anymore." He took a pair of leather gloves from his pocket and pulled them on.

With a roar of rage, fueled by the cocaine coursing through him, Gioia lowered his head and threw himself at DiVarco.

Not bothering to get up from the pit group, DiVarco reached out and grabbed a handful of Gioia's hair. He slid to one side on the couch and controlled the bigger man's headlong plunge.

Gioia smacked into the pit group, bellowing like a wounded bull. The furniture went over in a flurry of throw pillows.

Coming to his feet with the lithe grace of a dancer, DiVarco waved at Myron to put his gun away. The bodyguard did, stepping back from the immediate area.

"You'd be better off having him kill me!" Gioia screamed. "I'm going to break you in half!"

DiVarco flashed the man a tight-lipped grin. He felt good about what was coming as he watched Gioia push himself to his feet and prepare for another lunge.

"I kicked your ass when we were kids," Gioia said, stripping away his smoking jacket and shirt. "Then I spent years making sure nobody else did it."

"That was a long time ago, Jimmy G. Ain't nobody kicked my ass in years. And you aren't man enough to do the job anymore."

Gioia threw himself forward.

DiVarco blocked the big man's arms with a forearm sweep, then brought up a roundhouse kick that caught Gioia on the side of his face. Amazingly, the big man didn't go down. Blood seeped from a cut over his eye, then trickled down past his nose and bleeding mouth. Evading Gioia's grab, DiVarco planted a flurry of punches into the big man's midsection that took Gioia's breath away. As Gioia started to sag, DiVarco caught his arm, spun and set a hip, and pulled the big man over it. DiVarco kept hold of his wrist until bone snapped.

Gioia went down and landed hard on his back.

Looking down at him, DiVarco adjusted his leather jacket. He wasn't even breathing hard. "Times change, Jimmy G. I think your ass-kicking days are over. You should have come in with me like I asked."

"The way Bonnelli and Tracana did? Screw you, Sebastian. You didn't leave those guys nothin'. They busted their asses for what they had, and you took it from them by selling out to those goddamn gooks."

"I didn't sell out. It was just business."

"Once they have everything they want, they'll shell you like a peanut."

"We'll see." DiVarco motioned to the silent body-guard. Myron tossed him the Detonics Janus Scoremaster. Catching it one-handed, DiVarco flicked the safety off and pointed it at Gioia's head. "Good-bye, Jimmy G."

"I'll see you in hell, you bas—"

The gunshot cut off his words, and the heavy round slammed his head back against the floor. His eyes rolled up, as if contemplating the hole that had suddenly appeared in his forehead.

DiVarco sheathed the .45 and turned to Myron. "When my people get here, have them take this garbage out and dump it. I want a team in here tearing this pimp's paradise down, and I want an office that I can live with standing in this spot by tomorrow night."

"Sure thing, Mr. DiVarco."

"And tell the accountants I want a meeting with them concerning the books on this operation at two P.M. tomorrow."

Myron nodded.

DiVarco headed for the door. His own security people were waiting in the hallway to escort him to his car. He moved confidently across the parking lot, breathing in the night air. He thought about his next project. With the destruction of the jackal network in Atlanta, DiVarco was no longer willing to take interference from Omega Blue lightly. His partners were going to have to pony up to help put Wilson and his group out of the way. Otherwise, DiVarco intended to handle that job himself.

CHAPTER 7

Slade Wilson was pouring himself a coffee refill when he heard the door open and close behind him. He put the coffeepot away and turned to face the man he knew would be standing there. "Quinn Valentine."

"Yes, sir." Valentine was five ten and maybe one seventy. His hair was dark and curly and hung in ringlets down the back of his neck, offsetting his olive complexion. He was dressed in navy sweatpants and a V-necked watermelon-colored sleeveless sweatshirt that hung loosely on him and showed sweat stains. His feet were bare. A short gold chain glinted at his neck.

"Have a seat." Wilson waved to one of the chairs around the oval table in the center of the room. They'd taken a free office from the behavioral science section on one of the underground floors of the Academy in

Quantico. The Omega Blue unit didn't have set quarters. That was one of the rules Wilson had introduced when they formed the strike team. No headquarters meant no files to be rifled or destroyed or tampered with.

Not many agents hung around the behavioral science section. The monster hunters lurked there, the people responsible for tracking down serial killers and rapists, who preyed on the helpless, young, and infirm. The rooms were littered with the grisly remains of investigations, photographs of countless victims. No one walked away untouched.

Valentine sat, his eyes never leaving Wilson's.

Wilson was sure, though, that the young man had taken in the presence of the other members of the unit with his peripheral vision. "I assume you didn't have time to dress before this meeting, or was it that you figured you didn't need to?"

Valentine nodded at the manila folder that lay in the middle of the conspicuously empty desktop. "You have my file right there, sir. You knew I was in the gym, and you're the one who wanted me in here immediately."

Sipping his coffee, Wilson walked behind the desk, forcing the young agent to follow him and putting the rest of the team out of sight. It was a move designed to make Valentine self-conscious. "According to your schedule, you were off this morning."

"I work out at the gym every morning at seven A.M.," Valentine replied, "when I don't have morning classes. You have that in your file as well."

"You think I keep notes that good?"

"I know you do. I broke into your files and made sure you had an accurate schedule for me."

"When?"

"This morning. About two A.M. After I found out about Newkirk."

Wilson tried to control his irritation. He'd managed a little sleep on the private charter back from Atlanta, but nothing that had made a dent in his fatigue. He felt as though sandpaper had been glued to his eyelids. "I'd say that was pretty callous, Agent Valentine."

"No. I'm a realist, with a little ambition thrown in."

"Maybe with a lot of ambition thrown in." Wilson set his coffee cup down and flipped open the folder. "You've been at the top of your class consistently since you've been at the Academy. You're an overachiever."

"I work hard to be damn good at what I do. That's not overachieving."

"Why do you work so hard?"

"I work hard because I want to be good."

"You could go out into the field and become one of the best agents this Academy ever turned out." Wilson tapped the folder. "At least that's what this file says. Yet you applied from the beginning to be part of Omega Blue. Why?"

"Did anyone ever ask you bullshit questions about why you were as good as you were? I researched your files. You were near the top of your class when you graduated too."

"Near the top," Wilson repeated. "Not *the* top. You're too aggressive."

"I'd call busting a jackal network with only six people pretty aggressive."

"You weren't there. You can't call it anything."

Valentine's jawline tightened. "Yes, sir."

"You've got a juvenile record for assault and battery in Los Angeles that you didn't report when you applied for the Academy."

"I wasn't required to report it. Those records are supposed to be sealed."

"Those records were sealed," Wilson said. "But your neighbors' mouths weren't."

"You had someone canvass my neighborhood?"

"It may interest you to know that not everything I do is logged in the personal files of my computer. I can't afford for it to be. And I knew you were rummaging around in there four months ago. Remember the test scores that I 'accidently' transposed? I can give you the day and time, and the location where you were when you changed them back. The scores I changed were only a matter of a few points, nothing that would affect your ability to be considered for this unit. Yet you changed them back. It told me something about you." Wilson ticked off points on his fingers. "First, you're aggressive. Second, you're conceited. Third, you don't trust the system. And fourth, you're good at what you do."

Valentine remained silent, but his dark eyes showed that he was trying to work out exactly where he stood.

Wilson didn't let up. "How old are you?"

"Twenty-four."

Taking a seat beside the thin folder on the desktop, Wilson sipped his coffee again. It was significant that Valentine hadn't pointed out that his age was listed in the file. Eventually the young agent had realized there was no give and take to this interview on his part—only give. Behind Valentine, the rest of the team watched. Later, they'd have a chance to express their own views. Each of them—with the exception of Lee

Rawley—had been through the same drill. Rawley had been a gut call on surface evaluation alone. "What's your name?"

"Valentine, Quinn Michael."

"Not what you call yourself now. Your given name."

An angry blush stained Valentine's features. "Mique Valentas."

"When did you change it?"

"When I was eighteen."

"Why?"

"Personal reasons."

"You had two brothers in street gangs. Your oldest brother, Tito, was the leader of the East L.A. Warbirds. Clemente, also older than you, was a captain of the Midnight Rush."

"If you know that, you also know they're dead. This is history. Why are you digging it up?"

"This is you. If you're going to be up for this position, I need to know you. Where's your father?"

"I don't know."

"He left your mother."

"When I was fourteen. My brothers were already involved in the gangs."

"You worked to help support your mother?"

"And put myself through school."

"You graduated at the top of your class in high school in spite of that, and with honors from city university."

"Yeah."

"And you want to tell me you're not an over-achiever?"

"No. I just work hard."

Wilson paused a beat. "Where's your mother?"

"Here in D.C. with me. I brought her out after I was accepted into the Academy."

"Why?"

"I didn't want to see her die in that pisshole of a neighborhood."

"What did she say when you changed your name?"

"That's none of your business."

"But she didn't approve."

"That's not a subject for this conversation."

"Even if it means blowing this interview?"

Valentine erupted out of his seat. "Hey, fuck you, man! You're not going to come in here with any kind of bullshit and expect to blow me away when I got a chance at this. You got a legitimate reason to can me from this unit, trot it out and let's take a look at it."

"You're getting emotional."

"What I'm getting is tired of being fucked with. Ask me about my quals and training. Let's get this interview back in the arena where it's supposed to be."

"All right." Wilson closed the folder and picked it up. "It also says that you're a black belt in Tae Kwon Do. Can you defend yourself?"

"Against anyone in this room," Valentine said defiantly.

"Mac," Wilson said.

At the back of the room, Mac stood. He wore a fresh blue suit, but his shirt was unbuttoned and his tie dangled from a pocket. "Yeah."

Wilson looked at Valentine. "Try to subdue him."

"What if I hurt him?"

"You won't."

Valentine adjusted his clothing and shoved the table out of the center of the floor. Mac remained at his end of the room. January, Scuderi, and Rawley lined the opposite, their expressions neutral.

Wilson remained seated at the desk. He was tense, ready to move if things didn't happen the way he'd choreographed them to. Valentine was still a cipher of unknown and heated passions.

Valentine set himself and brought his hands up to defend himself. A cruel smile twisted his lips. "C'mon, old man, let's see what you've got."

"Sure, kid." In a smooth motion, Mac reached under his jacket and pulled out a gleaming silver pistol. He didn't bother to aim, just pointed and fired. Three liquid spitting noises filled the room.

Valentine tried to dodge, but two brilliant lime-green bursts of color dotted his chest, while a third materialized between his eyes and trickled down through his eyebrows.

"You're dead," Wilson stated. For a moment he thought Valentine was going to throw himself at Mac anyway; he braced himself to intercede.

Then Valentine visibly relaxed and turned to face him.

"Any questions, Agent Valentine?" Wilson asked.

"No, sir."

Wilson stood up and approached him. "Besides being something of an aggressive overachiever with a chip on his shoulder, you're overly confident of your own abilities. This unit is a team effort. Any attempts at being top dog in this outfit when an operation goes down will ensure that you end up as a one-night stand. If you don't get yourself killed, I'll bounce you off the team anyway." He paused to let his words sink in. With the facts he'd presented in the last few minutes, he knew Valentine was receptive but probably also felt a little like retaliating. "The only reason you're here now is because another man is dead. You need to keep that in mind."

"Yes, sir." Though the words were there, Wilson heard no regret in his voice.

Handing the manila folder over to the young agent, Wilson said, "As for your file being in here, it isn't. These are permission forms for the Walter Reed staff to perform the SeekNFire operations on you later today. You're scheduled for one o'clock. It's a six-hour surgery, but you'll be back on your feet by tomorrow morning. The hardware takes a little getting used to. I wish I had time to let you work your way into it, but I don't. Everybody on this team gets a crash course. You'll have most of tomorrow, but that's all."

"Yes, sir."

"I'm sure you think you're a quick study, but sometimes the SeekNFire doesn't take. You'll know within a few hours."

Valentine nodded. He made no effort to remove the paint stains on his forehead.

"Maggie."

Scuderi turned to Wilson.

"You're in charge of our new guy. Debrief him today about current operations and the team before the trip to Walter Reed. Once he goes under, you're on your own. Report back to the hospital at oh-eight-hundred hours tomorrow for the SeekNFire follow-up."

"I'll be there."

"Any questions now, Valentine?"

"I'll make a list as I go along."

"Do that. You people are dismissed until tomorrow morning." Wilson grabbed his jacket and led the way out the door. He felt Valentine's angry stare boring into the back of his neck all the way down the hallway.

"I had to let them go," Vache said.

"When?" Wilson demanded. He leaned across the liaison's desk and tried to curb his feelings of frustration. It was more important to understand than to lash out. They hadn't had time to interrogate the Asians in Atlanta, and he'd wanted to sit on that angle of the investigation for a little while before the media got hold of it.

"Ten, fifteen minutes ago." Vache remained calm behind his desk. Paperwork and clipboards littered the space in front of him and around his computer. "You were busy with Valentine and I chose not to interrupt. There wasn't a damn thing you could have done about it anyway. And I didn't need a goddamn international incident right here in my office."

"They couldn't have bonded out. Charges hadn't even been filed against them yet."

"They didn't bond out. A Korean ambassador showed up an hour ago with all the proper papers. Those guys are supposed to be part of the Korean Embassy staff. He acted surprised as hell that they'd be involved in shoot-outs in the streets of Atlanta. He also told me that as soon as he found out why those guys were there, he'd get back to me."

"He got them out on diplomatic immunity?"

"Yeah."

"What was this guy's name?"

"Look, Slade, this guy's a guy you definitely have got to stay away from. He had the director ready to shit sixteen-penny nails."

Exhaling deeply, Wilson turned from the desk and gazed at the familiar walls of Vache's office. Framed pictures of Vache with various Justice officials, as well as several presidents, over the years took places of prominence, along with the law degrees he'd garnered since moving out of field work. They were there to impress and intimidate first-time visitors to Vache's office. Wilson knew where to look for the real Vache. A half-dozen pictures were tucked around the room where the liaison could see them easily. Most of them were of Vache's family, small five-by-sevens of Vache at home with his wife and fishing with his three boys.

"I know how you feel." Vache reached for the electric coffeepot behind him. "Coffee?"

"No. I've had my limit." Wilson felt a pang of guilt as he stared at the spot where the picture of Blair and himself with a smiling Vache between them had been.

There was a new picture on the wall now, and he couldn't remember when Vache had placed it there. In it Kasey was five, a squirming bundle in Wilson's arms, with dark hair like her mother. Neither one of them was smiling. The pang of guilt blossomed into a sweet ache, and Wilson had to look away.

"So how did Valentine take the news?" Vache asked. "Turn any cartwheels, any cries of exuberant glee?"

"Actually, he's pretty much pissed with me. How do the Koreans fit into this?"

"I don't know. What's Valentine pissed about?"

"I think I disenchanted him."

"You're developing a real habit of doing that to people."

"This ambassador you talked to, did you get a feel for him?"

"Some."

"Did he feel like embassy staff?"

"No."

"Then what?"

Vache laced his hands behind his head. "He came in here, and his eyes were everywhere. I got the feeling he knew the names of my kids, could have pointed them out in the pictures and told me Carson was left-handed and wanted to play professional hockey when he grew up."

"Any explanation as to how he knew those people would be here?"

"No."

"And he didn't mention that the embassy staff had noticed they'd gone AWOL?"

"No."

"What about the weapons they were using in Atlanta? Has anything turned up on those yet?"

Vache flipped over a piece of paper covered with scribbling and gazed over the jotted information. "They're from a cache stolen from Fort Benning six months ago."

"What about NCIC records on the Koreans?"

"Nothing turned up. As far as NCIC, InterPol, or the terrorist tracking network are concerned. I even had them run through the foreign-fugitive files. Nothing. They're clean."

"Then where's the connection between DiVarco, who used to be nothing but small change in the Boston Mafia, and a hit team connected with the Korean Embassy and outfitted with endo-skels?"

"You're talking about an international conspiracy," Vache pointed out. "Any unsubstantiated accusations coming from you could lead to your dismissal."

Wilson looked at the man. "That sounds official."

"That's how it came down to me just a few minutes ago. Almost word for word."

"And—officially—what is Omega Blue supposed to do?"

"Keep its nose clean. That's a liberal translation. The director passed on some legalese and political threats that are much more impressive boiled down to the bone."

"We're not supposed to investigate?"

"No. But I've been assured the State Department will look into it."

"I'll bet the Korean Embassy is shaking in its collective boots at this very moment."

"You don't have to sell me on the sarcasm," Vache said. "At most, the State Department will administer a slap on the wrist, probably kick the parties we turned up in Atlanta out of the country and let it go at that."

"Where does that leave us with this investigation?"

"The Korean angle is strictly hands-off. And you know what the general consensus is regarding jackal networking."

"Despite what happened in Miami?"

"Especially despite what happened in Miami. I was also warned about that this morning. The director was told that further investigation by Omega Blue into the jackal networking would run the risk of a high profile that could cause a national panic."

"That's bullshit."

Vache nodded. "They were laying it on thicker than usual this morning. Of course, you and your team kicked a bigger hornet's nest than usual too."

"So what have we got to work with? Officially?"

"DiVarco. The files you recovered from Atlanta indicated some money laundering he's doing through the Cayman Islands."

"Can we do anything with that?"

"No. It's a dead end, but I'm not going to file it that way yet. I don't like cover-ups any more than you do. I also mind being politically correct a lot less than you do, but I'm not going to sacrifice this unit's power because some politicos are afraid of backlash in the media. Things aren't right on the Hill, and that's not our fault. But I refuse to be part of the ongoing problem."

"Officially we're working on the money laundering angle."

"Officially, that and the theft of government property."

"The guns from Fort Benning."

"Yeah."

"Any evidence that DiVarco was behind that?"

"No, but I've got some files that can reflect that he was by morning in case we need to present a case foundation." Vache sipped his coffee. "I want DiVarco as badly as you do if he was the guy behind Newkirk's death. Emmett was a friend."

"So we can go to work on DiVarco."

"Yeah, and if any of this other shit hits the fan, we'll deal with it then. I'm only going to be able to buy you a few days with this smoke screen we're putting together. Lamar Cashion's the second chair on the House subcommittee. He's one cagey son of a bitch, and he's been rooting around for dirt. If you people don't get something tangible—that isn't a political hot potato—soon, you'll be out of there so fast it'll make your head swim."

"Cashion's from Massachusetts, isn't he?" Wilson asked.

Vache's surprise was evident. "Yeah. How'd you know?"

"I keep abreast of things, Earl, I just don't get involved in things where I can't function." Wilson pressed on. "However, I find it interesting that as the unit has received more heat these last few months, Cashion's been moving in closer to the top. Could be we're not the only ones who've been laying groundwork on this thing."

"Conjecture," Vache said.

"Coupled with a healthy dose of paranoia. Whatever games you play with those people, play them a little closer to the vest these next few days."

"Yeah. Let me know if there's anything I can do."

Wilson nodded and opened the office door.

"You really think Valentine's going to work out?"

"If I don't have to bounce him from the team for insubordination, or put him in the hospital." Wilson let himself out. In the hallway, he glanced at his watch and found the time to be only a few minutes after eight. Emmett Newkirk hadn't even been dead twenty-four hours yet.

Wilson was bone tired. It was too early to visit Kasey. Mornings were always rough for her, and Wilson knew he needed to be feeling better himself before he went to the hospital to see his daughter. Guilt washed away his fatigue and leached into his nerves.

He hit the break room one floor up, ransomed a Diet Pepsi and a Snickers from the machines, and headed for the file room two floors down.

* * *

"Computer," Wilson called. He stood in the center of a small closet of a room that looked like the inside of an eight-foot cube. The dim outlines of the door barely registered against the dull gray finish of the interior.

"Computer on," a feminine voice responded.

"Access requested."

"Voiceprint."

"Wilson, Slade Ryan. Special agent in charge, Omega Blue unit."

There was a pause, then a familiar beep.

"Authorization request permitted, Agent Wilson. How may I help you?"

"I need a batch file on DiVarco, Sebastian Vittore." Wilson spelled it. "See attached NCIC file and reference all related materials." He gave the file numbers.

"Working."

Wilson waited. The acid of the Diet Pepsi burned his stomach, and the candy bar had only taken the edge off his hunger. But he knew better than to eat a meal until he was able to relax.

"File coming up," the computer said.

The lights in the room dimmed.

"How do you want the information formatted?"

Wilson studied the wall ahead of him as a head-and-shoulders shot of DiVarco came into view. "Standard play. Give me present stats on the subject, roll back for antecedent criminal activities—proven and suspected—then spread out from there to his known peer group."

"Highlighted names?"

"Prio, Harry. No known initial at this time. Also called Balls."

"I have a file on Prio, Araldo Picciotto."

"Aikman, Nelson Charles."

The photograph of DiVarco changed angles, then pulled back and became a full-figure shot.

"I'm sorry. I can find no file on Nelson Charles Aikman."

"References?"

"None."

Wilson nodded out of habit. The computer wasn't geared to pick up body language. It made sense that DiVarco would choose to bend an accountant who hadn't been popped yet. "That's fine for now. Start cycling them through."

"Commencing."

Wilson listened as the computer ran down the list of businesses DiVarco was known to control inside Boston and out. News footage was interspersed with footage culled from home camcorders, shot for media consumption and ongoing investigations by other law-enforcement agencies. He said, "Freeze."

"Freezing."

The onslaught of pictures and verbal information halted.

"Give me a three-D," Wilson ordered.

"Three-D coming."

The shadows in front of Wilson shuddered, then altered shape. Seconds later, a three-dimensional hologram of Sebastian DiVarco stood facing Wilson.

Wilson studied the man. DiVarco in the flesh was a couple of inches taller and a few pounds heavier. The man's hair was pulled back in a ponytail that left his face chiseled and hard. The dark eyes were merciless. The three-D was clothed in a long black coat, gloves, an open-throated polo shirt, and olive Dockers. The footwear consisted of polished Italian loafers. "Display armament," Wilson said.

"Known armament as follows: Detonics Janus Scoremaster .45 ACP is primary weapon, and is usually carried in a hip holster."

The pistol appeared on the image, as though Wilson had suddenly donned X-ray glasses. "Next."

The computer moved along quickly, establishing that DiVarco knew and used a number of weapons, of both Western and Eastern origins. He'd studied martial arts for some time since starting to work his way up the ranks of Boston's Mafia.

Wilson moved on through the files, trying to break the information down into categories in his mind, so that he could review it at a later date. Even without the Korean angle, DiVarco was going to prove a dangerous adversary.

Bob MacDonald pressed a palm to the indent plate set into the wall. A heartbeat later the door slid aside and allowed him access. When the door closed behind him, he stood in the darkness of the room, letting his eyes adjust.

The room was one of the firing ranges on the two physical-training floors. The old-fashioned Hogan's Alley still existed on the grassy fields outside the buildings, but most of the weapons training now was done in simulation tanks like this one.

"Mac," Lee Rawley called out from the shadows. "Over here. Goggles are on the wall to your left."

Mac found the goggles by feel and slipped them on. Despite the coffee he'd been drinking steadily since last night, and the blueberry muffins he'd taken time out for with Scuderi, January, and Valentine, he still felt worn down to the nub. All hollow, his grandmother used to say as she passed him more homemade butter and a pan of biscuits at breakfast time back on the farm his grandfather had maintained till his death. He'd been prepared to make the jaunt to his apartment in Alexandria, grab a few hours of sleep, and attempt to make a connection with either Robert or David. Both his sons had busy lives these days, and it was sometimes hard for Mac to remember he was a grandfather. Only on days like today did he ever feel that old.

He reached up and switched the goggles on.

Instantly the room came alive as virtual reality took over the walls, ceiling, and floor. The scenario was a jungle lush with tropical flowers and Spanish moss. Night had draped a cooling wind around trees that would have grown through the ceiling if they'd been real. Brush and undergrowth moved with the changing breezes while the limbs above clattered. The scent of crushed blooms and rotting beauty filled Mac's nose. Even though he knew the odors were only computer programming, it didn't seem any less real. He put a hand out and touched a nearby tree. The bark felt rough, solid, and a crawling insect scuttled over his fingers, leaving an itching sensation. He took his hand away and scratched.

Lee Rawley, dressed in jeans, boots, a Western shirt with pearl buttons, and the familiar Stetson stood in the center of a moonlit clearing with a Colt .45 government model in his fist. He smiled beneath the mirror sunglasses that for some reason didn't reflect the moonlight. "Jump on in if you feel like it. Won't take but a minute to get you into the programming."

"No thanks. For me, gunplay is much better as a spectator sport."

"Suit yourself."

Mac leaned against a tree and waited. The bark seemed to chafe against his skin through his clothing.

Rawley continued walking through the jungle with the Colt .45 at the ready.

Watching the other man, Mac felt slightly disoriented as his tree seemed to float along behind. He didn't press conversation. Rawley had invited him here. He thought about the years he'd known the man, and the gossip he'd heard about him. As far as he knew, Rawley had never asked anyone to join him anywhere. It was history in the making.

A man in camo clothing popped up suddenly with an AK-47 cradled in his arms. The harsh *aaaakk-aaaaakkk* of the Russian-made weapon on full auto filled the room. Brass glinted in the moonlight as it spun up over the muzzle flashes.

Mac had to check an impulse to duck.

Wheeling lithely, flowing like a big cat changing directions, Rawley went under the line of fire and landed in a prone position with the .45 extended in his hand. He fired twice.

The camo-covered guy went back as the computer registered both bullets striking the guy in the face.

Mac was impressed. Personally, off balance like that, he would have gone for the body, then tried a follow-up head shot only once he had some cover or some breathing space. But Rawley was good even without the SeekNFire programming. A glance at the LED toteboard floating in midair next to the crescent moon showed that Rawley wasn't using SeekNFire, and that he'd put down fourteen aggressors before this one.

Regaining his feet, Rawley slipped a fresh magazine into the .45. The rounds were specially fitted for the simulation tanks and were in no way lethal. "The investigation regarding the Asians was quashed a little while ago."

"How do you know that?"

The mirror shades were noncommittal. "I know."

Mac accepted that. Rawley had a means of getting information that sometimes didn't have anything to do with the FBI. "By whom?"

"The State Department. Turns out the guys we captured in Atlanta were part of the Korean Embassy team."

"Does Slade know?"

"He does by now. Vache pulled him into his office about an hour ago."

"Have you talked to him?"

"No. He's in for a session with records. Besides, I don't have anything to tell him. Yet."

"Yet?"

"Yet," Rawley repeated. He voice-commanded the simulations program to freeze, then crossed the jungle floor to face Mac. "I have a problem with that. I figure Slade's gonna go for the investigation however he can, but he's gonna be working with his hands tied. Me, I want to untie them some if I can. We owe Newkirk that much."

Mac nodded. It was really turning out to be one for the history books. No one had ever heard Rawley evidence any emotion about any of the other members of the team. Nor had he ever hit on Maggie, which was a mistake most new guys made when coming aboard. "How do you plan on doing that?"

"I'm going to call in some favors a few people owe

me in D.C. The places I'm going aren't exactly patronized for their atmosphere. I could use some backup."

"I take it the people you're calling the favors in
from won't be exactly amenable."

"That's a fair assumption."

"Why not go to Slade with this?"

"Man just lost a friend and a guy he was responsible for. He needs some time away to get his head together. He'll go see his little girl this afternoon, spend a
few hours with his dad. By morning he'll be chill, ready
to step back into the harness. Who knows, by then we
could have something for him."

Mac listened to Rawley's words, realizing they
were spoken with conviction, and from experience. It
made him wonder who Rawley had lost in one of his
other lives, and how that loss had come about.

"So," Rawley said, "are you in or out?"

"In. What time do we meet?"

"About eight. The people we're going to be talking to don't do sunlit hours. I'll give you a call, let you
know where."

Mac gave Rawley his home phone number, but felt
in the back of his trained investigator's mind that the
man already knew it.

Rawley said a curt good-bye.

Mac watched him go. Two camo-clad men came
into view, saw Rawley, and swiveled to fire on him.
Rawley put them both down without breaking stride.
Mac let himself out after hanging the goggles up and
losing sight of his teammate.

Rawley was an enigma. His interest in the simulations tank was legendary; usually, after any investigation by the Omega Blue group broke up, Rawley would
loosen up in the firing range. Or maybe it was to keep

himself in top form. Only once had Rawley forgotten to erase the score he'd made inside the program, and the ensuing rumors had become Bureau legend. But that incident of forgetfulness had come at a time when Slade Wilson had been looking to replace the team's armorer and makeup man, so it was possible that it hadn't been an accident at all.

CHAPTER 8

The limo glided into the RESERVED PARKING ONLY area roped off in golden braid in front of the restaurant. It was 10:30 A.M., and Sebastian DiVarco had beaten the lunch crowd.

The restaurant was three stories of dining opulence, walled on the outside with chrome and glass blocks. The glass blocks were shot through with thin wire in neon colors that alternated during the day as the sun moved across them. The effect helped the Crystal Palace earn its name, and the quality of the food and service kept the monied crowds coming back. With the economy the way it was, those crowds would have been thin if it hadn't been for the upscale criminals who patronized the place. Alexander Silverton owned the Crystal Palace and was a guiding force among Boston's elite. He'd had to make some compromises a few years ago to keep his flagship investment afloat.

"You're clear, Mr. DiVarco," one of the Kevlar-clad bodyguards said.

Carmichael held the door open as DiVarco climbed out of the limo, straightened his jacket, and stepped onto the red carpet beneath the mirror-bright awning. Two of his security people followed him.

He wore a three-piece blue-green sharkskin suit that glistened. The Detonics .45 was in a breakaway shoulder rig that the suit had been tailored to conceal. The gun barrel had been destroyed and replaced so the bullets that had killed Jimmy Gioia couldn't be traced back to him.

Stopping in the lobby, he purchased a *Globe* from the machine and folded it three ways till it formed a rough cylinder he could hold in one hand. It felt weighty and solid. Gripping it by the end, he walked into the main dining area.

A seductive hostess in a clinging blue chiffon dress intercepted him. Blond curls touched her bare shoulders. "Will you be joining us for lunch?"

"No," DiVarco said. "I'm here to see Silverton."

The girl shifted gears smoothly, showing her professionalism. "Is Mr. Silverton expecting you?"

"No. But he'll see me." DiVarco stared her down until she moved. He crossed the main dining area.

A few people were already having early lunches, either to avoid the rush or to conduct business out of the office. None of them paid him much attention. The tables were arranged to provide privacy; the low walls were constructed of highly varnished dark woods, with plants growing out of them and hanging from the ceiling.

The hostess stayed where she was, but DiVarco saw her twist the ornate bracelet on her arm.

"Alarm," the bodyguard on DiVarco's left said. The man was glancing at a readout screen that fit comfortably in the palm of one big hand. "They'll have someone waiting."

DiVarco nodded. "I don't want anybody hurt permanently, but I don't expect you to let Silverton's hired muscle make you guys look like assholes either."

"Yes, sir."

"Right, Mr. DiVarco."

Pushing through the ornate double doors covered with carved fairies and dragons in bas-relief, DiVarco made his way through the wait station and into the kitchen. The room was huge and gleaming. Refrigerators that resembled standing meat lockers stood like steel soldiers along the back wall. Cooks worked furiously at the huge cauldrons and grills. The smell of exotic spices filled the air.

"Hey!" a man's voice rang out.

DiVarco turned right and started for another set of doors. He'd never been in the rear of the Crystal Palace before. He'd only dined in the lunch and dinner areas. But money spread around in the right places had gotten him a complete schematic of the restaurant and let him know where Silverton's office was.

"Hey, jerkweed! You can't go back there!"

"It's a Pink," one of DiVarco's bodyguards sneered. "Kid don't even look like he's got his full growth."

DiVarco glanced at the Pinkerton security man. The Pink was in his early twenties, with a shock of punk-cut brown hair, wearing a blue coverall with built-in Kevlar jacket and tan jackboots. His hand was dipping under the waist jacket.

"Freeze it right there, buddy, or I'll ventilate you."

Blued steel showed in the Pink's hand as it started to emerge from the jacket.

"Take him down, Tommy," DiVarco ordered.

Tommy moved at DiVarco's right, and the dulled finish of a Taser filled his hand. There was the familiar *sproing* as the dart flew to its target, trailing the thin wires. When the electric current hit his system, the Pink jerked into a wild dance, then collapsed. The pistol went skittering from his hand and slid under a gas range.

"You people get back to work," DiVarco advised, "or lunch today is going to be delayed."

One of the chefs started bellowing orders, and two of the younger staff went to pick up the unconscious Pink as the rest of the crew followed DiVarco's advice.

DiVarco went through the doors. A hallway lay beyond, stretching for a short distance behind the one-way glass that made up the back wall of the giant fish-bowl where the floor shows were conducted during lunch and dinner. A scattered collage of enormous clam-shells, pink, white, and purple coral spiderwebs, and tall green plants covered the black rock of the fake sea floor. Bubbles spun and broke as they wandered lazily to the surface twelve feet above. A topless mermaid, latex fins encasing her lower body, hit the water in a sharp dive, then coasted to a stop on top of a clamshell. Her silver hair flowed out around her as she stretched sinuously.

Two other Pinks stood guard over the door leading to Silverton's inner sanctum. They stood their ground uncertainly.

"I'm here to see Silverton," DiVarco said. He was tense inside; he'd never before dared invade Silverton's turf. He didn't stop walking.

"Sorry," the nearest Pink said. "Mr. Silverton's not seeing anybody this morning." He stretched out a hand to make contact with DiVarco's chest. His other hand held a short-barreled automatic.

DiVarco waited until the man's hand pushed against him. Shifting his weight, he swung the rolled-up newspaper in a vicious arc. The heavy end smashed into the Pink's wrist and sent the pistol flying. Before the Pink could react, DiVarco swung the *Globe* again, whipping it into the Pink's unprotected groin and doubling him over. He raised a knee into the Pink's face, bringing the man's head back up, then shoved the end of the newspaper into the Pink's face.

The Pink's nose broke with an audible snap and he tumbled over backward, moaning with the blinding pain.

Stunned, the other Pink started to move, then found himself staring down the barrels of two handguns. The Pink let his weapon dangle by one finger, then slowly lowered it to the floor and raised his hands.

DiVarco tossed the bloodied newspaper on top of the disabled Pink, straightened his suit jacket and tie, then let himself into the office. He wasn't even breathing hard, and that pleased him.

Alexander Silverton was seated behind an ornate mahogany desk covered with brasswork. Almost sixty years old, the restaurateur was still tall and lean, with a patrician's features. Silverton wore an indigo suit that was pin-striped with turquoise lines. A turquoise ascot was knotted around his neck. His hair was snow white, carefully coiffed, and made his powder blue eyes seem even more brilliant.

In one of the matched pair of high-backed, over-stuffed chairs fronting the immense desk, Tonsung Min sat watching through a cloud of pipe smoke. His black eyes glinted like chips of obsidian in his wrinkled face. The Korean man was bald and moon faced, the symmetry of his features marred by a jagged knife scar that formed a V on the right side of his face, from his temple to the corner of his mouth and back to his earlobe.

"Hello, guys," DiVarco said, heading for the wet bar in the corner. "Hey, Alex, you don't mind if I fix myself a drink, do you? Looks like you guys are doing all right."

Silverton stood up behind the desk. "What the hell are you doing here? I told you never to come here."

"Why?" DiVarco demanded. "Because I might dirty the place up?" He finished pouring a brandy and worked at reining in his anger.

"You're risking everything by showing up here," Silverton said.

"I'm risking everything by keeping my ass out there on those streets," DiVarco replied. "While you sit in your little ivory tower and publicly deplore the violent side of this city in your media ads."

"Mr. DiVarco," Tommy called from the doorway, "we got more Pinks coming."

"Call off your dogs," DiVarco warned Silverton, "before somebody gets killed."

"Get out," Silverton said, "or I'll have you thrown out."

"Your choice, Alex." DiVarco freed the Scoremaster from the shoulder rig and started to bring it out.

"Sebastian," Min said in his accented voice. His words crackled with authority. "Don't pull that weapon. For your own protection."

A creeping unease scaled down DiVarco's spine. He glanced around and saw three Korean bodyguards wearing dark suits and sunglasses step into the room from two hidden doors.

A cruel smile twisted Silverton's lips. "Get out, DiVarco, while you still can."

"Fuck you."

A mottled red flushed Silverton's face.

Min interrupted. "Sit down, Alex, before you let this thing get out of control. At this point I think it's a good idea that Mr. DiVarco showed up. There are some topics we need to address with him after last night."

After only a brief hesitation, Silverton pressed a button mounted on the side of his desk and said, "Harrelson, pull your men back."

The hidden speaker sounded tinny. "Yes, sir."

DiVarco glanced at Tommy and the big man gave a short nod. He releathered the Scoremaster, then picked up his drink.

"Please," Min said, indicating the empty chair.

As Silverton resumed his seat, it was clear that the restaurateur wasn't happy.

DiVarco sat. "I didn't expect to see you here," he said to Min.

The Korean man took out a lighter and relit his pipe, puffing on it till a blue-gray haze haloed his head. "There were some things Alex wanted to discuss with me in light of the events last night."

Street paranoia kicking in, DiVarco wondered how many other such meetings had been arranged between the two of them without his knowledge. He made a note to ream out the surveillance team assigned to keep tabs on Silverton's comings and goings for him. "What events?"

"The jackal network that was discovered in Atlanta, Georgia, by the FBI last night." Min had never minced words. "They've traced it back to you."

"How?"

"Someone mentioned Mr. Prio's name."

"Who?"

"At this point, that doesn't really matter, does it?"

"This has happened because you got so damn greedy," Silverton said. "All you had to do was follow orders and concentrate your efforts in the areas we asked you to. But no, you had to start nickel and diming on your own."

"That jackal network was worth millions."

"And now it's worth shit. Worse, it's become a liability."

"Gentlemen," Min said, "this is getting us nowhere. I knew about Sebastian's involvement with the jackal network. Steps were taken to secure it last night, but the team I sent down was unable to completely eradicate the trail."

"You knew?" Silverton demanded. "And you didn't tell me?"

DiVarco looked at the old man in a new light. If Min knew that he'd transgressed the boundaries of their agreement, why hadn't the old Korean taken steps before? The only answer he could come up with was Min's own greed. Perhaps at a later date, the Korean would have tried to cut himself in for a share. He filed the theory away for later consideration.

"Not everything," Min said to Silverton, "warrants your attention. You have your hands full doing the things you're supposed to be tending to."

"I should have been consulted."

"And you would have said no. Sebastian is merely looking out for his own interests."

"And jeopardizing everything we've done to-gether."

"Not necessarily. I think that this unfortunate inci-dent can be contained. Jackal networking is not an issue eagerly brought into the view of the American public. The Justice Department will be under orders from Con-gress to shut down further exposure as soon as possible. It isn't conducive to anyone in a political place of power to admit that they can't protect the average person on the street."

"The Omega Blue unit broke the case," DiVarco pointed out. "Slade Wilson doesn't have a reputation for being a guy who can be controlled."

"If he can't be controlled," Min said in his deadly calm voice, "then Slade Wilson must be broken."

DiVarco smiled. "Those were my thoughts ex-actly. And that's why I'm here." He looked at Silverton. "You still own the number-two guy on the funding committee in the House, right?"

The restaurateur tried to hide his surprise.

Easing into the chair beside Min, DiVarco said, "C'mon, Alex, it's okay to brag a little in front of your associates. We won't hold it against you. You've had Cashion by the short hairs for three, four years now."

"Is that what you're here for?" Silverton de-manded. "To have us protect you from the FBI?"

"Actually, I'm only here to do some damage con-trol. I'm not afraid of Wilson or his goon squad. They're human despite all the bullshit floating around about them. One of them was killed last night. But if Wilson makes it into this town and starts stirring things up, this little ménage à trois we've been managing may make the headlines. I didn't figure you wanted something like that."

Silverton looked apoplectic.

"No," Min replied. "That's not what we want. You have something you want to suggest?"

"Silverton has political clout on the Hill," DiVarco suggested. "He owns Lamar Cashion, the Massachusetts representative warming the second chair on the House funding committee underwriting Omega Blue's operations."

"Is this true?" Min asked.

"Yes, but Cashion's in no position to do anything about pulling Wilson or his team back off an operation," Silverton said. "Keith Jarvis is still running the show, and he's hesitant about taking steps against Omega Blue that are too strong. A number of media outlets have tried to make folk heroes out of those people."

DiVarco sipped his drink. "Most of that committee key themselves off Jarvis's lead."

"Yes," Silverton said.

"So if Jarvis was out of the way and Cashion could take the lead, maybe they'd vote with him to suspend Omega Blue's caseload pending an investigation of abuse of power."

"You're gambling."

"The alternative is to bushwhack Wilson and his playmates when they hit the streets of this city," DiVarco pointed out. "How does that grab you?"

Silverton glanced at Min. "I told you we were making a mistake by involving him. He's street trash, and he'll never know better than to bite the hand that feeds him."

"Fuck you, asswipe!" DiVarco stood up suddenly and started to round the desk.

"Sebastian!" Min's voice was sharp, uncompromising.

The three Korean hard men shifted, bringing their weapons into view.

DiVarco reined in his anger but didn't back down. He stood the ground he'd already gained.

Silverton's finger was poised above the button on his desk.

"Don't give me that holier-than-thou spiel," DiVarco said. "At least I'm honest about what I am and don't try to hide. And don't you ever once think you could have pulled this thing off without me."

"There were a hundred other guys out there like you who would have jumped at the chance," Silverton said.

"Who knows? Maybe they still will. Get out there on the street and talk it up with them. But don't be surprised if they hand you your head. You haven't got what it takes to hack it out there on the street. That's why you got me in the first place."

"Sit down," Min suggested, "and let's talk."

Slowly, DiVarco turned and resumed his seat in the chair as Silverton took his finger away from the button.

"Sebastian's plan has merit," Min said.

"I don't like the idea of risking Cashion," Silverton said. "The man has proven valuable over the years, and his best years are yet to come."

"It's no risk," DiVarco said. "All I'm talking about here is a promotion. He's already been known for leaning on the Omega Blue unit anyway. No big deal. Business as usual for him."

"You can do this?" Min asked.

"As of nine o'clock tonight, sure. Piece of cake. It's already set up."

"And the Omega Blue unit is up for review tomorrow afternoon?"

Silverton nodded.

"In light of the apprehension of the jackal network against unwritten federal policy, it wouldn't be surprising for Wilson and his team to be temporarily taken out of circulation pending an investigation," Min said.

"Chances are we won't be able to shut the unit down," Silverton said. "If that could have been done so easily before, it would have."

"But it will buy us some time to maneuver," Min replied. He directed his attention to Silverton. "Call your man in Washington. Let him know he's going to move into the first chair overnight, and let him know what is expected of him." He pushed himself out of his chair. "Sebastian, do me the courtesy of walking with me to my car."

DiVarco downed the last of his drink and set the empty glass on Silverton's desk. He smiled as the restaurateur made a frantic grab to lift it from the polished wood. He followed Min out into the hallway, walking at the older man's side.

Min put on a pair of dark sunglasses. "I understand the fires that drive you," he said, "far better than I understand the ones that drive Alex. You're brash, bold, and you're just coming into your own. By setting up the jackal network and the other sideline businesses you've established, you're building your own fortunes."

"It could be I got a glance at how big the pie was," DiVarco said. "Maybe I didn't like the size of my share."

"There's always room for negotiation." Min fixed him with a black-lensed stare. "To a point. Remember that, Sebastian. Too often a man's eyes get too big for his stomach. Do you understand?"

DiVarco curbed his resentment, conscious of the

Korean guards surrounding them as they made their way out the side door of the restaurant. He nodded.

"With us, you'll have much more than you would ever have had on your own. Remember that when your ambition kicks in."

Not saying anything, DiVarco waited with Min as the Mercedes limo pulled into place before them.

"Take care to close in your street operations," Min said as he slid into the rear seat of the car. "In case Alex's man isn't able to accomplish everything we want. There are a lot of people in this city who would look forward to seeing you fall from the lofty perch you've scaled to these last few months."

"I will." DiVarco chafed at being treated like a child. He watched Min's vehicle pull away. Part of him was satisfied. He'd made himself the equal of Alexander Silverton in Min's eyes by forcing the issue, and he'd made the other men admit how much they needed him.

CHAPTER 9

Slade Wilson pulled his two-tone gray Jeep Cherokee into one of the rear slots in the parking area at the Schaeffer Center for Handicapped Children in downtown Washington, D.C. Across Potomac Street, he could see the Victorian facade of St. John's Episcopal Church rising from a cultivated lawn and manicured trees. To the west, the gothic spires of Georgetown University stabbed into the blue sky where a helicopter bearing radio-station markings flitted like a fickle dragonfly.

Schaeffer Center was a five-story building constructed of straight lines that seemed to hold an unforgiving intensity. Steel bars covered the windows. A playground had been built on the side facing Wilson, but the colorful toys and swings looked incongruous, an afterthought to soften the effects of the chain-link fence and security gates. A trio of khaki-coveralled men and one woman worked the landscape with lawnmowers and trimmers, reducing the play area to something that looked as though it had been covered with Astroturf. The cacophony of gasoline engines sounded harsh and alien.

To Wilson, it didn't look like a place where a child would want to play.

The dashboard clock showed that it was 2:57 P.M. The 8 flipped over as he switched off the key, extinguishing the welcome blast of cool air from the air-conditioning vents.

He shrugged out of his shoulder holster and shoved it under the seat, then added the Crain combat knife with its trick holster and the H & K VP7 0Z from his boot. He kept the Walther TPH .22LR in its paddle holster at the small of his back. Slipping out of the polo shirt he'd put on after his nap and shower back at Quantico, he reached into the rear seat into the overnight bag he kept there and pulled out the kelly green short-sleeved, brushed denim shirt that he always wore when he visited his daughter. He pulled it on, leaving the tails out to cover the Walther .22. The wrapped gift fit easily in one of his hands. He fluffed the big yellow bow so it stood up taller than before.

He signed in at the gate, spoke briefly with the regular security officer who recognized him from all his visits. As he neared the center's entrance, it seemed as though the weight of the building was settling onto his shoulders.

He hated the center, hated the thought of Kasey spending her days and nights there. But most of all, he hated wherever it was that Kasey spent her time, held in thrall by whatever it was she found there. He tried to shelve the depressing thoughts, but it was no use.

After signing in again at the second-floor nurses' station, he walked down the cold corridor to Kasey's room. Only a few people were in the hallway. During prime business hours in the nation's capital, not many parents came to see their children. It was expensive to keep a child there. Wilson knew. If it hadn't been for the insurance package that had come with his promotion to SAC of Omega Blue, he wouldn't have been able to afford it.

For a moment, Blair crossed his mind. Her memory brought a mixture of resentment and uncertainty, as it always did.

"Agent Wilson. Slade. Wait up."

Wilson turned around and saw Neil Holland, Kasey's usual caregiver, trotting up the hallway toward him.

Holland was a young, beefy guy with an easy smile. His center blues made his black skin look darker. He held a clown puppet with green hair and a red, bulbous nose on his right hand. "I wanted to talk to you a minute before you go in to see Kasey."

Wilson's stomach churned. "What's wrong?"

Holland slapped him on the shoulder. "Nothing's wrong. She's doing fine, but there has been a change. Not good or bad, just a change. The doc'll be along shortly to talk to you once I tell her you're here." The caregiver moved over to the dark window set into the wall of Kasey's room, and flicked the switch at the bottom.

Instantly the window cleared, allowing a view into the room. It was ten feet square, with an eight-foot ceiling. The walls were hung with padding in colorful patterns from old Walt Disney movies. Mickey Mouse and Donald Duck cavorted with the Little Mermaid and characters from *Beauty and the Beast*. In the middle of the room was a small table and chairs made of plastic and foam. A neatly made twin bed lined one wall. At the bed's foot was a padded toy box overflowing with stuffed animals.

Kasey sat facing the north wall, to Wilson's right. She was slight and slender for a five-year-old, all bones and thin muscle. She wore a blue dress with small yellow flowers that didn't hide the fact that she was also wearing a diaper. On her head was a helmet that looked like something a boxer might wear in a sparring ring. She was leaning forward, bouncing her head off the padded wall in a deliberate rhythm.

Wilson tried not to let his feelings of guilt and pain show in his voice. "What's that on her head?"

"Protective headgear," Holland answered. "This past week she's gotten in the habit of pounding her head up against the walls."

"Why?"

"Don't know. Doc Culley ordered the headgear to make sure Kasey didn't hurt herself. She didn't seem to like it at first, but now she's incorporated it into her actions. She hits the walls harder now than she used to, but the headgear keeps her protected. While you're in there with her, you might keep an eye out. A couple days ago she caught me not looking and popped me in the mouth. Loosened a couple teeth. She's a strong kid."

"Thanks." Wilson reached for the door.

"Hey."

"Yeah?"

Holland fished in his pocket and came out with a

plastic bag with chocolate chip cookies the size of half dollars. "She's had her lunch, but she might like the cookies to munch on."

Wilson took the cookies and nodded. "Appreciate it, Neil."

"No prob, guy. She's one of my favorite kids."

Wilson didn't figure there were any kids in the center who weren't one of Holland's favorites. He let himself into the room, aware of the smack of leather against plastic at once. "Hey, Kasey, how's Daddy's little girl." He made his voice light and kept talking to her the way Dr. Culley had suggested.

Kasey made no response, just kept thudding her head against the wall.

"Hey, kid, I missed you. And I brought you something, too." He tossed the gift onto her bed, then picked her up in his arms and held her close.

Kasey fought against him at first, using her hands and feet to pummel him as she tried to gain leverage to free herself. Her head swung wildly as she arched her back and twisted like a cat.

Wilson hung onto her with difficulty as he made his way to the bed. He sat down cross-legged on the floor with Kasey in his lap. She was agitated now, and began emitting a series of clicks and whistles that didn't sound human. "Hey, take it easy. It's Daddy. I came to see you like I told you I would. Just let me hold you for a little while."

She swung her head at him, bouncing it solidly off his chest.

He pulled her closer with one arm, felt her immediate response as she fought more, then took her hand in his and rubbed it along the brushed denim shirt. Kasey tried to pull her hand away, but he kept it there.

"Easy," he whispered, his voice tight with the emotion. "Easy. It's just Daddy. I love you. I love you, Kasey."

Gradually she calmed down. The bouncing of her head against his chest grew lighter until she just lay against him. Her hand, now free, trailed across his shirt, back and forth, as she was captured by the texture and feel of the denim material. He hadn't noticed, months ago, that she'd developed a fascination for the shirt until Dr. Culley had told him.

Still talking soothingly to her, he changed his daughter's diaper, then gave her the wrapped gift. He sat on the floor and held her, talking to her nonstop as he opened the package for her and revealed the stuffed dolphin. He squeezed its tail and showed her how the eyes lit up and dolphin squeaks issued from it.

Kasey held it in both hands without looking at it. Her fingers explored every inch of it.

Wilson kept up his dialogue. Autistic children were still a mystery to modern medicine. No one knew where autism came from or how it could be cured. He hugged Kasey frequently to let her know he was there despite the daydreams or nightmares holding her mind prisoner.

After awhile, tired from her struggles and stuffed with chocolate chip cookies, she slept. Wilson remained seated on the floor listening to Kasey's soft snores against his chest. He didn't remember going to sleep with his arms around her.

Dinner came at six.

Wilson ate with his daughter, taking time to make sure she'd eaten everything she wanted. Blair came in while he was clearing the dishes away.

His ex-wife was beautiful. Her dark hair cascaded to her shoulders, framing a heart-shaped face that was tinted with just the right amount of makeup. She wore a strapless white evening gown that showed off her legs and bare back and made her tan look even better. She stopped just inside the door and looked down at him as he piled the dishes on one side and kept Kasey and the dolphin on the other.

"I'm surprised to find you here," Blair said in an accusatory tone.

Wilson didn't rise to the bait. His ex-wife was still battling her own private demons, and he'd learned it was best to keep from getting involved.

"Slow day for crime?" she asked. She fumbled with her purse, took out a pack of cigarettes, and lit up.

"I thought we'd agreed you wouldn't smoke around Kasey."

"Wrong. You agreed. I didn't."

"It's not good for her."

"Neither is an absentee father."

Wilson finished with the dishes and pulled Kasey back into his lap.

"We all know how the absentee husband role played out," Blair said.

It had been almost two years since Vache had told Wilson about Blair's affair with a Washington, D.C.,–based agent. The pain had been blunted over time, but it hadn't completely gone away. It had taken most of that time for Wilson to learn to stop blaming himself. That was made a little easier by Blair's decision to put Kasey in Schaeffer Center six months after their separation. Once the divorce had been granted, Blair's attorney had arranged for child support and alimony that made sure his ex-wife could live in reasonable comfort in the house Wilson was still paying for. With her free life-style now out in the open and paid for, their daughter had become an inconvenience.

"Don't you have somewhere else you're supposed to be?" Wilson asked.

"Not for another hour and a half. Senator Tipton's throwing a gala bash at his house. A lot of celebrities supporting the Greening of America environmental movement are going to be there."

"Still moving in the upwardly mobile strata, I see."

"After you, there was nowhere to go but up."

Wilson wanted to walk away, but Kasey was clinging to the brushed denim shirt with both fists. He stroked his daughter's hair and felt her warm breath against the inside of his wrist.

"How long has it been since the last time you saw her?" Blair asked. "Five days? Six? Maybe a week or more? Do you even remember?"

"Go away, Blair."

"You can't tell me to leave. I have custody of her."

Wilson glared at her. "You had custody, but you decided to sign that over to this hospital."

"She was too hard to manage."

"On your schedule, I don't doubt it."

Blair smiled. "Oh my, can't we be catty when we choose to be?"

Wilson remained silent. He'd never achieved even a remotely tenable position when arguing with his ex-wife.

"These little sporadic visits of yours aren't doing her any good, you know," Blair said. "Every time I come in, I check the toy box to see if there's a new addition. That's how I know you've been here. All you're doing is trying to assuage your own guilt over your inability to commit to another person."

Wilson refused to reply. She knew he was trapped by a catch-22: if he accepted a demotion to spend more time with Kasey, his insurance would be cut and he wouldn't be able to make the maintenance costs on the center.

There was a rap on the door, then Dr. Davette Culley let herself into the room. She was a shade under five and a half feet tall, and was slender, with a runner's physique. Her sandy hair was pulled back in a French braid. Her brown eyes flicked around the room casually, and Wilson knew she could sense the tension there. The blue hospital scrubs she wore looked professional and flattered her figure at the same time.

Wilson could tell that Blair was aware that the doctor's slim build made her full-figured body look almost plump. It wasn't true, but it troubled Blair's ego.

"Mr. Wilson," Dr. Culley said, "I'd like to talk to you briefly about your daughter if I could."

"Sure."

"Mrs. Wilson, you're welcome to stay, but I won't be discussing any material that we haven't covered before."

"No thank you," Blair said. "I've got somewhere else I've got to be." She started for the door.

"There's no smoking in the halls," Culley said. "You'll find an ashtray just down the corridor."

Blair gave the doctor a hard glance as she left the room.

The smile Culley gave Wilson was warm and generous. He liked thinking that Kasey got to see that smile a lot. It beat the hell out of the plastic grins on the walls and what he feared Kasey got from her mother.

"There's no way you could have missed the headgear," Culley said.

"No," Wilson agreed.

"Let me put your fears aside on that first." Culley knelt in front of Kasey and touched her face softly. "There's nothing wrong with Kasey, but she has developed some new habits we haven't seen before."

"Why?"

"I'm not sure. It could be she's learning something about the world inside her mind, or maybe she's trying to break free of some of the things holding her inside. She's more emotional at times than I've ever seen her before. Last week I saw her crying."

Wilson tightened his grip on his daughter unconsciously. Kasey squirmed in his arms until he loosened back up. "Was she in pain?"

"No. Not that we could diagnose. But it could be a breakthrough of some sort. Good things sometimes happen out of the blue, as well as bad ones. Her condition isn't worsening, and we may even be gaining some ground."

"Is she responding any better to the therapy?"

Culley smiled sadly and shook her head. "It's so hard to be sure in these cases. I choose, however, to think positively. I want you to try to do the same."

He nodded.

"She really seems to appreciate your visits though. After you leave, the next morning when she wakes up, she usually makes her way to the toy box and lies on the stuffed animals for hours at a time. Neil has told me she gets very agitated if she's moved to be changed or fed until she chooses to move on her own."

Wilson swallowed with difficulty.

Culley sat cross-legged on the floor and took

Kasey's hands in hers. "I think she misses you when you're gone."

"I'm here as much as I can be."

A look of concern flashed through Culley's eyes. "Don't take that as a criticism. I know you've got a difficult job. What I wanted you to understand is that whether you've seen it or not, you've built a bond with your daughter that she doesn't seem to have with anyone else."

"I'd like to think so."

Culley smiled. Wilson decided that the woman was probably his age or a little younger. He wondered if she had children; he'd never seen a wedding band on her finger.

"I think her fixation with the stuffed animals is because your cologne is on them," Culley said. "I believe she identifies that smell with you, the same way she's learned to identify you by that shirt."

"Maybe you should have been a cop."

"Theoretical medicine and detective work have a lot in common." She smoothed a stray lock of hair that was sticking out from under Kasey's headgear. "I'm talking to a colleague of mine about an innovative new procedure regarding autism. You're familiar with virtual reality?"

He nodded. "We use some aspects of it at the Bureau."

"My friend is Dr. Richard Means. Lately he's finished devising a program that has been approved by the FDA for testing virtual reality on human subjects. If it works the way he expects it to, it might open a door for Kasey and others like her."

"What does it do?"

"It creates a world that will hopefully bridge the

gap between the one we live in and the one the autistic child is trapped by. Part of it comes from biofeedback we get on the subject's brain waves. The other part comes from guesswork on the part of Dr. Means and his associates. What it takes, though, is a young subject who's been able to bond with someone." Culley hesitated. "I've nominated you and Kasey to work with Dr. Means and his staff when the time comes."

Wilson was silent for a moment. "Why a young subject?"

"An older autistic person has dwelt too long in the world inside their head. In order to open them up to the world we have out here, it might be necessary to tear down the existence they've woven for themselves. It would take much longer to get results, and perhaps prove too emotionally unsettling for them to handle. Dr. Means feels that children would be the most resilient."

"How soon?"

"Maybe a matter of weeks." Culley paused. "There would be a certain amount of risk to yourself too. But there's no one else I see that could possibly guide Kasey out of her dreams."

"My ex-wife has custody of Kasey."

"We'll have to work that out with her before we can start."

"I'll find a way to convince her," Wilson said, wondering if that would be possible.

"Good. I've seen Dr. Means's work. When you have time, I'd like to show it to you. I think you'll feel even more confident about our chances. Just keep in mind that this isn't a quick fix. There'll still be a lot of work ahead of us."

"I'd like the chance to tell Kasey how I feel about her."

Culley patted Kasey on the head and smiled. "I'm sure she already knows."

Kasey's head started thudding against Wilson's chest as Culley got up to go. He watched the doctor leave the room and started ranking impossibilities in his mind. He didn't know whether to file them chronologically, or by degree of difficulty. Between the House subcommittee, the snarl of criminal activity spinning out from Sebastian DiVarco in Boston, bringing Quinn Valentine on-board the team quickly, and convincing Blair to give permission for the new virtual reality therapy, he figured his highest hurdle would be his ex-wife. At least with the other problems he'd been able to work out some strings he could pull. But of course that didn't mean the string pulling would turn out to be worth a damn. And he'd be reaching for the first string tomorrow afternoon.

CHAPTER 10

"**O**kay, guys and dolls, belly up to the center stage, because it's time for our evening Hot Buns contest!"

Bob MacDonald dodged through the crowd swarming toward the stage, holding his cup of black coffee as he headed for the last place he'd seen Lee Rawley inside the singles club. Mac wore a dress shirt, no tie, jeans, and a Toronto Blue Jays windbreaker covering the Delta Elite in a shoulder rig; he felt out of place among the other patrons.

Clad in shiny leather pants, a soft neon green silk shirt, and a bomber jacket with the collar turned up, Rawley fit in with the night crowd. His mirror shades were dulled and blank. "Wait long?"

"Only for service. What's up?"

"Guy that owns this place is named George Haldane," Rawley said as he turned and walked down a small hallway leading to the phone area and rest rooms. "Besides running a string of singles clubs along the East Coast, George is also known to traffic in false IDs and passports."

"The Koreans didn't have any ID on them."

"No." Rawley led the way to the end of the hallway, where a steel door was marked: NOT AN EXIT— EMPLOYEES ONLY. "But Maggie got the numbers of the license plate of the van that attacked her and January and the state police in Atlanta."

"I thought that plate couldn't be traced."

"It wasn't," Rawley agreed. "At least not by anybody at the Bureau. I know some people who've got better systems than the FBI does. I leaned on a couple of them this afternoon."

"Haldane fixed the van's plates." Mac put his coffee cup on a trash bin by the door.

"I don't know." Rawley reached inside his jacket and took out a lock-pick set. He had the lock open in seconds.

Mac slipped his hand under his windbreaker and gripped the butt of the Delta Elite as they went through the door. "Then what are we doing here?"

"This deal's big enough that if Haldane didn't cut himself a piece of it, he'll know who did."

"We don't have a warrant."

"If we tried to get one based on what I turned up, the judge wouldn't give us the time of day."

"Right."

"And Haldane has a fleet of lawyers who deal with shit like this for him."

"But Haldane owes you?"

"Haldane owes somebody who owes me."

"Oh." Mac resigned himself to the fact that part of Rawley's mystery was going to remain mysterious.

Three short flights of stairs led them up to the next floor. The hallway was softly lighted by low-wattage bulbs. Mac understood why when he saw the one-way glass tilted at a forty-five-degree angle overlooking the dance floor. A track ran around the inside and the panes of one-way glass were a continuous flow of silvery glaze. Speakers were mounted every twelve or fifteen feet and broadcasted the events taking place below. Mac wondered where the security personnel that should have been stationed at this level were.

Rawley hit the top of the stairs and instantly turned left.

"Okay," the speakers boomed as they walked past, "I got these lovely ladies up onstage just waiting for a judge to evaluate them and find out who has the hottest buns tonight. The first man who can bring me a woman's undergarment gets to be the judge."

A general roar issued from the crowd. Mac shook his head in disbelief as he saw one woman drop to her back on the floor and start shimmying out of her pants while the men around her urged her to move faster.

Ahead of him, Rawley was moving quietly through the shadows. A man coming the other way spotted them and yelled, "Who the fuck are you guys?" while reaching for the big pistol hanging under his arm. "Freddie, Mike, get your asses down here!"

Suddenly Rawley shifted gears from walking to full speed. He closed the distance between himself and the big man in only a few long strides, then hurled himself into the air. Two men came running up behind the first guard, and were caught in the melee as Rawley's impact drove his adversary backward. All four of them went down in a heap.

Leaving his gun in its holster, unwilling to increase the charges that could be leveled against them if things went down wrong, Mac broke into a run.

Rawley rolled out of the general confusion and came up on his feet. As the big man tried to stand, Rawley executed a spinning back kick that knocked the man's pistol out of his hand, followed by another spinning back kick that crashed into the man's face. The big man went stumbling away with blood spiraling from his broken nose.

Catching the second man's arm in his, Rawley spun and twisted the captured wrist. Bone snapped, followed immediately by the man's screams of pain. Coming back to face his opponent again, Rawley fired a boot into the man's forehead. The man's head jerked back and he collapsed.

The third man had a knife. Mac ducked under the wild swing and set his feet. He'd studied martial arts for a time, but couldn't break the boxing reflexes he'd counted on for so long. His right fist jabbed three times in quick succession, rocking the man's head each time. The man's knife hand whipped back and Mac let it go by. When the man swung again, he blocked the movement with his left arm, threw an overhand jab that caught the man's jaw and set him up, then followed it with a snapping left cross that dropped the guard like a poleaxed steer. Mac wasn't even breathing hard.

Yelling in pain and anger, and moving at an uncertain trot, the first man reached for Rawley.

A slight grin twisted Rawley's mouth. He captured the man's hand by the wrist, then pulled on it as he deflected the man's reach and stepped outside it. When the guard was close enough, Rawley twice smashed him in the face with his elbow. Before the man could fall, Rawley grabbed the back of his shirt, pulled him down, and met him with a knee to the ribs.

Mac could see the guard was out on his feet as the man fell backward.

"Cuff them," Rawley said, bending to the task. "Don't want these bastards coming back to haunt us."

Mac took a pair of plastic disposable cuffs from his windbreaker pocket. Rawley was an expert shot, but the man was clearly a trained killer in martial arts. Mac knew Rawley had had to hold himself back to keep from killing the two men he'd taken on.

Within seconds the guard team was cuffed. Only one of them was regaining consciousness.

Rawley took the lead again.

Trailing behind him, gun in his fist, Mac triggered the SeekNFire programming. Adrenaline spun his senses as his palm scanned the butt of the Delta Elite.

A door came into view around the sloping corner of the observation run. Rawley approached it with a flat card in his hand, ran the card through an electromagnetic reader, and stepped through when the door opened.

Mac covered Rawley's back as he followed.

The room was spacious and well lit, with a nautical theme. Books lined one wall, all of them leather-bound in colors that let the observer know they were sets. None of them gave the appearance of ever having been removed from the shelf. A brass ship's wheel hung on the wall opposite the bookshelves, and another wall was covered with sailing pictures.

There was a desk of glass and steel at the other end of the room. Four phones, a computer system, scattered notebooks, and a well-thumbed atlas covered the desktop. Behind the desk was a fat, bald man with a pencil mustache. He was on the phone. His dark suit was expensive, and he sported a yellow carnation in his lapel. The man took a pipe out of his mouth as he took in Rawley and Mac. The bittersweet smell of red satin filled the room. "Let me get back to you on that," he said, cradling the phone without giving the other person time to respond.

Rawley came to a halt in front of the desk. His pistol was still in his hand, and was aimed at the second button down on the fat man's shirt. "Haldane."

"Who the fuck are you wiseacres?"

"We're the guys who just kicked the ass of the security team you're hitting that hidden panic button for," Rawley said. "Me, I'm the guy interested in whether or not I can hit that second button of yours when I pull the trigger, in case we missed any of your guys."

"How many did you take out?"

"Three." Rawley held up fingers on his free hand.

Mac turned to keep an eye on the door. Haldane was putting up a good front, but the man was scared. His was the kind of business where a good dose of fear was healthy.

"You missed five of them," Haldane said.

"Then you better call them off before somebody gets hurt."

"You guys think you can waltz in here, threaten me, and waltz back out without a scratch? What are you after? The safe? Fuck you. Nobody takes nothing from me."

"We're just looking for conversation," Rawley

said. He took something out of his pocket and tossed it at Haldane.

The object hit the desktop with a glassy ring, then slid to a stop next to the computer keyboard.

Haldane picked it up and looked at it. Confusion twisted his features and he took an unconscious drag on the red satin–loaded pipe. "This is a 1933 Indian head nickel."

"Yeah," Rawley replied.

Two gunmen suddenly filled the doorway with drawn weapons.

Mac tensed involuntarily as the SeekNFire programming automatically trained the 10mm's sights on the gunman carrying an Uzi machine pistol.

"Put the guns down," one of the men commanded, "and back out of the room. Do it *now!*"

Haldane waved at the guards. "Get the fuck out of here, Crittenden, and take those other dweebs with you. When I get through talking to these guys, I want to talk to you and Barry about the security around here."

"Yes, sir."

Haldane juggled the nickel in his hand and gazed at Rawley in open speculation. "A coin like this you don't just come by."

"No," Rawley agreed.

"Not many people know what it means to me."

"No."

"Yet you got one."

"Yeah."

"I owe the guy who gave you this really big."

"Yeah. You gave him twenty of those nickels nine years ago."

"So you and I both know he doesn't give them back to me lightly."

"No. He owes me really big."

Haldane's eyebrows elevated in appreciation. "So what can I do for you?" He dropped the nickel into a vest pocket.

"Somebody's done some document work for the Korean Embassy. I want to know about it."

"What kind of work? Floating them into the country?"

"No. I think they got in on their own, but they've got walking-around papers since they've been here. A crew of them went down in flames in Atlanta last night."

"Are you FBI?"

"It's my nickel," Rawley reminded.

Still on edge, wanting a cigarette even more because of the smoke swirling around in the room, Mac let his gun arm relax but didn't return the Delta Elite to its holster.

"What do you want to know?" Haldane leaned forward in his chair and tapped the computer keyboard.

"Everything."

"That's going to take some time."

"We can wait."

It took an hour and twenty-three minutes. When Haldane settled back in his chair, mopping sweat from his brow after yelling at and intimidating almost a dozen people over the phone, they had a picture—of sorts. According to the information Haldane had turned up, several Koreans that were affiliated with the Korean Embassy had been outfitted with false IDs that would show them to be native-born citizens. Almost all of them were listed as residents of Boston and the city's suburbs. Haldane had no idea what the Koreans were doing there, but there were rumors about mob activity in the area starting to be dominated by Korean interests.

Mac took notes and pocketed the list of false IDs Haldane had been able to confirm.

"Anything else?" Haldane asked.

"No," Rawley answered.

"Then get out of here. You're wasting my time and I've got a business to run."

"Terrific." Rawley reached under his bomber jacket and pulled out a rectangular brick wired with a sophisticated detonator. He slapped it down on the glass desktop, then showed Haldane the compact device he had in his hand. "Plastic explosive. The only thing that keeps it from going off in your face is the fact that I've got my thumb on this button. You touch it, it goes up anyway. See this amber light?" He pointed.

His features stained an unhealthy gray, Haldane nodded. "Hey, you don't need no shit like this. Come on."

"Some of your playmates out in the hallway might feel like trying to get a pound of flesh when we try to leave. Like you, I don't have time to waste. And I don't have another nickel to make sure we get a safe walk out of here." Rawley pointed at the amber light again. "When this goes off, you can touch it. Get rid of it any way you like."

"How do I know you're telling the truth?"

"Because I made a promise to the guy I got the nickel from. He wanted you left intact."

Haldane nodded.

Rawley headed for the door. "In case you get any bright ideas about leaving the room and having your guys try to whack us anyway, just keep in mind the cocaine lab you're running on the floor above us. An explosion, even if all it does is destroy this room, is going to cause an official inspection. Do you think you can hide all the evidence before the authorities get here?"

"Get out," Haldane snarled.

Rawley went, brushing by the outside security personnel as Haldane bellowed orders for them to leave Mac and Rawley alone. Mac followed, but didn't put his gun away till they hit the dance floor. His stomach was tense. He'd been wondering how they were going to leave the club without another confrontation, but he hadn't foreseen anything like Rawley's play.

Outside the air seemed cooler and the darkness more complete.

Rawley headed for the parking lot, turning his bomber jacket collar up a little more. "You know somebody who can trace that list on the QT?"

"We can have Maggie do it."

"Maybe, but she'll be using FBI codes. I think our security has been holed. Until we plug the leak or know for sure it doesn't exist, let's take a shot at using different channels."

"Okay. I've got a guy who works out of the district attorney's office in Boston that I still swap Christmas cards with. I'll ask him to take a look."

"Sounds good." Rawley flicked off the arming switch on the detonator and pocketed it.

Mac opened the door of his sedan, then reached in and turned off the overhead light so they could stay in the shadows of the parking lot. "Haldane's really running a coke lab in there?"

"Yeah."

"For how long?"

"Beats me. I just found out about it this afternoon when I got that nickel and figured our way into and out of the building."

"What are we going to do about it?"

"Me? I'm not doing anything. I got what I came for, that's why I made the trip."

"You're going to leave him and his operation intact?"

"That coke lab is the problem of the Washington, D.C., police department, vice section."

Mac glanced back up at the building.

"Look," Rawley said, "if Slade said burn the guy, I'd burn him. Until then, Haldane isn't anything to me. Just a place to get information tonight. I'll probably never see him again. As far as the coke goes, don't expect me to buy your altruistic feelings. Nobody's putting a gun to an addict's head and making him buy that stuff. If you have a market for something out there, somebody's going to provide it. You can't save people from themselves. Trust me, I know. And in case you forgot, I turned off the explosive. Could be Haldane's boys will be out here any minute to pick up where we left off. We left a couple of them really hurting. Let me know if you find anything out with that list."

"I will." Mac dropped into the driver's seat and watched Rawley cross the parking lot and climb into a full-size Chevy truck. Mac scratched the license-plate number on his pad as Rawley wheeled the vehicle onto South Capitol Street. He didn't try to follow the man. No one had successfully tailed Rawley, and Wilson discouraged any curiosity that was out of place. Rawley was entitled to his privacy.

Turning the other way, taking the long way back to his apartment to give him time to work the car phone, Mac called the Washington, D.C., Department of Motor Vehicles, reached a policewoman he knew professionally and personally, and had her run the truck's plate for him. She said she'd get back to him within minutes.

He punched in a new series of numbers, got a friend of a friend in vice, and clued the guy in about the coke lab Haldane was operating above the club. The narco squad wouldn't be able to go in immediately, but they could set up surveillance on the building now that they knew about it. Within weeks Haldane would be out of the drug business for awhile—one way or another.

While he was waiting for the connection to Boston, he crossed the Anacosta River. Moonlight filmed a soft glow over the sluggish water, then leaked out over the fog already gathering along the banks. He reached his friend in Boston and was told to call in the morning to initiate the search for the names on the list. Mac thanked the guy and hung up.

The phone rang just before he took the left on Massachusetts Avenue. "MacDonald."

"Hey, Mac, it's Trudy. I found that truck you were looking for."

"Are you going to tell me, or just keep me in suspense?"

"The truck belongs to Hayden Scroggins." Trudy added an address from the northeast quadrant of the city. "It was reported stolen about ten minutes ago by the guy who stole it, then he called in and told us where to find it. Scroggins didn't even know it was missing. Is that what you were expecting?"

"No." Mac felt a frown darken his face. None of his ex-wives had ever liked that look. "But it makes sense. Thanks."

"Are you going to tell me the story behind this?"

"Can't. It's classified information. If I told you, I'd have to kill you."

"You sure know how to turn a girl's head. Well, if I don't get the story, you at least owe me lunch."

"Done. Give me another three or four days, and you can set up when and where." She agreed and he broke the connection.

Reaching inside his windbreaker, he took his cigarette pack out of a pocket and shook one free. He lit it, cracking the window to let the smoke get sucked away. He was tired. The few hours of sleep he'd managed in the afternoon had left him wanting more. Rawley got under his skin. The man played things too closely. The truck had been a subtle message tonight to leave well enough alone.

Not for the first time, Mac wondered how dangerous uncovering Rawley's real identity would be.

But it was a puzzle he couldn't resist. Rawley represented too many questions, and every question was punctuated with danger. Wilson wasn't satisfied with things either, but Rawley served a purpose, and Mac couldn't fault Slade for keeping that in mind.

In the early days of Omega Blue, there'd been some consternation that the special agents assigned to the unit would become just as bad as the criminals they were working to put away. In Rawley's case, though, Mac was willing to believe that the man had probably started out on equal footing, whether it was from training with a government agency or a background in the Mafia. He didn't like thinking about what would happen if Rawley ever turned on them.

CHAPTER 11

"In here."

Harry Prio followed the man ahead of him through the corridor of the third floor of the motel. The lights were dim, and people passing them in the hallway kept their eyes down. Prio didn't worry about being recognized. The Hotel Briscoe was where you went when you wanted to turn invisible. Media personalities and performers lounged there when they were in town and didn't want any of the tabloids dishing the real dirt on them.

The hard guy came to a stop outside room 328 and took up a position.

Glancing back down the hallway, Prio saw that three other men were there to control the situation.

"It's open," the security man said in a low voice.

Prio slipped his hand under his trench coat and

freed the silenced Colt .45 automatic from its belly holster. He entered the room as quietly as possible.

The living room area was dim. A television in the corner was tuned to a twenty-four-hour news channel. The light flickered over the lean assortment of furniture. The sounds of passionate moaning could be heard from the bedroom.

Prio eased into the bedroom, managed to stay out of sight of the two people performing sexual gymnastics on the round bed. The familiar anticipation of the voyeur filled him: his body reacted to the sights, sounds, and smells inside the room.

The woman was on top, her taut hips partially swaddled by the crisp white sheets. Perspiration gleamed along her body as moonlight from the partially open windows glazed it. She looked tanned and healthy, her blond hair tumbling halfway down her back.

Congressman Keith Jarvis lay underneath her, his hands pulling at her flesh as he thrust up against her. His complexion was pasty, and his hair—normally combed back—was in wild disarray across his forehead.

The woman was Angel Candless, a secretary in the congressman's office. She had a coke habit that DiVarco had found out about and exploited. She thought she was here tonight to let the congressman get caught with his face in compromising pictures or video footage.

Prio knew the woman wouldn't recognize her mistake until it was too late.

Without warning, Jarvis surged up against the woman and pulled her to him tightly. An animal moan escaped his lips. Candless laughed good-naturedly and whispered in his ear.

Prio stepped up and saw the congressman's smile

freeze uncertainly on his face. When Prio showed him the gun, Jarvis tried to shove the woman off. She screamed and fell to one side. The congressman couldn't get clear of the blankets.

Firing methodically, Prio put four hollowpoints— all within a space that could have been covered by a playing card—into the congressman's chest. The man's body slammed back into the bed as crimson droplets sprayed over the sheets. His legs jerked a couple of times, then relaxed.

Candless continued to scream, hunkering down into a fetal position against the wall.

Prio turned and fired the remaining three bullets. One of them caught her in the face and the screaming stopped immediately. Crimson smeared the wall as she slumped to the carpet.

After sticking a fresh clip into the pistol, Prio took an envelope from inside of his trench coat and dropped it onto the bed. Inside was a letter put together from newspaper clippings that read: HE SHOULDN'T HAVE TAKEN HER AWAY. THEY GOT WHAT THEY DESERVED.

The note would lead the homicide investigators through Candless's erratic life-style, and there were plenty of men to keep the detectives busy for a long time. Candless's habit had kept her bed hopping as she tried to make the down payments.

Another pocket yielded a current bill from a flower shop where an account had been kept in the congressman's name for the last three months, and one of DiVarco's men had paid for charges against it in cash. Every two or three weeks, a bouquet of flowers had been delivered to Candless at home or at work. Even if the homicide detectives were leery about establishing the relationship between the two through whatever records Jarvis might have left, the statement from the flower shop would put it out there for everyone to see.

Prio slipped the statement into the congressman's wallet, then headed for the door. Jarvis's death hadn't happened merely to insure that Cashion was pushed to the head chair position on the House committee responsible for the funding of Omega Blue. Jarvis was also a message from DiVarco to Cashion that results were expected, soon.

The house was a two-story split roofline less than seven miles away from Wolf Trap Farm Park, and was cut out of the forested area. A wooden deck ran around the front and east sides of the house. A soft yellow light gleamed from two of the windows on the lower floor.

Parking his Cherokee in the garage that was set apart from the home, Slade Wilson crossed the yard to the front porch. He could tell from the flower beds that his father had spent the day working outside.

The door was open and he went on through. He could tell as soon as he entered the living room, where the stereo was playing an old Bonnie Raitt music disc, that his father was still awake. He glanced at his watch and saw that the time was 10:42 P.M. An early riser, his father was usually in bed before now.

"Dad?"

"Kitchen," Chaney Wilson called out. "I was beginning to wonder if you were coming home after all."

"Sorry. I took my time and didn't push it. Had some things I wanted to clear out of my head." Wilson draped his jacket over a coatrack beside the door, then added the Delta Elite and Walther .22. He kept the

9mm in his boot, walked through the neat living room and dining area, past the stone fireplace, and into the small kitchen. Bonnie Raitt kept the background alive with her bluesy voice.

"Everything go okay with Kasey?" At one time, Chaney Wilson had been a big man. He sat in his wheelchair in front of the stove, stirring the contents of a Dutch oven. He had broad shoulders and dark hair that refused to go gray, despite his nearly sixty years. He wore a beard these days, part of his self-styled rebellion against the clean-shaven look he'd had to keep while patrolling a beat in Washington, D.C., but his hair was still clipped short. His skin was weathered from the sun and the time he spent outside working the landscape, tending the livestock he kept, and chopping wood for the fireplace. After almost thirty years of a cop's life and after surviving his wife's death seven years ago, he wasn't prepared to give in to the gunshot wound that had severed his spinal cord and paralyzed him from the waist down. He wore jeans over legs that were getting too thin for his barrel-chested build, and a black sweatshirt with the sleeves pulled up to midforearm.

"Yeah." Wilson's father already knew about Kasey's new headgear. Kasey received more visits from her grandfather than she did from him.

"You don't sound so good."

"It's hard seeing her like that."

"I know."

"Dr. Culley said there's a new procedure she wants to try with Kasey."

"Not drugs?"

"No. Something to do with virtual reality. She thinks there may be a way to tap into Kasey's brain."

"Not literally, I hope."

"No."

"She offers hope?"

"Yes."

"Are you going to do it?"

"Maybe. I'm going to want more information first, and even if I decide to go ahead with it, there's still Blair to contend with."

"True."

Wilson opened the refrigerator and poured himself a glass of iced tea, then freshened his father's glass. "I saw her this evening."

"Yeah?"

"Yeah. It went about the way you'd think it would."

"Sorry to hear that."

"You'd think I'd get used to it after awhile."

"You will."

Wilson sipped his tea and peered into the Dutch oven. "Smells great."

"Chili con carne. Cooked it earlier so all I had to do was heat it up once I knew when to expect you. You hungry?"

"Yeah." The food at the center hadn't begun to satisfy Wilson. It was hard to have an appetite while he worked with Kasey. It wasn't her fault, but all of his attention was on making sure she was okay.

"Let's eat." Chaney cut the heat under the pot, then used pot holders and a towel to rest the Dutch oven in his lap. He wheeled himself into the dining area. "Grab some bowls, spoons, and napkins. The crackers are in the pantry, and there's a garden salad in the refrigerator."

Wilson managed the items in two trips, adding their tea glasses and the pitcher as well. He sat and they focused on the meal. It had been over a week since he'd eaten with his father. He didn't realize how much he'd missed it until he was enmeshed in the small talk surrounding their lives. Gradually, the conversation worked around to what Wilson was presently investigating.

His father was a good listener, only interrupting to clarify a point or make a limited observation. By that time they'd cleared away the chili and salad and were working on the sliced fruit and cheeses from the tray Chaney had prepared.

"Boston's a hard beat," his father said when he'd finished. "Lot of old-time hard-liners up there who don't hesitate over territorial rights. Figure they got the grease in all the right places."

"I know."

"Even in the D.C. squads, you find a certain amount of graft, but Boston's been hit pretty hard lately with all the layoffs and street crime. I don't think it would be in your best interests to be counting on any help up there."

"I'm not."

"Any idea how long this is going to take?"

"No. With the Korean involvement, I'm not sure even what we're dealing with here."

"When are you leaving?"

"First thing in the morning. I've got some prep work to do before I crash the House committee meeting with Vache."

"How's that going?"

Wilson cleared the dishes and headed for the kitchen with them. "Better than I expected. Lamar Cashion is the number-two man on the subcommittee, and he's carrying a lot of weight these days."

"Is he for or against you people?"

"Against. Vache has been taking a beating from them lately. The thing is, Cashion hasn't seen all the cards in my hand yet." Wilson ran water into the sink, added soap, and started on the dishes while his father programmed in another music disc.

"Slade."

Wilson awoke with a start, slinging water out of the bathtub as he raised his arm in defense. He couldn't remember the nightmare that had claimed him, but Kasey had been part of it. He blinked, his eyes felt grainy and hard. The water was up to his chin, just starting to turn cool now. He pushed himself up and reached for the intercom toggle switch on the wall. "Yeah, Dad."

"Phone call. It sounds like Earl Vache."

"Thanks. I'll take it in my room." He pushed himself out of the tub, then grabbed a towel and wrapped it around his waist. He picked up the 9mm from its place on the soap dish and padded into his bedroom.

The room was almost as barren as a motel room. Once he'd moved in, after learning about Blair's infidelity, he hadn't tried to make the house a home. It belonged to his father. The only personal items were pictures of Kasey. His father had added a few things from Slade's early days, like the framed movie poster of Alan Ladd in *Shane* his father had found somewhere when he was still a boy.

He lifted the telephone and said, "Wilson," then heard the click of his father's phone being cradled.

"It's Vache," the FBI liaison said. "Somebody just whacked Congressman Jarvis."

"When?" Wilson checked his watch. It was a quarter to one. He'd slept in the bathtub almost a half-hour.

"They just found his body. An aide called it in. Couldn't be more than a couple hours ago."

"What happened?"

"The stupid son of a bitch was out at a hotel playing slap and tickle with a woman from his secretarial pool."

"Did he have a past history with her?"

"Yeah. The aide knew all about it, but you can tell she's trying to shove a lid over everything."

"Who pulled the trigger?"

"It looks like the woman had a jealous lover tucked away somewhere too."

Call waiting beeped in his ear before Wilson could reply, and he asked Vache to hold on while he switched to the other line. "Wilson."

"It's me," Mac said. "We need to talk."

"I've got Vache on the other line."

"It'll keep till you're finished. Call me." Mac broke the connection.

Wilson switched back over to Vache. "Have they got the jealous lover in custody?"

"No."

"Then how do they figure that?"

"There was a note."

"At the scene?"

"Yeah."

"That's pretty damned convenient."

"That problem belongs to Washington, D.C., homicide. My problem is the House subcommittee meeting tomorrow."

"That's still on?"

"Oh yeah. Lamar Cashion called me himself as soon as the news broke over the media to let me know I needed to be there tomorrow afternoon. And I can tell you right now that the call was definitely not a friendly one."

Wilson was silent for a moment. "It's interesting that the present investigation we're on is taking us into Boston at the same time a jealous lover decides to kill Jarvis, leaving Cashion—who's from Massachusetts—in charge of a committee that supposedly has clout with us."

"They *do* have clout with your unit," Vache warned. "Don't make the mistake of thinking for an instant that they don't. With Jarvis's murder, there're going to be a lot more people interested in that hearing tomorrow than would normally tune in. We're going to be in the goddamned spotlight."

"Think about the events that have happened."

"I am. Are you trying to hand me a conspiracy theory here, Slade? Christ, those things have been popular ever since Lincoln got whacked."

"They also tell me fruit never falls far from the tree."

"I don't need clichés."

Wilson ran a hand through his hair as the headache the long bath had almost gotten rid of came back in full force. "Then tell me what you need."

"What *we* need. We need to skate that House subcommittee interview tomorrow."

"I've got a good feeling about that."

"A good feeling?"

"I'll wear my lucky socks. Christ, loosen up. Wait and see what happens tomorrow. I've got to get back to Mac."

"Okay. If you hear anything, let me know."

"Bet on it."

Vache broke the connection.

Wilson cradled the phone, retrieved a pair of gray gym shorts from a dresser drawer, and pulled them on. He walked into the other bedroom where he kept his computer, a desk, and filing cabinets. Dropping into the seat behind his desk, he booted up the computer, tuned it to a media channel, and watched it without the audio portion as he dialed MacDonald back.

In terse sentences Mac explained what he and Rawley had turned up in Haldane's nightclub. "I got a call back from my buddy in Boston."

The video footage on the computer monitor showed a coroner's team taking Jarvis's body out of the hotel under a white sheet that was spotted with blood. One of the media cameras almost made it into the back of the coroner's wagon before a uniformed cop shoved the camcorder and photographer back. Wilson didn't bother saving the sequence in the computer's memory. The story was sure to play over the next few hours, becoming more elaborate as it was spun out.

"What did he say?" Wilson asked.

"The Boston PD's already working on the Korean angle inside the city."

"Any links to Sebastian DiVarco?"

"Plenty. Rumor has it that DiVarco's making a bid for control of a majority of the illegal action inside the city and the suburbs. The Koreans are supposedly fronting the muscle to get it done."

"Any ideas why?"

"No."

"A bona fide mystery."

"At least it's not a locked room," Mac said. "I'd rather figure out why somebody's doing something than how they're doing it any day. Why gets easy once you start tracking the money. How is usually the tricky part."

Wilson agreed, then rang off. He sat at the desk and watched the latest updates on Jarvis's murder. It all tied in somewhere, somehow. He was sure of that. But Mac had it right when he said that tracking the money would help them uncover the players as well as the motivations.

"Slade?"

Wilson reached for the intercom. "Yeah, Dad?"

"Is everything okay?"

"Just got a couple new wrinkles to work through. I'll probably be up for a little while."

"Anything you want to talk about?"

"No."

"Won't do yourself any good if you're worn out tomorrow."

"I won't be long. Good night, Dad."

"Good night." The intercom burped as the link was severed.

For a moment Wilson wondered what it would be like to simply reach out to a switch and tell Kasey good night. The thought hurt. He put it away and turned his mind to DiVarco, the Koreans, and Jarvis's murder.

CHAPTER 12

"A re you sure you want to do this?"

Slade Wilson glanced at Earl Vache as they moved through the labyrinth that comprised the House of Representatives. "More now than ever."

Vache hustled to keep up with him.

Wilson looked at the map he'd drawn for himself after getting directions from one of the pages circulating within the building. He took another turn, then glanced at his watch. It was 12:35 P.M., and he'd verified that Congressman Lamar Cashion was getting ready for the subcommittee hearing in a borrowed office.

"You want to tell me what you're going to say to the guy when you see him?" Vache asked.

"No."

"For Christ's sake. I'm in this too."

"Not this part of it."

"I'm here."

"Not by invitation."

"Why do I get the feeling that you're taking a chance on making things worse?"

"Because you know me."

"That really helps, Slade."

Wilson ignored Vache and concentrated on keeping himself together. Everything depended on presentation. Cashion was an egotistical man and couldn't be easily shoved, but political power was everything to the man. Last night's events must have given Cashion a real good look at the things that could be his if he played his cards right.

Taking two more turns, Wilson found the door he was looking for. He went through, waving the secretary back into her seat as she got up to intercept him. He showed her the ID pinned to his sport coat.

The woman reached for the intercom button, an uncertain look on her face.

Wilson entered the rear office before Cashion could answer his secretary's buzz.

The congressman was soft and balding. His blue eyes were light and watery behind the rimless glasses. The gunmetal gray suit he had on was carefully tailored. He pressed the intercom button. "Summon security, Ms. Travers."

"Yes, sir."

Cashion sat in the plush office chair and steepled his fingers before him, making a conscious effort to preen smugly. "What the hell do you think you're doing here, Wilson?"

"Lodging an informal request that we postpone this afternoon's festivities for a few weeks while we recognize the nation's loss."

"Bullshit. After a couple of days, Jarvis won't even be in the media, except for the tabloids, who'll probably list sightings of him with Elvis."

Wilson never had liked Cashion, but the callousness the man displayed now deepened the feeling.

"Jarvis got exactly what was coming to him," Cashion said. "Don't expect to buy me off with some sympathy ploy."

"I didn't expect to buy you off with that," Wilson replied. He was aware of Vache fidgeting beside him as he took a step toward the desk.

Cashion pushed himself back against the wall. "Lay one hand on me, Wilson, and I'll have you thrown in jail. This is what I've been talking about ever since I was put on this subcommittee: you people are losing sight of the line that separates you from the criminals you're supposed to be pursuing."

"I pursue criminals," Wilson said in a soft voice. "I've even been known to catch a few despite congressional interference and special-interest groups."

"Mr. Cashion," the secretary said over the intercom, "security has been notified, and they're on their way."

Cashion gave an oily smile. "I bet you can hold your breath longer than the time it'll take them to get here."

"In that case," Wilson said, "let me be brief." He reached under his sport coat and dropped a five-by-seven manila envelope on the desktop.

"What's that?"

"Transcripts on accounting done through a Zurich bank account over the last seven years," Wilson said. "You might recognize the account number." He gave it.

Color drained from Cashion's face as he involuntarily reached for the packet. "Where did you get this?"

"Does it matter?"

A uniformed security guard stepped into the room with his hand on his weapon. Two more men followed him. "Congressman, you reported some trouble?"

Wilson stood his ground and matched Cashion's icy stare until the congressman looked away.

"It was only a misunderstanding," Cashion said. "Please close the door on your way out."

The security people left, and the door was eased shut.

"You're not gaining any popularity points with the security people," Wilson said. "They hate false alarms."

"Where the hell did you get this?"

"From the bank."

Cashion turned to Vache, who had remained silent throughout their conversation. "What do you know about this?"

"Nothing," Wilson answered. "This is my deal to you."

"Vache."

"I don't know," Vache replied. "Let me have a look at it."

Cashion shoved the packet into his jacket and took a couple deep breaths. "No, just stay out of this." He looked at Wilson. "What are you going to do?"

"That depends on you."

"What do you want?"

"Some space. I want this subcommittee off my fucking back for awhile so I can finish what we started in Atlanta."

"You knew organ jackal operations were off-limits," Cashion said. "You knew that going in. There's too much political controversy over them."

"The homeless aren't recyclable people."

"Depends on your point of view. The government dole has already proven incapable of taking care of them. They're dying by the dozens every day of malnutrition, disease, and predators within their own groups."

"Then something needs to be done to fix the problem. They're not there to be preyed on or stripped for spare parts."

"Find a solution, Agent Wilson, and you'll be hailed as a great man."

"If I turn those records over to the media people I know, no one will even be able to find the bones of your career."

"That's what you say."

"Tell me different." Wilson stood his ground.

Reaching out, Cashion tapped the intercom button. "Ms. Travers."

"Yes, sir."

"Contact the other members of the subcommittee and let them know I've decided to postpone the meeting. Let them know I'll get back with them later for rescheduling."

"Yes, sir."

"I think we're at a standoff," Cashion said. "For awhile. You won't use those records against me because they'll complicate your investigation of the jackal network now, when you need to move immediately to take it out once and for all at the source. By the time you get started on your investigation in Boston, those records you have won't even be real anymore. You'll just have a fistful of worthless paper."

"I've also got your money," Wilson replied.

"Something less than three million and change. Before I came in here, I had it transferred over to another account that you can't touch. Screw with me and I'll make sure it evaporates. As long as my group is operational, your money's safe."

"You're lying."

"Call your bank. But I wouldn't suggest doing it from here. Calls out of congressional buildings are logged and kept on file." Wilson turned and led the way out of the room. The burden weighing him down felt lighter, but Boston was going to prove a deadly little game before it was over with. The traffic in the hallway was more dense now as people returned from lunch.

"Slade." Vache tried to get his attention.

"Yeah." Wilson kept walking, going over the mental notes he'd made himself last night concerning the unit's insertion into Boston.

"Did we just blackmail the head of the House subcommittee responsible for our funding?"

"No. I did it."

"But I was in the room."

"If we get caught, I'll take the rap. I tried to back you out of it."

"How long do you think that's going to work?"

"With any luck, long enough." Wilson made his way to the front of the building. Outside the air tasted fresh and clean. There was still a lot of green in the yards and on the trees, but it was only temporary. Winter had already put its mark over the land. From the steps he was able to see the Grant memorial at the foot of the hill at the eastern end of the Mall museums. The giant bronze statue showed the former president seated on a horse.

"How did we blackmail him?"

"A gift from Newkirk," Wilson said. "He rummaged through Cashion's financial closets till he came up with that Zurich banking skeleton. He couldn't find anything on Jarvis. We were hoping to get Cashion to help us leverage Jarvis into backing off. With Cashion chairing the subcommittee, things worked out even better."

They started down the steps toward the underground parking entrance, knowing it would take less time to clear security from the outside because most House members would be using the inner exits to avoid the media and lobbying groups.

"Who's paying Cashion off?" Vache asked.

"I don't know. Newkirk traced some of the funds to Boston banks, but the trail disappeared. I've got DiVarco figured for it."

"DiVarco hasn't been a big enough dealer for the seven-year period you're talking about."

"He could have picked up Cashion's chit from someone else. DiVarco's cutting through the local mob circles."

"That explains DiVarco's ability to put together a jackal network running up the East Coast."

Wilson gave his ID a workout at the security counter, then he and Vache were passed through in just under three minutes.

"Where's Cashion's money?" Vache asked.

"It was received as a donation to Help the Homeless Foundation in Miami this morning in Cashion's name, with a note that the donation is to remain unmentioned."

"That'll last all of two or three days, then Cashion's going to know you double-crossed him. He'll be after you harder than ever."

Wilson unlocked his Cherokee, climbed in, and unlocked Vache's door. "That gives us two or three days. By that time I hope to have a handle on DiVarco's organization. I've already got some angles for us to work on. With any luck, when we pull down DiVarco, we'll take Cashion with him."

Vache pulled his seat belt tight as Wilson roared out of the underground garage and followed the access roads leading to Constitution Avenue. "And if you don't?"

"Taking DiVarco and his organization out is our job. If we can't get it done, we deserved to get busted by Cashion."

"And to do it, you'd even commit a felony like the one you just pulled off?"

Wilson didn't hesitate. "Yes."

Vache sighed and turned away, sinking into his seat. "You know, Cashion may be right when he says Omega Blue is blurring the lines between cop and crook."

"Bullshit, Earl. The only problem these days is that it's getting harder to save people from themselves. They still have to make that decision on their own. I'm just trying to make sure DiVarco and guys like him don't get big enough to take that decision away."

Standing behind Quinn Valentine, Maggie Scuderi put her hands on his shoulders and straightened them. "Relax," she advised. "Let the programming do the work. Don't try to force it. Just accept it."

Valentine stood in a stall at the indoor shooting range at the FBI Academy. He had a two-handed grip on the Delta Elite and was peering over the sights at the silhouette target downrange.

Guns banged constantly around them as other shooting classes obeyed the harsh bark of their instructors.

Scuderi breathed in the harsh scent of cordite, satisfied herself with Valentine's stance, then released him. She was dressed in cowboy boots, jeans tucked into them, and a yellow oxford shirt with the sleeves rolled up over a long-sleeved black sweatshirt.

"This is ridiculous," Valentine said. "Hell, I was a better shot before the operation." He wore black Dockers with a pumice-colored fashion pullover with the sleeves pushed up to his elbows. A white gauze patch covered the incision on the back of his neck where the microsurgery had been done the day before.

"That's because you're fighting the programming," Scuderi said as she adjusted her ear protection.

"I know how to shoot."

"You have your way of shooting. The programming has its way. Once you learn to go with the programming, it won't matter what your stance is, or what kind of position you're shooting from. The SeekNFire will give you optimal results at all times. Now, shoot."

Valentine squeezed off all seven rounds, then pushed the button to reel the target in. When it arrived, two of the bullets were out of the black and one of them had missed entirely. The rest were scattered across the torso of the silhouette.

"Shit," Valentine said in disgust.

"Just loosen up."

"I have loosened up, damnit."

"No you haven't." Scuderi made her voice hard. She adjusted her amber-colored shooting glasses and stepped forward. Raking another silhouette target from the rack on the stall wall to her left, she pulled the last one down and replaced it.

"I suppose you can do better."

"Hell yes, I can do better."

"Then let's get it on. Show me."

Scuderi curbed her impatience and anger. She could well remember the frustration Valentine was going through. Letting out a deep breath, she pushed the button that sent the silhouette winging back out to the distance necessary for the exercise.

Valentine reloaded, then released the slide and snapped the first round into place. He stood behind her in the stall.

Whirling suddenly, Scuderi locked her fists in Valentine's shirt and yanked him toward her. "Shoot the damn target in the head! Now!"

Valentine tried to aim.

She shifted her weight and yanked him off balance again.

"Damnit! Quit!"

"Shoot!"

"I can't like this." Valentine tried to use his free arm to brush her grip away.

Scuderi elbowed him in the ribs hard enough to knock the wind out of him. "Shoot!"

He swiped at her again.

Headbutting him, she popped his head back. "Shoot, goddamnit! You either get this today, now, or you'll be staying here when we leave tomorrow!"

Valentine's nose trickled blood across his lips. "Fucking bitch!" He raised his gun arm and pointed.

"Don't aim, just look. Ignore those sights, look at your target." Scuderi kept yanking on his clothes, keeping him off balance. "Look at the head. That's your target. Don't let me catch you aiming or you're going to be singing soprano tonight. Now shoot, goddamnit!"

Valentine emptied the clip in a roll of thunder as she kept pushing at him. He was breathing hard when the slide blew back empty.

She released him carefully, all too aware of the ball of resentment Valentine carried around. Wilson had warned her that he might try to retaliate, despite her seniority. Scuderi stepped back. "You okay here?"

Glaring, Valentine nodded, then swiped at the blood leaking across his lips. It left a crimson smear.

Without a word, Scuderi punched the target retrieval button and the silhouette jerked forward. A group of cadets and instructors had come to a halt around them and were watching the developments intently. A red-shirted security man started over. "Beat it," she told him. "We're chill here."

The guy nodded and moved away.

Shots started ringing out with more frequency as everything returned to normal.

Scuderi stripped the silhouette from the hooks and showed it to Valentine. All seven shots were centered in the target's forehead and could have been covered with a drink coaster.

"Son of a bitch." Valentine took the target in surprise. He held it up to let the light shine through the holes. "I did that?"

"You and the SeekNFire system." Scuderi took her purse from the shelf built into the stall, rummaged inside, and came up with a package of tissues. She handed a couple to Valentine.

He took them and wiped his face, then tossed them into the trash can outside the stall. "So all I have to do whenever I need to use my gun is think about how pissed I was at you. Terrific."

"No. What you need to do is trust the programming." Scuderi stored her ear protectors on the shelf and walked away.

Valentine caught up with her. His pistol was tucked inside his belt. "So where are we going? We can't be through."

"In here we are. You're too conscious of the target range." Scuderi passed through the doors into the bright afternoon sunshine. She took the path leading down to the outside shooting areas flanking the Hogan's Alley setup. The absence of gunfire made it seem as though her ears were packed with cotton.

"What the fuck is it with you people?" Valentine demanded. "Wilson reamed my ass the first time I met him, and I haven't heard shit from him since. Nobody else has even talked to me. And you use me for a god-damned punching bag when you're supposed to be teaching me to use this new system."

"I am teaching you." The trail petered out at a clearing set up for a rifle range. Tall trees ringed the area.

"Bullshit. Teaching is something that's done in a more relaxed environment." He wiped at his nose. The flow had already stopped.

Scuderi stopped and gazed at Valentine. "You don't have a relaxed job." She paused. "Nobody wants to like you. Besides having an abrasive and hostile nature all on your own, you're a neophyte to this unit. Your life expectancy isn't worth shit. In the history of this unit, four people never made it out of the probationary stages. They were people who had a hell of a lot more experience behind them than you do. Nobody wants to buddy up to you because you could be gone tomorrow. If your macho attitude doesn't get you killed, your lack of training could. You understand?"

"Screw it. I can take care of myself."

"That's the kind of attitude I'm talking about, you pompous little prick. Nobody can just take care of themselves in this group. You've got to take care of everybody else, and know when to let someone take care of you. You'll get somebody else killed while you're trying to take care of yourself."

For once, Valentine didn't have anything to say.

"Get your weapon ready," Scuderi ordered.

Valentine readied the 10mm with a snap.

Opening her hand, Scuderi showed him the seven quarters she'd taken from the roll in her purse. "I'm going to throw these into the air. You try to shoot them before they fall."

"You're kidding."

"No. If you let your reflexes go to the programming, you'll be able to do it." Without giving him any warning, Scuderi threw the coins into the air in front of them. They glittered and spun.

Valentine's pistol emptied in a steady drumroll.

"Oh for seven," Scuderi said when she picked up the fallen quarters. "Reload."

Taking rounds from the hip pouch he'd been given inside the gun range, Valentine reloaded. On his second attempt he got two of the coins. It took him ninety-eight rounds to shoot away the roll of forty quarters. On his last attempt he'd shot the last five quarters with six rounds.

"You're coming along," Scuderi said as the sounds of the last gunshots faded away. And it was true. Wilson would be glad to know that Valentine was actually integrating with the SeekNFire programming more quickly than was usually expected. But she couldn't tell Valentine that because of the guy's cocky attitude.

"Wait," Valentine said.

Scuderi turned to face him.

He smiled cruelly. "I've heard a lot of shit about how good this system is. You've been cramming it down my throat all morning long. How about you giving me a demonstration?"

Scuderi folded her arms across her chest. "I don't demonstrate anything."

"Then how about a wager? You pop all seven coins, I buy dinner. You miss even one, you buy dinner. You're so sure of yourself, this should be an easy dinner, right?"

"What's the catch?"

"No catch. I just want to see if you can back up what you say."

Scuderi pulled her pistol out of her purse. "Go for it."

"And they're dimes, not quarters." Valentine smiled and opened his hand to show her.

"That's fine." Scuderi reached behind her jaw and triggered the SeekNFire circuitry. It juiced her system in heartbeats.

Valentine stood beside her, then made a show of tossing the coins into the air.

Scuderi watched them sail up, glittering and spinning, arcing across the blue sky. Her gun came up, then she felt Valentine smash into her from the side. Pain racked her and she went with the force of the blow, falling and rolling, the Delta Elite extended in her hand. The SeekNFire circuitry pinged as target acquisition was achieved. Two of the dimes disappeared with the pair of shots she managed as she cushioned her fall. Another winked out as she rolled on her stomach. Two more followed as she continued her roll. The sixth sparked away when she was pushing herself to her feet. She was standing again when she saw the seventh dime at almost shoulder level. She squeezed the trigger again and the last coin skipped out of sight. As she turned around, she reloaded the 10mm. "Dinner's on you."

A smirk twisted Valentine's face. "Either way it was a bet I couldn't lose. I'm hoping you'll prove a more talkative dinner companion than teacher."

Scuderi turned and walked away. "I'll take dinner tonight," she said. "At Duke Zeibert's." She stopped. "Oh, and make sure it's a reservation for one. I don't want to spoil my appetite."

The string of curses that followed was passionate and gender specific, but Scuderi didn't think any of it was particularly unique or original.

Graveside services for Emmett Newkirk were held at seven P.M. at Arlington National Cemetery, and the list of guests was small. The agent was buried in the land annex that had been added when the cemetery filled up in 2008.

Standing under the canopy spread over the site, Slade Wilson stared out over the precise rows of tombstones. From his position he could see the flickering flame that marked President John F. Kennedy's grave. Twilight was heavy now, and he could barely make out the members of the Third U.S. Infantry Regiment that stood guard over the Tomb of the Unknowns. Even though he couldn't see them clearly, he knew the guards would still be carrying out the twenty-one-step, twenty-one-second-pause pattern that had been going on for decades. His father had taken him there as a small child to visit the grave of an uncle he'd never known, and he'd been fascinated by the routine of the guards.

He listened to the priest's words as the final prayer was said, trying to find solace in them. There was none. Newkirk wasn't the first friend he'd buried.

Earl Vache stood behind the priest. Darnell January and Bob MacDonald stood under a tree together just in back of the small group of mourners. Quinn Valentine stood alone to their left. Wilson reflected that he hadn't even said anything to the younger agent, and made a note to take care of that. Things were getting tense enough without straining them further.

Wilson sat with Newkirk's surviving family of three daughters in the line of folding metal chairs closest to the casket. Vivian, the oldest, had only known Wilson superficially, but had invited him to sit with them. Maggie Scuderi, wearing a simple black dress, sat beside him with tears glinting on her cheeks. She kept her hands in her lap.

There was no sign of Lee Rawley.

The smell of fresh earth filled Wilson's nostrils as he looked at the gleaming metal casket. Normally graveside services weren't done this late in the evening. At this time of year the cemetery closed at five P.M. Despite the planned assault on Boston that would begin in the morning, Wilson felt tired and empty, and he knew part of the reason was that familiar smell of turned earth.

The service finished and the priest closed his Bible.

Wilson said a small prayer to himself for Newkirk, then stood up. The husbands of Newkirk's daughters took their wives away, some of them holding small children in their arms. Vivian said good-bye, then took the single white rose her husband had clipped for her from the wreath on top of her father's casket and walked away.

Silently, Wilson walked up to the casket and touched it lightly. Scuderi was at his side. His voice was tight when he spoke. "I don't know what to say anymore. You know?"

"I know," Scuderi said. She linked her arm through his as support. "Just keep in mind that it doesn't end here. Emmett wouldn't have wanted that."

Wilson nodded. A small spark of lightning was reflected in the chrome finish of the casket's trim. Instinctively, he turned and pushed Scuderi down, falling over her body. They rolled against the carpet-covered mound of dirt waiting to cover the casket.

Flame sizzled from the metal surface of the coffin, and the sound of a heavy-caliber rifle shot echoed across the cemetery a heartbeat later.

Pushing himself to his feet, his Delta Elite in his hand as he used his other hand to trigger the SeekNFire circuitry, Wilson yelled, "Sniper!"

The rest of the team had already bolted into action, moving out to push the rest of the mourners to the ground. The priest dropped out of sight on the other side of the coffin. Vache had drawn his gun as well.

A rapid series of rifle shots raked the grounds, clearly focused on Wilson.

Scrambling for position, Wilson scanned the tree line for muzzle flashes. He slipped the T-jack from his pocket, activated the electromagnetic pulse that adhered it to his jawline, and blew into the mike. "Does anybody have a fix on that guy?"

"No," Darnell January radioed back.

"The trees," Quinn Valentine said. "I'm on him."

Wilson glanced at the position where he'd last seen the younger agent. Valentine was in motion, streaking for the tree line while trying to hug the ground.

The rifle shots continued.

"Cover him!" Wilson said. He located the sniper's position and started firing but knew it was too far away for pistol fire to be effective. The guy had them pinned down.

The sound of a different rifle cracked through the air.

Straining his eyes against the encroaching darkness, Wilson saw a prone figure drop from the trees.

"He's down," Lee Rawley's calm voice said over the T-jack.

"Was he alone?" Wilson asked.

"Yes."

"Rawley?" Scuderi asked. She was only now getting her T-jack in place.

Wilson nodded.

"Guess he made it after all."

"Yeah." Wilson saw Rawley's slim form separate from the shadows of the tree line in the distance and move toward the fallen sniper. He guessed that Rawley had actually gotten there before the mourners and set up to wait, but whether the man had come to pay his last respects to Newkirk or to spring close the trap he'd set up, Wilson didn't know. A lot of times with Rawley it was better to view the results of an action than to speculate on the motivations behind it.

He holstered his weapon, switched off the SeekN-Fire circuitry, and moved out to help reassure the mourners and evacuate them from the immediate vicinity. If the team didn't make the jump into the Boston war zone the following morning, it looked like the war zone was fully prepared to come to them.

CHAPTER 13

A cold, gray fog filled with spitting rain rolled into Boston before dawn. Slade Wilson and the Omega Blue team followed it in, touching down at Logan International Airport only minutes later as other airline arrivals were starting to get stacked up. They unloaded the special gear for the operation from the transport jet into the three Ford vans waiting for them, including the four military-style Kawasaki KLR-250 Enduro motorcycles Wilson had requisitioned. Boston traffic was notoriously hard to get around in and he wanted the team to have mobility.

By eight o'clock Wilson was at Boston Police Headquarters. The seven-story building looked old and hard, and weathered well past its years. Wilson and Scuderi walked into the building, leaving the others to work out the parking. They were to stay with the equipment and the vehicles to ensure that nothing was tampered with.

After showing their IDs on the bottom floor and confirming their appointment with Police Commissioner Cyril Isaacs, they were escorted up to the sixth floor by a PR woman who seemed to have had a smile grafted onto her face. Uniformed officers who were caught staring at them quickly shifted their gazes.

Wilson ignored the attention. He was sure the police force knew about the arrival of the FBI agents, and if the rest of the city didn't know about it yet, they would before lunch.

The PR woman left them in the hands of Isaacs's personal secretary, who offered them coffee and Danish. Scuderi and Wilson opted for the coffee but passed on the sweets.

Seventeen minutes later, they were ushered into Isaacs's personal office.

Police Commissioner Cyril Isaacs was a florid-faced man with hands that looked like shovels and a military haircut. His blunt features showed that the last fifty-plus years had been hard ones. He wore a well-fitted double-breasted dark brown suit and smelled of bay rum.

"Special Agent Wilson," Isaacs said, extending his hand.

Wilson took it. The man's grip was impressive. Wilson introduced Scuderi.

Dressed in a midthigh-length skirt, a simple white silk blouse, and a business jacket under her yellow raincoat, Scuderi looked like window dressing, which was the impression they'd wanted to give. While she occupied a large portion of Isaacs's attention, Wilson would have a better chance of observing the police commissioner.

Isaacs had a good record. At least nothing had ever been filed against him successfully. But there were a lot of questions, and Wilson needed some good guesses about the answers before he trusted the man.

"Have a seat," Isaacs said, waving to the pair of chairs in front of his spacious desk. He tried not to be too obvious as he watched Scuderi cross her nylon-encased legs.

Wilson gazed around the office, taking in the Boston Celtics basketball trivia. Pictures hung in neat frames, showing the police commissioner shaking hands with various players who'd been on the team and were acknowledged to be the best in their field. But the office was not the work of a fan. It looked more like a showcase of winners, and that attitude was reflected by the man behind the desk.

"What can I do for you?" Isaacs asked.

"We're here to investigate Sebastian DiVarco," Wilson said.

"On what grounds? Your office was kind of vague about that."

"A jackal network was uncovered in Atlanta, Georgia. DiVarco was pulling the strings."

"You're sure about that? DiVarco has been strictly small-time for years."

"That's in transition," Wilson replied. "And, yeah, I'm sure about the jackal network. I was there. One of my people died there."

Isaacs settled back heavily into his chair and it squeaked under his weight. "Have you got anything to back you up on that?"

Reaching into his briefcase, Wilson produced the

packet of information he'd prepped for the meeting, then dropped it on the desk.

The police commissioner opened the manila folder and started sifting through its contents.

Wilson tried to wait patiently. Twelve minutes later, Isaacs pushed the folder back across the desk. "What you've got there is a laundry list of circumstantial evidence and creative supposition."

"What I've got," Wilson corrected in a soft voice, "is a foundation for the case I'm going to be building."

Isaacs leaned forward and clasped his hands over his stomach. "I hope you didn't come to this office looking for help."

"No."

"Because if you blow this investigation, the FBI is looking at a hell of a lawsuit."

"I don't think so."

"Every man's entitled to his own opinion, but my advice to you, son, is to do a little poking around, then— if you don't turn up something quick—pack up and get the hell out of this city."

"I'll keep that in mind."

"You do that. And you keep something else in mind." Isaacs pushed himself out of his chair and sat on the corner of the desk, leaning over into Wilson's personal space. "When I heard you and your little entourage were coming to Boston, you could say I was less than thrilled. People have a way of getting hurt around you, Wilson. Your investigations have a tendency to run a high profile, run high in property damage and in lives lost."

"We've never lost a civilian."

"Yeah, but what the hell is a civilian to you people?"

Wilson let the barb pass unchallenged.

"I don't want that kind of grief to descend on my city. The people here depend on me to protect them, and I will. Even if it has to be against you. Sure, you come here with your warrants and your Justice Department credentials, but overall that doesn't count for diddly. I run this town when it comes to the streets."

"At some point I'm going to need some help processing the collars we make. Holding cells. Paperwork. Interrogation room. Maybe even some backup if that's not too much to ask."

"Make your case first, then come to me. If you're legit, the PD will be there. I do a damn good job when it comes to policework. Check my record."

Wilson reached into his briefcase and came up with another file. "Yeah, you've got a great record on the surface. Your arrests are netting you an eighty-two percent conviction rate through the DA's office."

"We've got a good working arrangement with the DA's office."

Wilson glanced at other figures on the page. "You've also got a twenty-nine percent unemployment rate in this city. Judging from national averages, even though your conviction rate looks impressive, the police department here is making less arrests than comparable cities with the same area and population."

"Arresting a suspect and keeping a criminal off the streets are sometimes two entirely different things. I figured the FBI would have taught you that. My team plays hard, and they play to win. We get an iffy case, we let it slide and only make arrests when a conviction looks pretty good."

"That kind of reasoning makes me wonder what else you let slide."

Isaacs's face purpled. "You're out of line."

Wilson shrugged. "I am. I apologize."

"I hear any of that shit filtering out through the media of this town," Isaacs warned, "the Bureau's going to be served a defamation suit stemming from this office."

Wilson nodded, gathered his papers, and shoved them back into his briefcase. He stood up but didn't offer to shake hands. "I think we're through here."

"We *are*." Isaacs thumbed the intercom button and hailed his secretary. "Get someone up here on the double to escort these agents out of the building." He turned to the newspaper and coffee on his desk.

A uniformed policeman picked them up in the outer office and silently escorted them to the street. Wilson used his T-jack to find out where the team had parked, and struck off in that direction.

Inside his vehicle, he paired up with Rawley, leaving January with Valentine, and Scuderi partnered with MacDonald. "You have your assignments," he told them over the T-jack frequency. "We're still not sure exactly what it is we're up against, so if there are any doubts, trust your instincts." He shrugged out of the suit and reached for the street clothes he had in the back, along with the Kevlar-lined motorcycle jacket. "Don't depend on the police department to back you. For now, just think of the team as being on its own."

The team radioed back their acknowledgments, then rolled toward their destinations.

Wilson dressed, then started stashing his weapons on his body. He could smell the gasoline coming from the motorcycle engines in the rear of the van. The plan was to shake up the perimeter of DiVarco's organization and see what fell out. There was nothing fancy about the operation—yet. He'd found over the years that the simplest things worked best. Later, he felt certain, there would be more to work with.

Rawley accelerated as Scuderi's van cleared the area. Wilson slid a pair of amber-tinted aviator sunglasses on to block the midmorning sun. For better or worse, the battle had been joined.

"There she is."

Darnell January looked at the crowd already milling in front of the copper-domed Quincy Market building. They were seated on some of the benches built around the huge flowerpots and areas roped off for individual trees. Canopies of glass and bright canvases shrouded the Bull Market, and some of the vendors had wheeled carts that sported gaily striped umbrellas with the name of their business or wares hanging from cards underneath. Voices filled the air between the three buildings linked to Faneuil Hall, some of them advertising what was to be had, and others calling out orders.

"Do you see her?" Valentine asked.

The younger agent was excited. It showed in the suddenly sharp lines of his body. But his age, January knew, would also make people ignore the interest he was showing. It was nothing out of the ordinary for a young man to be caught staring at a woman.

"Where is she?" January asked.

"At that deli. She's wearing jeans and an orange-and-white patterned top. Cream-colored jacket. Her hair's shorter than what we saw in her NCIC picture."

Casually scooping another portion of chow mein from the paper container in his hand, January looked in the direction Valentine had indicated. He found the woman easily. "Chill out. You don't want her to look back over her shoulder and catch you watching her."

Valentine shifted his attention back to the cherry-stone clams in the paper dish he held on his thigh.

January surveyed the woman in a series of quick glances as she pointed out what she wanted to the cashier and stepped to the till. Her peroxided hair, sallow skin scarred by a childhood bout of chicken pox, and hunched shoulders proved that life hadn't gotten any easier since her picture had been logged by the NCIC computers. She'd dropped about ten to fifteen pounds that she really couldn't spare.

Her name was Cynthia Hollister. She'd turned up in further investigative questioning of the young jackal MacDonald and Rawley had broken in Atlanta. She hadn't been involved directly with the jackals, but the man had given Hollister's name as being the current love interest of Mitchell Dodd, one of the black-market medtechs that had performed the organ strip in Miami. Dodd was a known Boston resident, but none of the Bureau's computers could find a current address for him.

Hollister had been a different matter. After checking her Social Security file, they'd found out she was currently working at Browser's, a used-book store around the corner. The address they'd gotten on her—an apartment complex in West Roxbury—was no longer in use.

January finished his chow mein and crumpled the carton as the cashier creased the top of the brown bag and handed it to Hollister. She gave the cashier a grin and a quick good-bye, then moved through the crowd in the direction of the book store.

"Two chili dogs," Valentine said with sarcasm. "The breakfast of champions."

Without commenting, January stood and tossed his empty containers in a nearby waste receptacle. He knew from the way Valentine had eaten his yogurt and bran flakes this morning—and opined against the sausages and eggs most of the rest of the team had had—that breakfast was something his teammate took seriously. But then, Valentine seemed to take everything seriously.

January set up the pursuit pace, trailing casually behind the woman.

"How do you want to handle this?" Valentine asked. Dressed as he was in faded black jeans, a baseball shirt with CHICAGO CUBS printed on the pocket, and a midthigh-length khaki-colored safari jacket, he didn't stand out in the crowd thronging the marketplace.

"I think we should stop somewhere short of a flesh wound," January replied dryly. When Browser's had opened up earlier that morning, Valentine had wanted to go inside and flash his badge at the clerk and demand to know where Hollister lived, not thinking that the clerk might call as soon as they left and tell Hollister about the two FBI agents who'd just stopped by asking directions to her home. The kid had a lot to learn about subtlety, and he wasn't going to be a willing student. Nothing about Valentine appeared to be subtle. January grinned to himself as he thought about it. Valentine was only six or seven years younger than himself, and he was thinking of the guy as a kid. Instead of bracing the clerk, January had found a pay phone, called Browser's, and asked to talk to Hollister, saying he was supposed to talk to her about a book she was going to order for him. The clerk had told him that she was coming in at a quarter to eleven to help with the noonday lunch crowd and tourist rush.

"I'm getting kind of tired of the bum's rush you guys seem to enjoy dishing out all the time," Valentine said.

"That's because you don't know how to just go with the flow. This isn't like what they teach you back in the Academy. Hell, Quinn, you've done time on the streets. You know that badge in your pocket don't amount to jackshit when somebody pulls a gun on you. You keep wanting to rush in where angels fear to tread. There's a natural rhythm to every investigation. It's your job to figure out what it is, then step in cadence to it. The name of the game is pursuit, and the only time you should make a move that's going to make your quarry recognize you is when you figure it's too late for that person or persons to stop you."

Knowing his height already made him stand out among most passersby, January had learned to stoop when he walked, dropping almost three inches from his height. He was dressed in warm-ups colored with swatches of purple, red, and white. The jacket was cut loose enough to conceal the Delta Elite in its shoulder rig. The T-shirt belonged to his high-school basketball days.

"So what have you got in mind?" Valentine asked.

"We lean on her. Tell her if she doesn't let us know where Dodd is we'll let her parole officer know she's been shacking up with a felon. She knows about violations, knows all that guy has to do is yank the string and she's back in a correctional facility like a yo-yo. She won't put Dodd's safety and security over her own."

Hollister had spent some time inside prison and jail on counts of prostitution and check kiting. She'd just gotten out almost a year earlier after an eighteen-month stay, and wouldn't be ready to take a chance on a trip back.

"Cindy!"

Hollister came to a stop and looked back over her shoulder.

"Keep walking," January said in a harsh whisper. He followed his own advice, closing on the woman as the voice hailed her again from behind them.

A confused smile spread across her face, then she turned and walked back toward the FBI agents.

January let her pass, then dropped to one knee beside the wall of the North Market building to retie his shoe. Valentine came to a stop beside him. As January watched, Hollister ducked through the crowd and homed in on a man almost running toward her.

"Dodd," Valentine said.

"I see," January replied.

Dodd was lean and lanky, with shoulders almost too wide for his frame. He needed another thirty pounds to look healthy. Greasy locks of dark hair blew over his face and he hadn't shaved in days. He took Hollister by the elbow and guided her to a spot under a pair of short trees out of the way of the heavy traffic areas. As he talked, he kept throwing furtive glances in all directions around him.

Gazing through the sea of faces that flowed between Hollister and himself, January saw the woman's face go from ecstasy to uncertainty to fear. She nodded, then reached into her purse and took out a handful of currency. Dodd took the money, then grabbed her by the shoulders, kissed her, and started to move away. She called him back long enough to give him the bag of hot dogs.

"He's running," Valentine said.

January nodded. "Let's take him. Easy. No guns unless you don't have a choice. This guy doesn't have a record that shows him carrying heat."

"What about the woman?"

"Let her go. We can pick her up later if we need to." Reaching under his jacket, January took out a pair of disposable cuffs and hid them in his palm. He moved out, a couple steps behind Valentine, flanking his partner and finding his own way through the crowd.

Dodd careened through the crowd, still glancing in all directions and ignoring the sharp invectives that followed him.

Almost at a trot himself, January straightened and took advantage of his size. The crowd parted before him. He reached into his jacket pocket for the T-jack, then adhered it to his face. He blew on the mike. "Quinn."

"I'm with you."

Dodd pulled to one side of the cobblestoned thoroughfare. A quick turn, and he was running through one of the narrow alleys flanking Faneuil Hall, stumbling through the press of patrons carrying their lunches out of the line of small shops inside the building.

January's feet slapped against the smooth pavement of the alley as he ran inside. The sound echoed hollowly in the enclosed environment. On the other side of the alley, Valentine had broken into a full run as well.

Dodd glanced over his shoulder and saw them coming after him. He dropped the brown bag and charged forward.

"Dodd!" January yelled with authority. "We're FBI! You're under arrest! Halt, *now!*"

Ignoring the command, Dodd cut inside Faneuil Hall and disappeared.

January was on the man's heels, a half-step ahead of Valentine as his partner made the swing back across the alley. He pushed himself through the crowd, scattering apologies in the general direction of anyone who might be listening. Ahead of him, he saw Dodd's head bobbing through the press of human beings.

Abruptly, Dodd came to an uncertain halt as three Asian men in dark suits stepped out from a doughnut stall in front of him.

"Quinn."

"I see them."

January kept moving, closing the distance. There was less than thirty feet between them when one of the Asian men put an arm on Dodd's jacket and dragged him forward. One of the men noticed the FBI agents and alerted the other two. The one holding Dodd turned and yanked the medtech toward a side door, leaving his two comrades to cover their retreat. Both of the men reached under their jackets as people between them and the FBI agents screamed, cursed, and got out of the way.

"Gun!" January roared, intending it more as a warning for the marketplace patrons than for Valentine. Still on the run, he scooped a five-pound smoked ham from a large tin barrel at his side in the center of the floor. He cocked his arm back, thinking back to his days on the college gridiron, then threw the ham like a short, over-the-line pass with all his strength.

The ham caught one of the Asian men in the face and knocked him backward against a fruit display. Carefully stacked oranges rained down on him as he crashed to the floor. The pistol he'd been reaching for went skittering away, immediately drawing another series of screams from the people still trapped inside the marketplace.

Valentine went airborne in a flying kick. His opponent ducked under the attempt as Valentine went over, and came around in a roundhouse kick that January knew was going to nail his partner. But instead of landing on his feet, Valentine let himself collapse to the ground, showing that the telegraphed flying kick had only been a feint.

Swiveling on the ground, Valentine slipped one foot behind his opponent's pivot leg as the roundhouse kick came nowhere near him, then lashed out with his other foot at the man's knee. Bone and cartilage splintered with a nasty, rending sound, punctuated by the man's screams of pain. When the man fell, Valentine was on top of him, rolling him over and snapping the disposable cuffs in place.

The man January had put down with the ham was struggling groggily to get to his feet. January drop-kicked him in the face and splayed his unconscious body out. He blew into the T-jack's mike, switched frequencies to the one used by Boston patrol cars, and called for a back-up unit and an ambulance.

"I'm relaying your request now, Agent January," the dispatch officer said.

"How long will it be?" January slipped through the display cases and tables strewn across the middle of the floor and crouched at the doorway where Dodd and the remaining Asian had exited.

"I can't say. The units in that area are busy."

"Doing what? I'm in the middle of a damn firefight here."

The woman's apology sounded cool and professional.

When January attempted to peer around the corner, a pair of bullets ripped long wooden splinters from the door frame. He ducked back inside and drew his pistol. Valentine dropped into place behind him as he triggered the SeekNFire circuitry. The adrenaline flowed through his veins as the programming locked into his reflexes.

"Cover me," January said, letting Valentine move into his place.

Valentine took a two-handed grip on his pistol, then gave a tight nod.

January bolted from the entrance, racing for the Dumpster on the other side of the street against the building. A couple of rounds whined off the pavement and another caught him in the ribs with enough force to throw him off-balance. Managing to turn his fall into a dive, he rolled up behind the Dumpster with his back to the sheet metal. He checked his abdomen, making sure the body armor had stopped the round. It had, but he still felt like he'd been kicked by a horse.

He glanced down the street and saw the Asian man hustling Dodd toward a dark blue sedan that came to a rubber-screaming halt with two wheels over the curb. A pair of gunners stepped from the passenger-side door and one of the rear doors. Machine pistols yammered and 9mm parabellums chewed into the sheet-metal sides of the Dumpster, driving January back to cover.

"Dispatch, this is Special Agent January of the FBI. How long on that backup at Faneuil Hall Marketplace?"

"There are no units available, Agent January. I'll notify you as soon as there are."

January cursed and peered over the top of the Dumpster as he brought the Delta Elite up. He fired as quickly as he could, letting the SeekNFire circuitry home in on his chosen targets. He put three rounds into the back of the man shoving Dodd into the vehicle and knew from the way the man acted that he was wearing Kevlar under his jacket. The other five shots took out the right rear tire, the back glass, and caught the port-side gunner in the neck well enough to drive him to shelter.

The quick bark of Valentine's weapon sounded in a rapid drumroll as it emptied.

Shoving a fresh clip into his pistol, January looked around the Dumpster and saw the man on the starboard side of the sedan going down with his black sunglasses embedded in the bloody flesh that had been his face.

The sedan pulled away from the curb, rocketing into the street and catching a red subcompact by surprise. Metal ground as the vehicles crashed. Without breaking pace, the sedan continued to surge into the smaller car until it bulled it out of the way and moved forward again.

Vacating his position behind the Dumpster, January ran in pursuit of the car, swinging his arms hard at his sides as he lifted his knees up high like he was back in preseason training. For a moment it looked like the heavy traffic might be able to hold the car long enough for him to close the distance. Then the sedan went up over the shoulder and sped away despite the flat tire.

The faint sounds of approaching police sirens were only now beginning to color the street noises.

Valentine was kneeling over the man he'd dropped. He glanced up and shook his head. "No ID.

Bet it's the same with the two we got tied up back in the market."

"No bet," January said in disgust. He turned and walked back through the mass of spectators starting to ease cautiously out into the street. Dodd's name had been in the paperwork Wilson had given Police Commissioner Isaacs less than two hours ago, and Dodd must have known someone had ratted him out. It would be hard to point the finger, but January didn't like the way things were shaping up. It was no stretch of the imagination that DiVarco's organization had infiltrated the Boston PD, but he had to wonder how high up the payoffs went.

CHAPTER 14

"I want to see Avery Hobart," Maggie Scuderi said.

The secretary regarded her for a moment, then said in a precise voice, "Is he expecting you? May I have your name?"

Scuderi took her badge case from her purse and let it drop open to expose her shield. "Agent Scuderi. FBI."

"Do you have an appointment, Ms. Scuderi?" The secretary made a show of examining the list she'd retrieved on her computer.

The office was on the main floor of the Whesphal Bank on Marlborough Street in the downtown section. Through the bulletproof windows on two sides of the spacious cubicle, regular banking business was taking place in single-file orderliness. Three blue-shirted security guards armed with shotguns formed a rough perimeter on the three sides of the floor that weren't teller cages. Plants grew beautifully in floor pots and hanging baskets.

The secretary was silver haired and colorless, almost fading into the simple blue dress she wore. As she waited for an answer, she reminded Scuderi of dozens of other secretaries who vigilantly defended the integrity of the powerful men above them, primarily because part of that power rubbed off on them.

"No, I don't have an appointment," Scuderi said, squinting to make out the name badge pinned to the woman's dress, "Ms. Fulton. However, I do have a warrant for Mr. Hobart's arrest."

The secretary blinked. "Mr. Hobart is in a stockholder's meeting now. He can't be interrupted."

Scuderi leaned over the desk. "He's going to be interrupted. Tell me where I can find him."

"Fourth floor. The conference room. Four-thirteen."

"Who's the head of security?"

"That would be Mr. Ebersol."

"Get him in here."

"Yes, ma'am."

Scuderi straightened and glanced at Mac who stood beside the door, wearing a gray suit with no tie. After the meeting with Isaacs earlier, Scuderi had changed into jeans, boots, and a plaid flannel shirt with the sleeves rolled up over a red long-sleeved sweatshirt, which concealed the slim-line body armor underneath.

Hobart's name had surfaced in the files they'd been able to break in the core dump from the office of Nelson Aikman in Atlanta. According to the information they'd retrieved, Hobart had been responsible for laundering money from the jackal network back through legitimate enterprises owned by DiVarco.

In less than two minutes, Ebersol was in the room with them. The man looked like an ex-cop to Scuderi. Ebersol was of medium height, with a belly starting to show the effects of too many beers in front of the sports channel. He had a round face with deep-set dark eyes, thinning hair that was carefully brushed back, and a gunslinger mustache. He didn't go with the athletic warm-ups he wore.

"So what's going on?" Ebersol asked.

"FBI," Scuderi said, then introduced herself and Mac. "We're here to arrest Avery Hobart."

"Can I see the paperwork?"

Scuderi handed it over.

After a brief inspection, Ebersol handed the papers back and said, "Laundering money?"

"Yeah," Mac replied.

"I never did trust that guy," Ebersol said, "even after they made him a senior partner."

"Mr. Ebersol," the secretary said, "your lack of loyalty will be noted—"

"And duly filed in triplicate. Yeah, yeah." Ebersol waved the threats away. "Blow it out your ass, Wilma. The guy's dirty. The FBI don't go around arresting innocent people. Jeez o'cripes." He reached to his hip and adjusted the pistol he had holstered there. "C'mon, let's go get your bad guy."

They took the elevator to the fourth floor and followed Ebersol's lead. The conference room was at the end of the hall. At the doorway, Ebersol had Scuderi and Mac wait, then went inside and whispered to Hobart while the meeting continued. Hobart followed the security chief out into the hallway.

"What's this all about?" Hobart asked.

"Sebastian DiVarco's jackal network down in Atlanta," Scuderi said. She captured the bank president's arm, pulled it behind him, and secured the cuffs.

"What's that got to do with me?"

"You were laundering profits for him." The other cuff snapped easily into place. "We've got enough evidence to put you away."

"There must be some mistake," Hobart insisted. He was a slight man, balding and showing the beginnings of a paunch despite the best efforts of his tailor.

"No mistake," Mac said. "We've got enough on you to send you away for a long time."

Ebersol was smiling as he trailed along behind.

"Look, maybe we can work some kind of deal," Hobart said. "Mind you, I'm not admitting to anything here, I'm just free-associating possibilities."

Scuderi punched the button for the elevator. "We want DiVarco. We can get you, but so far we can't touch him. The prosecuting attorney is interested in bigger fish, so if you scratch our backs, we can scratch yours."

Hobart's face hardened but seemed on the verge of crumbling. "I want to speak with my attorney."

Grabbing the man by his shirtsleeve, Scuderi pulled him into the elevator. "No problem."

Mac and Ebersol boarded the elevator as well, then the security chief punched the button for the main lobby. The doors closed and the cage dropped with a mechanical whine.

The elevator stopped at the third floor and a handful of people tried to get on. Ebersol flashed his badge and ordered them back, and they went grudgingly. The bank security chief's walkie-talkie crackled for attention on his hip as they continued uninterrupted to the lobby.

"About this deal," Hobart said nervously, "what will the prosecuting attorney want?"

"Records," Mac said, "that link DiVarco to the false companies handling the jackal network profits."

"What else?"

"You'll have to testify."

"I can't."

Ebersol slipped an earjack from his pocket and shoved it into his ear. Scuderi tried to overhear but couldn't.

"Your testimony would be one of the foundation blocks in the DA's case," Mac said.

"DiVarco will have me killed," Hobart said with real feeling. "You don't know how powerful the people are that he's connected with. They can—"

Ebersol reached under his jacket and pulled his gun as he looked at Mac and Scuderi. "A group of armed men just invaded the lobby. They killed all three of the perimeter guards."

Drawing her 10mm, Scuderi punched at the elevator's emergency-stop button. Before she could hit it, she heard the soft ring of the arrival bell. As the doors opened, she flung herself to one side and reached for Hobart. Her fingers closed in the material of his jacket.

Then a withering blast of autofire jerked him from her grasp and drove him up against the back wall of the elevator. A bloody line of bullet holes showed across the immaculate white of Hobart's shirt.

"Jeez o'cripes," Ebersol said, hunkering in one corner of the cage.

Bullets sprayed into the cage and ripped holes in

the back wall. One of them caught the bank security chief in the thigh and toppled him to the ground.

Mac punched the button for the second floor as an Asian man attempted to push his way into the elevator.

Without hesitation, Scuderi dropped the Delta Elite beside the man's temple and pulled the trigger as the guy raised his Uzi. The pistol recoiled in her fist and she saw the pattern of burnt flesh stark on the man's face as his head snapped backward. His blood was warm against her cheek.

Mac knelt beside Hobart's fallen body, placed two fingers against the man's neck, and glanced up at Scuderi. "He's dead."

"Shit," Scuderi said.

Ebersol groaned in the corner as the elevator bumped to a stop on the second floor.

"They have two options," Scuderi said. "Either they'll pursue to make sure the hit on Hobart went down right, or they'll pull out."

Mac nodded.

Scuderi pulled her T-jack out of her pocket and adhered it to her face, then reached behind her jaw and triggered the SeekNFire function. "You stay here. I'll cover the retreat."

"Keep in touch," Mac said. He flipped off the power to the elevator.

Scuderi ran from the elevator, mentally accessing the compass in her mind and finding the front of the building. For the team to invade the main lobby of the bank, they'd have had to come in through the front. Keeping the assault simple, they'd have parked out front too so the retreat could move quickly.

Halfway down the hall, she selected the office door she wanted. Stepping back, she fired two rounds into the locking mechanism, then slammed her foot into the door. It gave with a wrenching screech. She followed it inside, dodging quickly around the sparse furniture of the outer office, then into the rear room.

She shoved the venetian blinds to one side and saw five Asian men trotting down the steps toward a waiting green-and-white Chevy Suburban. Wheeling, she laid her pistol on the desk, grabbed the swivel chair behind it in both hands, and threw it over her hip toward the big window with a yell to focus her strength.

The chair smashed through the glass, catching in the venetian blinds and tearing them away with it as it fell.

Instantly, Scuderi fisted her 10mm, felt the SeekNFire circuitry reconfirm the weapon as one designated in its memory, and ran for the window. She arrived in time to see the whirling mass of chair and blinds strike the steps only a few feet from the armed men.

Before they could react, she knelt on the ledge with one hand wrapped around the window frame. She fell forward, letting her weight depend from her supporting arm. The rough brick exterior of the building abraded her cheek as she slammed full-length against it. A line of bullets chipped stone splinters to her left. Grimly, she released her hold on the window and dropped.

She heard the gunfire pick up in intensity as she fell, and saw puffs of brick smoke stirred up from the impacts. She landed in a flower bed, her boots digging into the soft loam as she went into an automatic roll to lessen the sudden stop.

The street scene blurred as she rolled over on her back. Her gun arm tracked the targets the circuitry picked out. She fired three times in quick succession, continuing her roll till she was able to get her feet under her. She tasted dirt from the flower bed when she opened her mouth to breathe.

Two of the Korean hit men were down and wouldn't be getting back up. A third was limping toward the waiting escape vehicle.

A burst of gunfire cut branches from the hedge next to Scuderi. She shrank away from it, but locked onto her next target. Even with the SeekNFire circuitry, when a target was in motion it was hard to hit. Her bullet took the man she was aiming at in the shoulder but didn't stop him from scrambling into the Suburban. She put the final two rounds through the side glass of the big truck in an effort to rattle the driver.

"Maggie," Mac called over the T-jack.

"Go."

The Suburban roared away from the curb.

Sprinting, changing magazines on the run, Scuderi made it to their van parked illegally in front of the bank. A parking ticket fluttered under the wiper.

"The bank security people have got everything under control in here," Mac said. "I'm on my way out."

"I don't have time to wait." Scuderi keyed the ignition and yanked the column shift into first gear. The van responded with plenty of power from the V-8 short block. The rear wheels dug into the pavement with a growl of tortured rubber.

The fleeing Suburban was almost at the end of the block.

Scuderi accelerated and shifted, then shifted again, running the tach up into the red each time. Despite the rack-and-pinion steering, she thought the van handled sluggishly. She wished she had a pursuit car worthy of the name, but grimly handled the rolling stock she had to work with.

By the time she started to enter the intersection the Suburban had raced through without slowing down, she thought she was beginning to catch up. A half-dozen bullets ricocheted from the bulletproof windshield, leaving spiderwebbings of cracks but not penetrating.

She heard the keening shrill of police sirens just before she saw the patrol cars come roaring from each direction of the cross street and brake to a stop, cutting her off. She braked to a halt and stuck her head out the window with her badge case. "FBI, goddamnit! Get those fucking vehicles out of the way!"

Instead, the drivers of the prowl cars got out with shotguns and crouched behind their open doors. "Out of the van!" one of the men ordered.

"You're letting them get away!"

"Get out of the vehicle," the cop commanded.

For a moment Scuderi thought about ramming her way through the V-shaped barrier of the two patrol cars, then discarded the impulse. Provided she didn't disable her own vehicle, the action would further strain the already tense relationship between Omega Blue and the local PD. She switched off the engine and set the emergency brake as she watched the Suburban take a right turn and disappear. She cursed in disgust and opened the door.

"Put down the gun," the police officer ordered.

Placing the 10mm to one side, Scuderi moved away.

"Facedown on the street, your hands behind your head."

"I'm an FBI agent."

"Do it!"

Scuderi complied. Her bruised cheek stung as she lay on the street and smelled the salt-air scent trapped in the dust. "I've got a badge."

Both men moved on her with their shotguns at the ready. One of them scooped up her badge case where she'd thrown it. The guy was young and cocky. "A real badge. What do you think about that, Minske?"

"Could be fake," the other cop said. He was older, with worn crow's-feet surrounding his eyes. "We need to frisk her to make sure she's not carrying anything besides that gun."

"The assassination team that just hit Avery Hobart at the Westphal Bank is getting away while you two assholes are amusing yourselves."

"Wow," the young cop said. "She sounds a little hot under the collar to me."

"I'll let you know as soon as I finish this frisk if the collar's all she's hot under," Minske said.

When the older cop's hands kneaded her buttocks in a degrading fashion, Scuderi figured, screw the PR. With him standing straddle-legged above her, she lifted one leg and kicked him hard in the crotch.

The cop grabbed himself and choked out a cry of pain that sounded like a hissing tea kettle.

Still in motion, Scuderi reached up and grabbed the barrel of the shotgun in one hand, yanked it forward, then slammed it back into the young cop's face as he tried to pull it back. It discharged, blowing out a tire on one of the police cruisers. Hanging onto the shotgun, Scuderi got to her feet, slid a hand down the barrel, and flipped the safety on, then gave the young cop a forward snap-kick that caught him in the face and knocked him on his ass.

As Minske came for her, she swung the shotgun like a baseball bat, coming off her shoulder in good form, and caught the cop solidly behind the ear as he turned to avoid the blow. He grunted with the impact, then sagged into the street, unconscious.

After picking up her badge and gun, Scuderi took time to cuff the unconscious cops with their own cuffs, then climbed back into the van and drove to the bank to sort through the mess that had been left there.

CHAPTER 15

"**H**ands flat against the wall as you lean into it, gentlemen. You know the routine."

Slade Wilson leaned against the wall, conscious of the .45 only inches from the back of his head. He kept his face impassive and stared at the two-tone white paint covering the concrete-block wall in front of him.

"Where're you carrying?" another man with garlic breath asked as he put his hands on Wilson's upper arms.

"Shoulder rig," Wilson replied. "Paddle holster at my back. Boot gun in my left boot. Combat knife along my forearm rigged for a quick release."

In quick succession, the weapons were removed and Wilson was allowed to turn around. He stood against the wall as the men continued working on Lee Rawley. By his count the Mafia security men took nine weapons off of Rawley, but Wilson knew they at least missed the little dagger concealed in Rawley's belt buckle and the concussion grenades built into his boot heels. How many others there might be, Wilson had no way of knowing. They'd missed the weighted cord around his own throat that resembled a necklace but had pulled double duty as a garrote on occasion.

"Anything else?" the head security man asked as a short-handled throwing dagger from Rawley's arsenal was dropped into the cotton bag containing their weapons.

Rawley grinned. "I swallowed an Airweight Bodyguard .38 on the way in. Figured I could shit it out later, show it to Mr. Triumbari, and really screw up the cushy job you guys have got here."

"Fucking wiseacre," Larry Gambini said. He was a hulking monster of a man, built along the lines of a professional wrestler, with a child's face and eyes the color of granite and twice as hard. He turned to one of the four men standing behind him. "Joey, if this son of a bitch even looks like he's going to take a shit at Mr. Triumbari's table, blow his head off."

Joey nodded.

"Happy now, wiseacre?" Gambini asked. "Hope you don't get indigestion."

"If Mr. Triumbari's holding up lunch on us," Rawley said calmly, "he's going to be pissed at how long you're taking."

"Let's go." Gambini took the lead and Rawley fell in behind him.

Wilson went next, memorizing the back rooms of the restaurant as they passed through them. The room where they'd been admitted at the rear of the building had held racks of paper goods and condiments. Next came the kitchen proper, where the smells of Italian spices and herbs made his stomach growl. The main dining room was furnished in rich dark woods, and a string section played opera music.

Armando Triumbari was seated outside in the open café under a dark blue awning that blocked the sunlight that had finally burned away the last of the morning fog only minutes ago. The Mafia don was old and frail looking. Viciousness and hardness clung to him in spite of his thinning gray hair and his palsied hands, which rested comfortably over the wooden cane in front of him. His gray eyes were as emotionless as gun sights.

The outer dining area had over a dozen tables covered with red-and-white-checked tablecloths. It was separated from the street by a low wall topped by strands of shiny chains that looked decorative but served as a protective barrier as well. The other tables were empty. Ristorante Costansia was in the heart of the North End on Richmond Street. A small private parking lot was southeast of the restaurant, and they'd been allowed to park the van there.

The man sitting beside Triumbari was younger and athletic, built like a good shortstop. His hands were carefully manicured, but they were working hands, too. He wore a dark, double-breasted suit that was cut open so he could reach inside the jacket easily.

"Sit," Triumbari said, motioning to the round-backed, wooden patio chairs on the other side of the table.

Wilson kept his ground and noted that Rawley did the same.

"Is something wrong?" Triumbari asked.

"I came to this meeting in good faith," Wilson re-plied. "I was told I could meet with you concerning affairs of ours that have overlapped. I believed that. Instead, I find myself held at gunpoint and stripped of my weapons. Somehow, I don't think that's the way you treat your guests."

"I'm looking out for my own interests."

"So am I."

"And if I refuse your terms?"

"Then the meeting's off." Wilson returned the hard glare full measure.

"May I interject something here?" the young man said. "While you're with Mr. Triumbari, I assure you, you couldn't be better protected."

"Who are you?" Wilson asked.

The man stood, smiled, and offered his hand. "Craig Ericson. I'm Mr. Triumbari's lawyer."

"Sit down and shut up, Counselor," Wilson said. "Nobody pulled your chain."

With an uncertain look on his face, Ericson sat.

Triumbari sipped from the glass of red wine before him. "I was warned that you were impudent."

"If I'm wasting my time here, let me know now."

"Ah, the fires of youth. No, Agent Wilson, you're not wasting your time." Triumbari looked past Wilson's shoulder. "Larry, bring their equipment."

Minutes later, with his gear stowed back in place, Wilson sat across from the Mafia don as a waiter poured wine in fresh glasses.

"A toast," Triumbari said, raising his glass. "To the destruction of our common enemy."

Wilson sipped in response.

"Who contacted Jo-Jo Manetti?" Triumbari asked.

"I did," Rawley said.

"Do I know you?"

"We've never met."

"Have I ever seen you?"

"You wouldn't remember."

Triumbari squinted as he studied Rawley's face. "You've had plastic surgery."

Rawley nodded. "Yes."

"So perhaps even if we'd met, I wouldn't know you."

"Perhaps."

Wilson watched the exchange carefully. Rawley's scars from the plastic surgery were there to see for anyone who knew where to look. Wilson did, and had. But Rawley had also offered to set up the meet, without saying how he was going to manage it. Wilson wanted to see how Rawley was going to be treated by the Boston Mafia lord.

"Manetti is a very old and dear friend of mine," Triumbari said.

"I know," Rawley said.

"He vouched for you, but he could not tell me who you were, except that the name you now wear is not your own."

"I asked someone who is a friend of Mr. Manetti's to intercede on my behalf."

"That's what he said. He also told me this person is his friend, but couldn't answer any questions about you."

"I like my privacy."

Triumbari smiled. "As do we all. Yet I find it fascinating that you can see your way to my table during these times of trouble without anyone knowing more about you."

"I'm a man of my word."

"Of that, I was assured."

"And it could be that these troubles we're experiencing are the only things that could have ever brought us together."

"You speak so smoothly."

Rawley grinned and lifted his wineglass. "It's the atmosphere, Don Triumbari, and the interest of a good host that brings out the skill of conversation."

Triumbari laughed lightly and shifted his gaze to Wilson. "And you. What do you know about this man?"

"That he keeps his word once it's given," Wilson replied. "That's enough for me."

"You," the Mafia don said, "I know much more about. You're also a man of your word. And can be very hard and demanding of yourself and others. Very desirable qualities for a leader to have."

"This isn't a mutual-admiration society," Wilson said bluntly. "I came here to discuss Sebastian DiVarco with you. If you don't have time for it, let me know so I can move on to more productive events."

Gambini started forward from behind Wilson. The FBI man shifted in his chair, readying himself for whatever might come.

A scowl darkened Triumbari's lined face as he waved Gambini back. "Besides impudent, you're also ill-mannered."

"Whatever," Wilson said. "I'm a cop, you're a crook. In the eighties and nineties, you moved the local family action into legit businesses to avoid the clash with the Jamaicans, blacks, and Colombians. Then when the U.S. and world economies went belly-up twenty years later and your legitimate enterprises bit the dust, you started moving your people back into the streets. You're back to struggling to make your living the same way you did when you started in the loan-sharking and prostitution rackets, and protection. The only difference between then and now is that now you have somebody else break a guy's legs when he's late on his vig instead of doing it yourself."

Triumbari leaned back in his chair, his face a cold mask of hate.

Rawley broke open a roll from the basket in front of him and started buttering it.

"My client doesn't have to listen to any of this. None of these allegations has ever been—" Ericson said, getting up from his chair.

"Sit down," Triumbari ordered.

Ericson sat.

"You view your world in a very black-and-white fashion," Triumbari observed.

Wilson shrugged it off. "It keeps things a lot simpler."

"Even so. Some things are meant to be intricate. Such as your friend's ability to arrange a meeting between us in the first place."

"No. You want DiVarco out of the way, and so do I. You don't want to go head-to-head with him yet, and I need to find legal means to take him off the streets."

"And the people behind him," Triumbari said.

"And the people behind him."

"Yet you don't want to bend your rules about consorting with what you see as the enemy."

"Not any more than I already have," Wilson agreed. "Right now, between you and DiVarco, I see dealing with you as the lesser of two evils."

"At another time that might not be so."

Wilson didn't hesitate. "Yeah."

"And anything we do now won't affect your decisions at a later date regarding me?"

"No. I can't afford to let it."

"You're a very unimaginative man, Agent Wilson."

"I prefer to think of myself as a guy not easily swayed by the convictions of others."

Triumbari seemed to consider that as he sipped his wine. "Your two previous attempts at managing a handhold on DiVarco have failed."

Wilson didn't say anything. He'd already heard reports from January and Mac, and the teams were still ironing out the wrinkles with the Boston PD in both areas. However, he was surprised that Triumbari already knew about them.

"So that leaves you with me."

"It leaves me starting with you," Wilson amended.

"You have other pressures on you as well. I've been told that your arrangement with the House subcommittee now under Congressman Cashion isn't expected to be long-lived."

"You're well-informed."

"That's why you came to me. My problems with Sebastian DiVarco could wait for months. It appears to me, though, that you only have a matter of days in which to prove your investigations fruitful before you are forced to dismiss your interest."

"Maybe only hours," Wilson said. "I have to keep that in mind while I'm talking to you." He glanced at his watch. "You've got five minutes to make your pitch, then I'm out of here."

"Craig." Triumbari snapped his fingers.

The attorney reached into the briefcase at his side and handed over a manila file folder.

Wilson took it, opened it, and began scanning the information it contained.

"There are eight businesses on those pages," Triumbari said. "All of them belong to DiVarco, and all of them are very lucrative. If you take them out, you'll guarantee retaliation on DiVarco's part and draw him more out into the open. The man is emotional. He'll make mistakes. All you have to do is capitalize on them."

Wilson was already counting on that. "I'll need witnesses to back up the warrants I'm going to be asking for."

"You'll get them. Whenever you need them, simply call Craig. He'll arrange it. There are already several professional witnesses standing by willing to admit they worked for DiVarco or his people in return for protection from legal harassment."

"I can fix it."

"See that you do. I've given my word to these people."

Wilson folded the papers and stuffed them inside his jacket. "One other thing. What can you give me on Isaacs?"

"Boston's illustrious police commissioner? Nothing."

"He's clean?"

"No. Somebody owns him, but I don't know who."

"DiVarco?"

"I doubt it."

"Isaacs has not been very supportive of our involvement here."

"Look beyond DiVarco. I've heard that there are other people involved in his schemes."

"Besides the Koreans?"

"Yes."

"Who?"

"That remains a mystery. But I'll keep my eyes

and ears open as well. If anything turns up, I'll let you know."

"Where do the Koreans fit in?"

"They're shoring up DiVarco's territorial bids."

"Why?"

"That's another piece of the puzzle, Agent Wilson. An interesting mosaic should take form in the next few days. I'll be fascinated to see what it looks like."

"Nobody does anything for free," Wilson said.

"I know. Figuring out the Koreans' butcher's bill would probably prove very instructional as well. I find myself at a loss to guess what DiVarco could have possibly offered them for their actions on his behalf. One other thing I feel I must tell you."

Wilson listened closely.

"Even after Jo-Jo Manetti acted as go-between for this meeting and for this arrangement, there were reservations between myself and the men I represent. There was much thought that we needed to take care of Sebastian DiVarco ourselves. The man raised himself out of the gutter, for which he is to be commended, but he failed to leave gutter thinking behind him. He has allied himself with foreigners against the families, stood with filth against his own blood, and killed his friends. DiVarco is an abomination, and must be dealt with. But if we tried to do it ourselves, blood would cover these streets and we would weaken our own organization. We elected to side with you in this because you represent the possibility of getting this over with quickly. The federal government can expel the Korean vermin from our streets and use military units to enforce that decision."

"Leaving your people ready to wade in and pick up the pieces," Wilson said.

Triumbari spread his hands.

"I can promise you right now," Wilson said, "that when we take down DiVarco's businesses, there won't be anything left standing to build from."

"Nature abhors a vacuum, Agent Wilson. Something can be worked out that will benefit us."

Wilson knew that was probably true, but whatever it was, it had to be less deadly than the plans DiVarco was putting together. If not, he and the team would return and put down Triumbari as well. The thought was small consolation, but it was all he had.

Triumbari waved a uniformed waiter over. "Will you be joining us for lunch?"

"No." Wilson pushed his chair back and stood up.

"You're missing truly excellent cuisine."

Before Wilson could reply, one of the security guards shouted a warning and sprinted for the table.

Out on the street, an engine suddenly revved up.

Wilson tracked the sound as he reached under his jacket, at the same time triggering the SeekNFire circuitry along his jawbone. The whining engine belonged to a beetle-shaped black Porsche that sped toward the restaurant.

The security guard launched himself into a flying leap that covered Triumbari and bore the old man to the ground under his body.

A passenger leaned out the window of the Porsche, holding a short tube over his arm.

Wilson recognized it at once and went to ground near the low wall. "Rocket!" He heard the warhead shriek through the air, thought he heard the impact of it hitting the building, then his hearing was lost in the explosion a heartbeat later.

Glass and wood and burnished steel rained over

the outside dining area. The canopy collapsed, already covered with a sheet of flames.

Choking on the thick smoke trapped under the burning canopy, Wilson struggled out from under a pile of debris and tracked the Porsche as it headed the wrong way down the one-way street. It had stopped for a moment as if to observe the effects of the rocket, then quickly got underway again. Wilson shoved the remaining wreckage away and got to his feet, only noticing then that his pistol was still in his hand.

Ten feet away, Rawley stood up, dusting his Stetson off on his jeans automatically. A cut seeped blood high up on his cheek.

A half-dozen gunners from the restaurant had fanned out and were taking shots at the retreating car.

"Get those sons of bitches!" Triumbari shouted as the bodyguard helped him up.

Wilson ran toward the low wall separating the dining area from the parking lot and used his free hand to vault it. He saw Rawley coming hot on his heels. Slapping the remote control unit wired into his motorcycle jacket, he watched the van's rear doors electronically release and open. A ramp extended from the undercarriage and dropped into place before he reached the vehicle.

Standing outside the van, he reached inside and pulled out one of the Kawasaki Enduro 250s. It came slowly, then gained momentum. He controlled it with effort, then swung a leg over. The key was in the ignition and the engine kicked over with the first touch of the electronic starter.

Rawley was pulling himself onto the other motorcycle.

"Going down Richmond that way leads out onto

Atlantic Avenue," Wilson yelled above the high-pitched whines of their engines. "After that they have a choice between north or south. I'm taking north."

"Let me know how it turns out," Rawley said as he adhered his T-jack to his jaw.

Wilson twisted the accelerator and felt the motorcycle's rear tire start to spin out from under him, then it grabbed traction and shot him over the curb. He was airborne for a moment, riding it out and bringing the rear tire down first. He swerved to miss an oncoming car, then shifted gears with his boot toe. His 10mm rode in his jacket pocket.

The wind slammed against his face like an invisible wall as he pushed the bike up to seventy miles an hour. On the straightaway, the sports car's top-end would have left him behind, but Boston traffic didn't allow for such speeds. He stayed low behind the handlebars, eyes roving over the traffic.

He downshifted and cut across traffic at the corner of Richmond and Atlantic. Popping the clutch, he brought the front wheel up and powered over the curb in a wheelie. The front wheel came slamming back down as the rear wheel caught the curb. He controlled the wild swerving and roared down the sidewalk for a moment until he could regain the street headed north.

Weaving in and out of traffic, he spotted the Porsche as they were nearing the Lewis Wharf area. He blew onto the T-jack's mike. "Rawley."

"Go."

"They're here."

"I'm on my way."

Wilson zipped around two cars, stayed within the narrow margin between the two lines of traffic, and hovered thirty yards from the sports car's rear bumper.

The guy in the passenger seat saw him first, reaching over to the driver and grabbing the man's jacket with enough force to cause the Porsche to momentarily jerk out of control. The driver recovered, downshifted, and cut across traffic onto a side road leading into North Square.

Forced to use the front brake, Wilson made the turn less than two car lengths behind. He gunned the motorcycle as he came out of the turn, using the bike's greater speed to close the distance.

The Porsche's four-wheeled base gave them an advantage on cornering, and the driver knew it. He made two more turns, then pulled onto North Street.

Wilson called the directions out for Rawley.

Hitting the straightaway again, the Porsche vibrated with the cobbled street under the tires. The passenger leaned out the window with a MAC-10.

Wilson leaned to the left, swooped over on the driver's side of the Porsche only a car length and a half behind, forcing the passenger more into the open. When the guy opened up, Wilson knew the man had to be sitting on the door frame, making a hasty retreat out of the question.

A line of bullets stitched the cobblestones in front of the Kawasaki as Wilson tapped the brake and cut back to the right. The FBI agent reached under his jacket and brought out his 10mm. Being left-handed, he could manage the accelerator with his right hand and take advantage of the SeekNFire circuitry built into his palm. The programming seized the target and he squeezed off three shots in rapid succession.

All of the rounds took the gunner in the chest in spite of the bumpy road. The man dropped from the Porsche and went rolling across the narrow street. A quick glimpse confirmed Wilson's earlier impression that the man was Korean.

Without warning, the driver locked his brakes as a car came by in the oncoming lane.

Knowing he couldn't hope to stop the motorcycle completely before colliding with the braking sports car, Wilson shoved his pistol into his jacket, downshifted, and hit both brakes to shut down the Kawasaki's speed as much as possible, then waited to the last second. With impact only feet away, he released the brakes, gunned the engine, and popped the clutch. The front wheel reared up obediently, riding up onto the sloped back of the beetle-shaped sports car. His forward momentum and the driving rear tire with all-terrain knobby tread carried him on top of the Porsche, then he was over it, coming down into the street all wrong.

He managed to land on the rear tire instead of the front by throwing his weight backward. For a second he thought he had it, then knew from the way the bike was weaving that he didn't. Choosing to cut his losses, he laid the bike over on its side and kicked free of it. He slid across the cobbled street, picking up dozens of bruises before he came to a stop. He got his bearings quickly. Paul Revere's two-story wooden house was to one side in a line of residences that looked almost as old, and was mirrored by similar structures on the other side of the street.

Forcing himself to his feet, Wilson ignored the Delta Elite lost somewhere inside his motorcycle jacket and went for the H & K VP7 0Z in his boot. His hand closed around the pistol. There was a small electric discharge when the SeekNFire programming changed gears, then the 9mm was jumping in his hand as the Porsche streaked toward him.

Horns blared now as the constricted Boston drivers realized someone had screwed up their timing with an accident.

Wilson put eleven bullets through the windshield before the sports car was on top of him. He dodged to the side, went down to one knee, followed the passing car with the barrel of his pistol, and surged in pursuit.

The Porsche missed the overturned motorcycle lying in the middle of the street and slammed into a tall wrought-iron fence. Partially crumpled from the impact, the fence had folded over the top of the car.

The driver was also Korean, and he was dead. It didn't look as though any of the eleven shots had missed.

Rawley coasted to a stop beside him and put a leg out to balance the Kawasaki. "You about finished here, amigo?"

"The other one?" Wilson asked as he went to check his bike.

"Dead."

A cursory inspection of the Enduro 250 revealed no lasting damage, and it appeared roadworthy. A quick tune-up later would put things to rights.

A siren sounded only seconds before a blue-and-white-striped Boston police cruiser came squealing onto North Street. It came to a rocking stop only a few feet in front of the wrecked Porsche.

"Looks like the local talent has arrived," Rawley said.

"Yeah," Wilson said as he turned to face the two armed officers getting out of the car with shotguns. "Late, as usual."

"You got to give them points for consistency, though."

"Right."

* * *

Balancing three wedges of cold sausage pizza, a cup of coffee, and a yellow legal pad, Slade Wilson crossed the floor of his borrowed office in the Boston FBI field office and answered the telephone. "Yeah."

"I see you had an exciting premiere today," Earl Vache said. "If it hadn't been for that jetliner crashing at Salt Lake City and killing over half the passengers, you'd have made the national news."

Wilson dropped into the typist's chair behind the desk and tried in vain to find a comfortable position. Bruises had already started to cover his body. Finding the remote control in the desk, he switched on the TV, changed channels to CNN, and left the sound off. Through the plate-glass window behind the television, he could see the rest of the team operating in the bull-pen to finish their assigned tasks. As each pizza box was emptied, it was pushed aside and the next one opened. The Boston FBI division had volunteered legmen and secretaries, but Wilson had politely turned down the offer.

"The premiere's not over yet," Wilson said. "So far DiVarco's only seen the teaser. The opening act starts at ten o'clock."

"Triumbari paid off?"

"Like an inside straight." Wilson managed a couple of bites of pizza and took a sip from the coffee beside the legal pad.

"How did Rawley do it?"

"I don't know."

"You didn't ask?"

"No."

"You really need to start playing him a little closer to the vest."

"Later you can tell me 'I told you so.' "

"I will. I only hope you're there to listen. Mitchell Dodd and the bank vice-president were scrubs?"

"Yes."

"So you've got no real case against DiVarco?"

"Not the kind you can take to a prosecuting attorney."

"What are you going to do next?"

"Start hitting DiVarco's businesses, starting with the ones that will cost him the most cash."

"You're crossing over into territory occupied by the Boston police department. It's their responsibility to investigate gangland activity within their city. If you can't prove that the strikes you're contemplating are part of some greater whole, you'd be better off not doing them."

"I know." Wilson pushed his unfinished pizza away.

"You went to Boston trailing a jackal network that was supposed to be off-limits, to try and build a case against DiVarco. Both your possible witnesses are out of the picture. If you can't make your case on the evidence related to the jackals, you don't belong there. Isaacs will be within his rights to ask for you to be pulled out of his territory."

"Has he done that yet?"

"He's been calling. So far I've been out each time, but it won't be long before he decides to bother the Director with it. When it gets that far, there's not a lot I can do for you."

"Can you work anything up regarding the Korean

angle? Anything that will keep me in place here until something breaks?"

Vache sighed. "Even if I could, I don't know if I would. You're in the middle of no-man's-land up there, guy."

Wilson leaned back in the typist's chair and it creaked under his weight. "I'm at the eye of the storm. DiVarco's got fingers in every crooked pie in this city, and the Koreans have helped him put them there. I want to know the reason."

"So do I. But sometimes you've just got to wait until you get a better swing at the ball."

"How much time do we have?"

"With your potential witnesses both dead? I'd say hours. Unless you can turn up someone else to support the jackal investigation."

"That's doubtful."

"Have you got anything else working?"

"Not yet. We impounded Hobart's personal records at the bank, and Valentine is sorting through them now. He's turned up some files, but they're in code. He's still trying to sort it out," Wilson said.

Vache grunted.

"Is there any way I can get some leverage with Isaacs?" Wilson asked.

"Everything I've looked at concerning the man shows he's clean."

"According to Triumbari, Isaacs is bought and paid for."

"Not surprising, but it might be harder than hell to prove. Triumbari couldn't give you a handle?"

"No."

"Then I'd say sometime tomorrow morning you're going to be shit out of luck, kid."

"Unless I can make something break tonight."

"Yeah."

"I'm thinking that Isaacs gave up my witnesses to DiVarco's people," Wilson said. "Both of them were hit only a short time after I dropped the paperwork off with him."

"I've already thought of that. Find a way to prove it and I might be able to leverage you enough weight to investigate that conspiracy you've mentioned. But I'm betting Isaacs is keeping his ass covered. Push him to the wall on it, and there's probably a secretary or pencil pusher somewhere he can lay the blame off on who'll be willing to take the heat."

Wilson considered that and realized Vache was right. Until he had something solid on Isaacs, he had no business bracing the police commissioner.

"Another problem's cropping up on the horizon," Vache went on.

Wilson listened.

"Cashion's coming around a little faster than you thought. Obviously he's thinking he's more politically invulnerable than you wanted him to believe. He made a few off-the-record comments earlier in the day to a reporter friend of mine that the Omega Blue unit was coming under review before long, and that he thought the controls in place were way too lenient. Once he finds out the money you were using to hold over his head is gone, he's going to be pissed and more than willing to shut you down for restructuring."

"I'll keep that in mind. But there's not a hell of a lot I can do about it."

"Hang in there, kid. We haven't gotten beaten by too many of these last-minute situations. I'm going to be rattling cages all night myself to see if I can't find something you can use up there. Somewhere in this town, there's got to be somebody who knows something we could use and who owes me their life or their first-born child. If I'm hard to get hold of, keep trying."

Wilson said he would, then broke the connection. His mind swirled as he tried to fit the Koreans, DiVarco, and Police Commissioner Isaacs together in anything that made sense. After a few long minutes, when a fresh headache started, he gave it up. There were no short-cuts.

Maybe Vache was right and the team needed to back off to take a fresh tack. But he had the feeling that they'd tumbled onto DiVarco's action too late. If he was wrong, there was every chance that Cashion would get him pulled from the unit, especially in light of the scene on the Hill yesterday afternoon. And once he was re-leased from the Bureau, he could forget about the insur-ance that kept Kasey at the center, and write off any possibility of freeing his daughter from autism using the procedures Dr. Culley had suggested.

So many things hung in the balance, and on either side he was gambling with the lives of other people. But how many people would continue to be hurt by DiVarco and the Koreans if they weren't stopped?

He glanced out at his unit, all working diligently at the different tasks they'd been assigned, finding infor-mation and collating it into some kind of arsenal they could use when the time was right. The Omega Blue unit hadn't been designed to back down. Once Wilson started doing that, the unit's edge would be blunted, and everybody on the team would know it.

Scuderi rapped on the door and interrupted his thoughts.

He waved her in.

"It's time," she said. "If we're still going."

Wilson saw that she knew what was going through his mind. "We're still going." He finished his coffee and shoved the pizza into the wastebasket.

"Was that Vache on the phone?"

"Yeah."

"I assume it wasn't good news."

"No news is good news," Wilson reminded her.

"He's thinking about pulling us since we lost Dodd and Hobart."

"Plus Isaacs is working to make sure the Director gives him no choice," Wilson said.

"Shit. Whatever this is," Scuderi said, "it's big. You can feel it out on the street."

"I know." Wilson took his jacket from the back of the chair and shrugged it on. "How's Valentine coming with Hobart's files?"

"I don't know. He's a cocky little bastard, but I watched him while he worked with it. He's good, fast, and he's creative. I'd put my money on him."

"We are. Have any of Isaacs's detectives asked for Hobart's files yet?"

"No, but maybe they don't know about these."

"They will, and when they do, they'll scream until they get them. Officially, they're more entitled to investigate Hobart's homicide than we are to check into Hobart's link to the jackal network. I want to hang onto those original records as long as possible before we have to give them up. Have back-up copies been made?"

Scuderi nodded.

"Let's roll." Wilson glanced up at the clock on the wall. It was 8:14 P.M.

CHAPTER 16

A cool breeze blew in from the Atlantic Ocean and ghosted around the tall buildings in downtown Boston, stirring up debris in the streets and making the few homeless people clustered in the shadows turn up their coat collars.

Slade Wilson viewed the target through infrared binoculars from his perch atop the office building across the street. Clad in a special cybernetically enhanced SensiSkin camouflage night suit, he was indistinguishable from the stone wall behind him as long as he didn't move quickly. Woven from silicon-based polymers chosen for their refractive properties and sensitivity to computer circuitry, the SensiSkins were programmed to imitate their surroundings in the same fashion a chameleon did. However, the shadowsuit had a much broader palette than the lizard. It came equipped with boots, gloves, and a pullover hood that covered the entire face, all of which were wired into the computer-assisted protective coloring systems. Second Chance armor plates, designed to shield the major organs, were sewn into the fabric. Wilson carried the Delta Elite on his left thigh in a counterterrorist rig made of the chameleon material, while the H & K VP7 0Z rode in his boot, and the Crain combat knife was strapped to his forearm. A .12-guage South African Striker shotgun was sheathed down his back so he could reach it easily. Concealed pockets in the SensiSkin held additional magazines for all his weapons, plus a few incendiary surprises that he'd thought might be needed.

The target was a five-story building that housed a number of independent businesses above two floors of furniture and household appliances in a large sales office. The furniture store had closed at five. Most of the other businesses had closed by six, and none later than eight. The travel agency, carpet cleaners, and lawyer's office had been the last to close. A one-man detective agency had advertised twenty-four-hour availability, but the windows of the office were dark.

The bookmaking operation Wilson was after had opened at three o'clock to take advantage of the last-minute bettors who'd gotten a lucky feeling before the opening kickoff of the game that night. According to Triumbari's notes, the handle for the operation fluctuated between a million and a million and a quarter on a good night, after taking on some of the laid-off action stemming from the Midwest and West Coast. As Darnell January had pointed out, tonight's game between the Dallas Cowboys and Philadelphia Eagles was highly speculative because of severe injuries sustained by both teams during last week's games.

Whatever the handle ultimately was, Wilson knew it would hurt DiVarco financially. He waited, perched on the edge of the building, and scanned the interior of the room on the third floor.

Even with the infrared binoculars, he couldn't see much. The actual bookmaking operation was beyond the corridor in suite 313, the biggest on the floor. Two men patrolled the hallway and occasionally looked through the plate-glass windows over the city. They didn't try to conceal the hardware they wore, and Wilson had to assume they were licensed to carry.

The T-jack crackled, and Maggie Scuderi's voice followed. "Slade."

"Go."

"We're on green. Vache just called to confirm."

Already not trusting circumstances in the city, Wilson was prepping each request for a warrant only minutes before pulling the actual raid. Vache had to pull in some markers to get the warrants issued this late, but this system cut down on the number of legal channels and meant that they didn't have to go through Isaacs.

"Hit it!" Wilson ordered. He raised the long CO_2 rifle from his side and made sure the tribladed piton was locked into the barrel. It was heavy and unwieldy, not meant to be used quickly. Shouldering it, he checked the distance gauge he'd preset, sighted on a place on the building's wall a foot above the window fronting the corridor near room 313. He squeezed the trigger, rode out the shoving recoil, and heard the explosion of escaping gases.

The piton sparked as it cored into the stone wall. The tensile wire trailing from it, leading back to the coiled reservoir inside the CO_2 rifle, was one-third of an inch in diameter and capable of supporting almost half a ton.

Working quickly, aware that one of the guards had approached the window to check out the resulting thump and the spark, Wilson looped the wire through the stake he'd already planted in the wall behind him. He pulled it tight, then clipped on the safety harness he wore over the SensiSkin, and stepped off the building's edge.

He dropped immediately, taking up the slack he'd programmed into the reservoir's release, using his hands and feet to keep from smashing into the side of the building he was leaving. Dangling from one hand clasping the safety harness, he slid quickly toward the target building, but not so fast that he had no control over his movements. His fingers tightened on the hand brake.

Reaching over his shoulder, he drew the .12-gauge Striker and flicked off the pistol grip safety with his thumb. At eighteen inches, the combat shotgun's barrel had already been short. Wilson had modified it to ten inches, chopping it off just ahead of the forward grip.

Twenty feet from the window, as the SensiSkin frantically tried to adjust to the landscape of shadows, he saw the guard become aware of him. The guy's mouth opened as he shouted a warning, then his hand reached under his jacket for his pistol.

Wilson dropped the shotgun into target acquisition and pulled the trigger. With the revolving cylinder design, the weapon had a long trigger pull, but he was still able to get off three rounds.

The double-aught buck shattered the window and dropped gleaming shards inside and outside the building. After chewing through the glass, they punched the guard backward and turned his shirt bloody.

Wilson was trying to bring his second target into his sights when the safety harness caught on the stop block he'd clamped onto the line to help him keep from smashing into the building. He was jerked off balance and felt a pistol round smash into the Kevlar armor covering his chest. The force took his breath away.

Already swinging forward because of his initial momentum at the end of the safety harness, Wilson released the catch on the harness and threw his free arm across his face. He smashed through the weakened safety glass filling the window, tearing it out of the frame. The glass draped itself over him as he fell on the floor. The spiderwebbed remains of the window felt like a heavy cape that tried to contain him. Somewhere in the confusion he'd lost the Striker.

The remaining guard brought his pistol to bear in a two-handed grip. The muzzle flamed.

Aware of the bullet digging into the carpet somewhere only inches to his left, Wilson charged forward, loosing a martial-arts yell to rattle his opponent. The SensiSkin's hood might have the mimicking properties of the suit, but it had none of the bulletproof armor. It was a gamble, but a better gamble than if he'd gone for his pistols locked into their holsters.

The guard fired again, but Wilson whipped to one side. The round skated off his protected ribs and jarred him with its passing.

Closing, Wilson grasped the man's gun arm and threw an elbow forward. Already, the SensiSkin was starting to take on characteristics of the man's clothing as protective camouflage. The elbow connected with a meaty crunch and popped the guard's head back. Bones broke in the man's arm as Wilson twisted and triggered two rounds from the man's own gun into his stomach.

The gun fell from nerveless fingers as the man staggered back and slumped against the wall. The eyes flickered, then glazed over.

Footsteps sounded in the hallway behind Wilson, and he turned to face the new threat.

An alarm was sounding behind the door of suite 313, and men's voices were yelling frenzied orders at each other.

Wilson saw the Striker lying on the ground at the same time that he saw the two armed men closing in on him. He dived for the shotgun just as they opened fire. He was aware of the SensiSkin patterning itself after the carpet as his hand closed around the Striker's grip. Rolling, he came up on his elbows firing. Four rounds cleared the hallway and left the air stinking of cordite.

Mac's voice broke in over the T-jack frequency. "Slade."

"Go."

"We're in place."

The message was quickly repeated by the rest of the team, except for Rawley, who came into view as Valentine cleared the channel.

"Do it," Wilson said.

Rawley fell in beside the door and shoved the shaped charges Darnell January had prepped into position. Wilson nodded, and Rawley touched off the electronic detonator.

A backdraft of wind filled with smoke and debris whipped over Wilson and Rawley. The door was flattened inside the suite.

Cradling the Striker in both hands, aware that he only had five rounds left, Wilson stepped into the room and yelled, "FBI! Put your weapons down, your hands on your head, and move back against the wall!"

The room was filled with tables, looking like an obstacle course for a corporate executive. Every table had at least a half-dozen phones with nearly as many lines per unit. The twenty-plus men and women working the phones were in rolled-up shirtsleeves and didn't look like the kind that would be predisposed to firearms. One wall was nearly filled by a large-screen projection monitor showing the betting line and the numbers taken by the bookmaking operation.

"Do what the man says," Rawley called out as he stepped through the destroyed doorway as well.

Mac and Valentine halted the trickle of warm bodies easing their way toward the back door by stepping through it themselves. Both carried CAR-15s. They looked like something out of a nightmare, as their SensiSkins kept trying to pattern themselves after the eddying smoke and the wall behind them.

Scuderi and January were holding positions at the elevators and fire escape.

Aiming at the ceiling, Wilson triggered the Striker. The double-aught pellets ripped the track lighting down and scattered pieces of the tiles in all directions, leaving a gaping hole that revealed electrical wiring and concrete supports.

Guns hit the floor as the men obeyed the instructions and lined up around the walls.

Wilson blew on his mike to access the T-jack. "Maggie."

"Go."

"The situation?"

"One down. No more in sight."

"Alive?"

"No. He didn't give me a choice."

"Darnell?"

"I'm clear here."

"Okay," Wilson said, "close it in and let's process these clowns. Maggie, call in the support troops and let them know where we are."

Unwilling to have to depend on the police department, Wilson had put the Boston FBI team on standby, not filling them in on what or where the operation would be going down, in case DiVarco had someone placed inside their bureau as well.

Minutes later, everyone in the room was handcuffed and lying on the floor. The weapons had been collected in a rolling linen basket January had found in a janitor's closet. The building security guards had come up to see what was going on, but Wilson had frozen them out of it immediately. Even if they weren't on DiVarco's payroll, he didn't want them around.

Valentine seated himself at the mainframe computer logging the bets, bettors, and amounts, and attached his portable computer. A pocket-sized modem hooked his computer to the phone line and mainframe computer in the command van parked a few blocks away. He began downloading and transmitting at once.

January found the office safe that was built into the floor in the corner farthest from the main entrance. There were money-drop slots under the false flooring so the safe wouldn't have to be opened much, but there was no time lock on it. That would have required the bagmen to show up at a certain time every day and would have turned them into certain prey for free-lance hijackers aware of what actually went on in the building.

"Who's in charge here?" Wilson demanded.

Nearly a dozen hesitant fingers pointed out a man in a gray shirt and white slacks.

"What's your name?" Wilson asked.

"Lewis. Art Lewis."

"Get your ass over here, Lewis."

"Yes, sir." The man gingerly crawled out of the pile of handcuffed bodies, then rolled over and tried to get to his feet.

Reaching down, Wilson grabbed the man by the back of his collar and hoisted him to his feet.

"I'm not really in charge," Lewis said nervously. "I just run the operation. I work for Mr. DiVarco."

"I knew that," Wilson said. "What I want to know next is whether you can open this safe."

"Yes, sir."

"Then do it."

"Yes, sir."

January escorted the man to the safe and watched him conduct the procedure. Some safes were programmed with self-destruct devices that would destroy their contents; Wilson had decided against having January blow it unless no other recourse remained.

"Slade."

Wilson glanced over at Scuderi. "Yeah."

"Fischer's here with the backup." She'd been monitoring the Boston FBI's progress on a separate channel.

Changing channels, Wilson contacted Fischer himself. "Get your teams deployed, first at street level, then bring them into the building. Every one of these people is a potential witness against DiVarco. I don't want to lose any of them. Put countersnipers in the surrounding buildings. I'll be sending a man over to take command of those people." He nodded to Rawley.

Rawley touched the brim of his hat and faded out of the room.

"Make sure the transport trucks are well-protected

too," Wilson continued. "Split some of the prisoners up among your mobile units. That way if we lose a truck, the survivors might be more inclined to talk."

"Do we want to use the local police on this?"

"Have they been in contact with you?"

"Yes, sir. Only a couple minutes after we started rolling on it."

From across the room, Scuderi said sarcastically, "Their response time is improving."

"They were monitoring your frequencies," Wilson said.

"I suppose so."

Wilson hadn't mentioned that they were cutting the local PD out of the operation. Fischer would be used to that, though. The Coast Guard, DEA, and Boston Police Department were usually at loggerheads regarding who was entitled to drug cases and who actually broke them.

"Keep them out of it for now," Wilson ordered.

"Yes, sir."

Across the room, January was reaching down into the mouth of the floor safe.

"One other thing, Fischer," Wilson said.

"Yes, sir?"

"You're familiar with the local media?"

"Yes, sir."

"Find me the three best reporters out of the crowd that'll start showing up at any minute. I want two television people, and one press reporter who has time to get the story in before the morning edition."

"You mean you're going to be giving exclusive interviews?"

"Yeah." Wilson broke the connection.

Scuderi raised her eyebrows in surprise.

With his prisoner's help, January began taking stacks of banded money from the safe and dropping them in a clear trash bag. Wilson figured the cash would make a hell of an impressive visual aid in the news stories.

He glanced at Valentine and found the young agent apparently engrossed by what he was turning up in his computer search.

"Slade."

Wilson turned his attention back to January.

The big man was holding up a kilo bag of white powder.

"Cocaine?"

"Maybe. We'll have to analyze it to be sure."

Switching to Lewis, who was still on his knees beside the safe he was supposed to be protecting, Wilson asked, "Is it?"

"Yes."

Mac smiled, maintaining his vigil over the bookies lying on the floor. "Sounds like we might even have enough to build a conspiracy to distribute charge against most of these people. That being the case, I think we'll be able to seize all monies running through the book-making end of this operation as probable drug profits."

Wilson nodded. The bust was shaping up better than he'd figured and was going to give them leverage in areas they hadn't counted on. With the drugs involved, and a foundation like the one Mac had mentioned, they would be able to take more out of DiVarco's coffers than the office change fund.

"Hey, Wilson," Valentine called. His animosity hadn't gone away yet.

Wilson crossed the room to the computer mainframe. "Yeah."

"Got something here."

Gazing at the jumble of letters and numbers running across the screen, Wilson asked, "What?"

"Everything's in code pretty much the way we figured it would be," Valentine said. "But a quick scan of today's sports section for games that were scheduled today and a list of the horse races is going to allow me to break the code with just a little time investment on my part."

"Okay."

"The interesting thing," Valentine tapped a line on the monitor screen, "is that one of the accounts being used here is one that turned up in Hobart's personal files."

"Hobart was laundering money for the bookmaking operation?"

"No." Valentine consulted a pocket-sized notebook, verified his findings, and put it away. "But Hobart was tapped into this account."

"He was monitoring it?"

"I think so."

"Why?"

"I don't know."

"Where's the account?"

"I don't know that either."

"Where does this account fit into the bookmaking operation?"

"Across the board," Valentine said, "they were dumping eight percent of the accumulated monies the house was raking in off bets into this account."

"That would be a large chunk of liquid capital."

"Yeah. Given the figures Triumbari quoted you."

"Where were the rest of the profits going?"

"I've got three different accounts here. All of them

were in Boston. Probably laundered through different businesses."

"Was Hobart interested in any of those?"

Valentine shook his head.

"Let me know when you find something out."

"Sure."

Wilson turned to go as the local FBI agents wearing black jackets started pouring into the room with drawn guns. Wilson knew he was going to have to ride herd on the proceedings to keep anyone from getting accidently hurt.

"Hey, boss."

"Yeah, Valentine."

"So, am I living up to your expectations? I mean, I'm busting right through these computer programs in the time it would take a lot of other hackers to just get started good."

Wilson glanced at the young agent and hardened himself. Despite his feelings for Valentine, he couldn't cut the guy any slack until they managed to squelch his cocky attitude. Scuderi had briefed him about Valentine's behavior on the firing ranges. He liked the kid, but Omega Blue was a tough racket. "Yeah, you're living up to my expectations. Just make sure you don't live down to them, too." He turned away before Valentine could react.

The T-jack buzzed in his ear, letting him know he had a communication waiting on the Boston FBI channel. He clicked over.

"Agent Wilson," Fischer said.

"Go."

"Police Commissioner Isaacs is here."

"I guess he didn't go home tonight."

"No, sir. It doesn't look like it."

"What does he want?"

"To come up."

Wilson glanced at Mac, January, and Scuderi, who were monitoring the frequency as well. "You told him this was a crime area restricted by the FBI?"

"Yeah. He told me he doesn't give a shit."

"He's going to come up anyway?"

"I get the feeling that Isaacs would have to be physically restrained at this point, and his people outnumber us."

"Have you got those reporters lined up for me yet?"

"The other television reporter I wanted hasn't made it here yet."

"Move on to your next best choice. Send Isaacs on up, and make sure the reporters are hot on his heels."

"Sir?"

"You heard me. Wilson out." Despite the fact that he wanted the scene secured, Wilson was hoping the presence of the reporters would negate the presence of the police commissioner. Whatever Isaacs was doing there, it couldn't be good. "Valentine."

"Yeah."

"Can you get me a list of smaller books running their numbers back into this mainframe?"

"The street guys?"

"Yes."

"Sure. No prob."

"Then get it done. I need it yesterday." It would buy some time. Wilson hoped it would buy enough.

CHAPTER 17

A knock sounded on the door.

Coming awake instantly despite the post-coital tranquilizer nature had supplied, Sebastian DiVarco rolled over in bed, knocking Alyssa off his arm as he reached for the Detonics .45 stashed under his pillow. The other side of the bed felt cool, as did the metal of the pistol. He flicked the safety off at once.

"What is—" Alyssa started to say.

DiVarco clamped a hand over her mouth. The only thing he could see in the darkness filling the whole room were the LED numbers of the clock on the television against the opposite wall.

Alyssa struggled against him, not really awake yet.

He cuffed her lightly when she tried to bite his hand. He realized he was at Alyssa's apartment, and memory of the room's configurations dropped into his head.

The knock was repeated.

Dropping the sights of the .45 onto the door limned in light from the hallway outside, DiVarco said, "What the hell is it, Vinnie?"

"Take a look at the TV. The FBI just busted Fat Gerry's book. I thought I'd better wake you."

Cursing, DiVarco sat up in bed and fumbled for the remote control on the nightstand. He found it, pushed himself into a sitting position against the headboard, and thumbed the television on. "What channel?"

"Any of the locals."

"Shit," DiVarco said with feeling.

Alyssa put her arm on his. "What's wrong?"

"Business. Leave me alone and go back to sleep."

"Fuck you, asshole." She rolled away from him, gathered the twisted sheets with one hand, and pulled them over herself to clothe her nudity.

DiVarco knew she was trying to stare holes in the side of his head but he ignored it. "What happened, Vinnie?"

"Nobody knows."

The picture cleared, then revealed an exterior shot of the building where Fat Gerry had made book. A sea of flashing lights lapped at the shores of the office building. The display windows of the furniture stores along the bottom floor were hung with huge red-on-white SALE posters. Yellow tape held back a curious neighborhood as prisoners were escorted out by FBI agents.

"Nobody's been able to get through to Fat Gerry," Vinnie went on.

"Get somebody down there," DiVarco ordered. "Somebody who won't be connected with Fat Gerry."

"Right." Vinnie's shadow left the transom of the doorway.

DiVarco recognized a few of the people being taken to the waiting armored vans in handcuffs. He cursed again. He'd only taken the bookmaking operation over seven months ago, but he'd arranged for a lot of the small bookies in the neighborhood to go out of business during that time. As a result, last month they had nearly doubled the beginning figures. It would take a long time to rebuild something like Fat Gerry's book. Another thought struck him and he reached for the phone, dialing a number from memory.

The man who answered at the other end sounded sleepy.

"Martin, this is Sebastian DiVarco. Fat Gerry just got busted. I need to know how protected I am from this shit."

"Depends." Abraham Martin was DiVarco's personal accountant. "Who busted Fat Gerry?"

"The fucking FBI."

"The local guys?"

"No. Omega Blue."

Martin's voice instantly became more alert. "Let your lawyer know tonight, Sebastian. Those guys are good. If they got Fat Gerry's computers before anyone could erase them, you're screwed."

"How screwed?"

"If they break those files, everybody's going to want a piece of you. And the IRS is going to be the least of your worries. Get your legal people working on this now. Maybe they can get the evidence overturned before it ever gets to court. We have some time here to work with."

"Get on it," DiVarco ordered. "Get me some options on moving that money away from Fat Gerry's."

"I don't think that—"

"Goddamnit, Martin, I don't pay you to think negative thoughts. Get your ass on it." DiVarco broke the connection, then called his lawyer and interrupted a romantic interlude. He didn't care; he got the man back on track immediately. There were some angry female sounds in the background.

The television continued to show footage of the FBI bust, and the reporter was promising a one-on-one interview with Special Agent in Charge Slade Wilson, celebrated head of the unique Omega Blue unit, regarding the arrests.

DiVarco's next call was to Alexander Silverton's private residence. A manservant took the call. DiVarco timed his wait. It was seven minutes before Silverton picked up the extension.

"How the hell did you get this number?" Silverton demanded.

"Don't get your panties in a wad," DiVarco said. Unable to stay in the bed anymore, he pushed his way out of the plush bed and paced the length of the phone cord. "You've got bigger problems than me having your private number."

"What?"

The air conditioner kicked on and raised goose bumps over DiVarco's nude body. The news station was doing a brief background review on Slade Wilson's career and the success of Omega Blue. "Wilson and his wrecking crew just crashed Fat Gerry's."

"The bookie?"

"Yeah."

"I fail to see what that has to do with me."

"Fuck you! Have you forgotten about those little accounts you and Min insisted on?"

Silverton didn't reply.

"My accountant just told me that if Wilson is able to crack the computer codes on Fat Gerry's book, we're all in the soup."

"If that's true, it's your fault for not being more discreet."

"Fuck discreet! We're talking about illegal money here. You can't be very goddamned discreet about that. You know that yourself."

Silverton remained silent.

More stock footage rolled on other Omega Blue cases.

"I thought you and Min were going to get this guy off my fucking ass."

"Things have gotten complicated."

"No shit. You're the one with the representative in your pocket. A representative, I might add, who got a promotion thanks to my campaign management. Where the hell has he been during all of this?"

"He'll be here in the morning to put a leash on Wilson."

"It may be too late by morning."

"I think you're overreacting."

"And I think you've got your head up your ass. Does it look dark from where you're standing?"

Silverton's voice got an edge of steel in it. "Don't presume to tell me how to conduct my affairs, you son of a bitch! If you hadn't let greed grab you by the nose, no one would ever have even known we existed until it was too late."

"If you can't take care of this guy, I can."

"Stay out of it. You'll only make things worse. Min is handling things if Cashion can't."

"Wilson's taking down my businesses. I'm not

going to wait and be standing in the ruins of what I built while you and Min cover your own asses."

"Everything is under control."

"Then I better see it," DiVarco said. "Damn quick." Breathing hard with emotion, he broke the connection before Silverton could reply.

On television, the station cut away to go live to the interview with Slade Wilson.

DiVarco remained standing to watch.

Slade Wilson stood in an empty office next to the suite used by the bookmaker, going over the notes he'd made on a yellow legal pad Scuderi had scrounged for him when Cyril Isaacs shoved his way into the room.

The police commissioner didn't look happy. He'd moved the door with enough force to break the translucent glass filling half of it, embedding the knob in the wall. He was in a different double-breasted suit than this morning, but blue appeared to be his color of choice.

"What the fuck do you think you're doing here, mister?" Isaacs demanded.

"My job," Wilson replied. "You ought to try it sometime."

Without warning, Isaacs rocketed a huge right hand in a vicious hook that caught Wilson in the cheek and corner of his mouth.

Wilson turned back to face the Boston police commissioner. He hadn't tried to dodge. Smiling crookedly, tasting blood, he tested his jaw. A couple of teeth had been loosened. For a desk jockey, Isaacs still threw a hell of a punch. "Fat Gerry's has been in operation for a lot of years," he said. "And from the handle they were bringing in every day, it's going to be apparent to a lot of people that your department should have taken them down a long time ago."

"I couldn't ever get anything on them."

"Maybe you weren't looking in the right places."

"You mean Triumbari?"

"You do get around, don't you?"

"If you made this bust on trumped-up charges, the defense lawyers are going to make mincemeat out of you."

"That's my problem, isn't it?"

"I may be looking into the situation myself."

"Look all you want." Reaching into the SensiSkin, Wilson took out a thin folder. With the camou programming turned off, the shadowsuit was a uniform charcoal gray. The bulletholes in the outer layer of material revealed the Kevlar body armor underneath. He knew the photographers would bring them a lot of attention. In fact, he was counting on it. Signs of violence would cue the reporters to reflect more on that than on the legalities involved. That was also why he didn't make a move to wipe the blood from his face. "Those are sworn depositions from people who've been assaulted by leg breakers in Fat Gerry's employ."

"This was a case for the Boston Police Department, if anything."

"Wrong. Some of the monies I'm tracing back from the jackal network wound up in Fat Gerry's cash flow. There's also enough cocaine on hand to freeze all the assets connected with this operation and confiscate them."

The T-jack clicked for attention in Wilson's ear.

"Go."

"The reporters are getting restless," Scuderi said, "and I saw Isaacs make his grand entrance."

"Send them," Wilson replied. "Should make for a good show about now."

"Who are you talking to?" Isaacs demanded.

"Straighten your tie," Wilson said. "You're about to be interviewed."

Isaacs reached for his tie. "This isn't over."

"I'm counting on that, and on your help."

"Hell will freeze over first," Isaacs promised. "I'm not going to be part of any harebrained shenanigans you're pulling."

The three reporters filed through the doorway after Scuderi. Two of them were women. An equal number of photographers trailed behind them. The room was suddenly lit up by the floodlights from the camcorders and disc camera.

Scuderi raised her eyebrows when she saw the fresh blood leaking down Wilson's chin.

Wilson didn't answer her unasked question. The reporters were too alert for body language, and he didn't want to give the idea that he and Isaacs were anything other than compatriots.

As the questions flowed, Wilson answered them succinctly, aiming to give the electronic media people sound bites of information that would be readily replayed over the next few hours, adding momentum to the investigation, and hopefully a little more solidity as well. He sketched in a story about how diligent work on the part of a number of FBI agents had unearthed the bookmaking operation after acting on tips supplied by people who'd been hurt over the years by the people who ran it. Gradually the questions went away, and interest turned to the police commissioner.

"Did you know anything about the bookmaking business located here, Commissioner Isaacs?" Kelly Lange of Station 29 asked. She was a redhead with a smattering of freckles that makeup couldn't hide. Her questions had been direct and to the point.

"No comment," Isaacs said.

"Actually," Wilson interjected. "Cy was just telling me that the file I gave him duplicated a lot of work his detectives had already conducted, it's just that we were able to get the witnesses to come forward. After we explained to them how the tragedy down in Miami was connected to the bookmaking business here, most of them said they felt obligated." He reached inside the SensiSkin again and took out more papers. "And, as every good vice cop knows, the bookmaking didn't just go on here. There were dozens of outlets scattered over the city. Too many for the small FBI squad assigned here to cover."

"You expect more arrests to follow, Agent Wilson?" Lange asked, extending her mike toward him.

"Yeah," Wilson said. He passed copies of the papers he had out to the reporters. "Police Commissioner Isaacs has volunteered his department to finish bringing these people in."

When he handed the paper to Isaacs, the police commissioner looked like a man who'd just found a cat turd in his slipper by feel rather than sight.

Addressing the reporters again, Wilson said, "The list you have there is a duplicate of the one Commissioner Isaacs has. It has every known contributor to this bookmaking operation on it. I'm sure you may be able to work out some arrangements with the commissioner to cover some of the arrests as sidebar material."

Instantly, with the promise of possibly filming actual arrests being made, the reporters turned their full attention to Isaacs.

Before the commissioner could act, Wilson seized the man's hand, shook it, and said, "Good hunting. Let me know if I can be any help." He left the room before Isaacs could untangle himself from the reporters.

"Now that," Scuderi said as they headed down the hallway to rejoin the rest of the team, "is what I call poetic justice. Forcing Isaacs to bust the very people he's been protecting."

"At least it's some kind of justice," Wilson replied. "And if Valentine can come up with the goods—"

"He will."

"—it'll just be the appetizer for what's to come."

CHAPTER 18

Cuddy's Warehouse and Storage was in the heart of the Combat Zone in Boston's theater district. Just off of Tremont Street and Boylston Street, the building was a ramshackle three stories with a peeling paint exterior and boarded windows. The neon of the red-light district provided soft, glowing bubbles against the harsh and angular shadows of the neighborhood. Only a short distance to the west, the Colonial Theatre was hosting a Broadway tryout that—Scuderi had mentioned—was getting good reviews.

Pausing at a ten-foot-high chain-link fence topped off with strands of barbwire running across a small alley between two office buildings, Slade Wilson let the Sensi-Skin soak up the night. The camou program even emulated the look of the fence behind him.

He pulled back a glove and checked the time. It

was 10:45 P.M. Only twenty minutes had passed since they'd left the bookie's place of business.

The T-jack crackled in his ear.

"Go."

"We're green here," Quinn Valentine said.

"What did we get?"

"Warrants for search and seizure for property or properties stolen and transported across state lines. John Doe warrants for whoever may be on the building's grounds, and for Michael Flynn and Carmine Zender, who are the registered owners of Cuddy's."

"Anything from Vache?"

"Yeah. He mentioned that a lower profile at this point might allow you to stay in the game longer. Also Judge Shoemake doesn't look favorably on the possibility of his being interrupted all evening long."

Wilson used the night glasses to scan the warehouse grounds again. Cuddy's was sandwiched in behind a defunct transmission-repair shop and a six-story pay-by-the-week apartment boarding house. Graffiti in neon-colored spray paint stained the walls. There were only three ways into the building, discounting the possibility of someone inside prying the boards off the windows and allowing them to dive through. Wilson didn't think that would happen. He'd checked the windows himself and found they were securely covered. A docking area at the back of the building allowed trucks to unload easily. Three eighteen-wheelers were parked there now, with nine men working around them to off-load the freight using hand trucks. Forklifts were out of the question, Wilson supposed, because that would have given the impression that Cuddy's Warehouse and Storage was a lot more profitable than it was meant to be. The light coming from inside the warehouse was subdued and didn't extend much past the edge of the dock. Insects pinged off the bulbs and hoods covering them.

"Okay," Wilson said, hooking his fingers into the fence. "Move in." He scrambled over the fence lithely, and the SensiSkin mimicked the play of moonlight and shadow. On his feet again, he drew the Striker .12-gauge from the holster across his back and rushed for the nearest truck. He came up hard against the bumper of the tractor and kept his back to it as he slid toward the docking area. His left-hand glove was off so the SeekN-Fire programming would respond to the chipped information in the shotgun's pistol grip. He blew into the T-jack's mike. "Rawley."

"Go."

"Are you in position?"

"Me and God," the man replied, "we got your back door."

Wilson went on. This wasn't like the assault on the bookmaker. The warehouse crew had a standing guard meant to protect the area from the smash-and-grab artists roaming the Combat Zone. The flesh peddlers held sway in the area, but burglary was still considered a big step above prostitution. And armed robbery of the sex-for-sale crowd was a favorite pastime that saw the professionals through the lean periods between big scores.

"I've got movement," Darnell January called out.

Freezing in place, Wilson glanced down at the bottom of the target eighteen-wheeler's trailer as light sprayed out around the tires over the pavement. Rubber purred as it rolled across the docking area. "Can you take it out?"

"Negative. Not without being seen on the approach."

"I've got it," Valentine said.

"No," Wilson ordered. "Stand down. Mac?"

"I'm on it," MacDonald answered.

"Christ, Wilson," Valentine said, "I could've taken one lousy driver."

"You hold your position," Wilson said. "You're the only guy I trust with the computer records available during these strikes, and I need you in one piece to do me any good. Unless you have something constructive to say, stay out of the com loop."

The big truck rolled down the alley, its diesel engine clattering like some prehistoric monster with indigestion.

Wilson caught a glimpse of Mac springing from the shadows and catching a ride on the tractor. The man's SensiSkin blended him in with the striped paint job almost immediately. "Mac?"

"Go."

"Leave the truck in the alley. If any of the others try to go mobile from this point, they'll be blocked."

"Roger."

The truck's door came open, and Mac whipped around the side with his pistol in his fist. A heartbeat later the truck's forward momentum stopped and the engine shivered and died.

An orange glowing dot appeared at the side of the trailer by the dock as Wilson edged back silently. He identified it as a cigar by the acrid scent in the air. Before the potbellied man standing there saw him, he reached up, caught the guy by the belt, and spilled him to the hard ground.

The guy groaned from the impact and fought to get to his feet.

Wilson put the barrel of his Striker under the man's

chin. "FBI. Spread 'em and you get to stay around after we bring down the curtain."

The man complied, eyes wide with fear.

Using disposable cuffs and a roll of ordnance tape from the pockets concealed in the shadowsuit, Wilson chained the guy to the undercarriage of the eighteen-wheeler and gagged him.

Shuffling feet came out onto the dock, louder than the squeak of the hand truck wheels. "What the hell is the matter with Bobby?" someone asked.

Wilson saw four men as silhouettes against the lighted mouth of the warehouse. He fell into position beside the four-foot-high dock and shouted, "FBI! You're all under arrest!"

"Raid!" one of the men yelled. "It's a fucking raid!"

The four silhouettes shifted, and hard-edged weapons came into view.

Wilson raided one of the concealed pockets on the shadowsuit and came away with a M470 Magnum concussion grenade. He pulled the pin and tossed it onto the dock, where it went skittering inside the warehouse behind the men. "Fire in the hole!" he said into the T-jack's mike to warn the team. He covered his eyes and ducked as bullets chipped flakes from the concrete edges.

The grenade went off with a thunderous boom and a brief nova flare that turned everything stark white and shadow.

Wilson swung back, coming up over the edge of the dock and seeing the last fiery wisps of the cardboard shrapnel go spinning away and wink out of existence. The gunfire from the warehouse guards picked up again, and a ricochet bounced off the body armor covering Wilson's chest. He squeezed the shotgun's trigger and saw one of the men go down.

The other three staggered and were slapped away as if by a giant hand. A moment later, and the booming echoes of Rawley's .50-cal sniping rifle rolled over the alley.

Wilson pulled himself up onto the dock, negotiated the crumpled bodies of the men there, and charged into the warehouse. In places the concrete flooring still reflected the overhead lights, but most of it had been worn away by years of constant usage that had left deep scars furrowed along the heavily trafficked areas.

Using a stack of wooden crates as cover, Wilson surveyed the interior of the warehouse. They'd already pulled the blueprints from Boston courthouse records and power company files, so he was familiar with most of the layout. He accessed the T-jack and found out that Scuderi, January, and Valentine were inside the building. Sporadic gunfire rolled around him.

He gazed through the tops of the stacks of crates around him and found the office built at what would have been the second floor if the structure had had a second floor. A narrow flight of wooden stairs crawled up to the flimsy door. Two men were running up the steps.

Wilson shoved himself into a run for the office, knowing the men intended to erase all records of the illegally received goods from the computer memory. As he crossed a walkway formed between stacks of crates, a burst of autofire chewed the corner from a large wooden box. Splinters snowed out ahead of him and he threw himself into a baseball slide to go under the danger area.

Before he could get to his feet, the gunner came racing around the corner.

Lying on his back, Wilson squeezed the Striker's trigger, aiming for the guy's legs because he was unable to get a clear shot and didn't want to take a chance on the guy wearing Kevlar. The double-aught pellets took the gunner below the knees and dumped him to the concrete.

Wilson got to his feet and kicked the Uzi out of the man's hand, then sprinted for the office.

The lead man was already working on the door as Wilson placed his foot on the first step. The gunner covering his back was a big, beefy guy wearing Kevlar and a bulletproof security helmet.

Gray scars screamed across the walls beside Wilson's head, and concrete dust became a fog in front of him. He flipped the shotgun's buttstock out and pulled the Striker into his shoulder. The SeekNFire programming found target acquisition and he went with it, pulling the trigger as he worked his way up the steps. He kept the shotgun centered on the man's chest. The fabric covering the Kevlar armor was torn away and left a pitted black surface beneath. The gunner shuddered as each charge hit him, taking steps backward till he was pinned against the wall of the office. The MAC-10 machine pistol in his hand etched a line of fire across the ceiling.

After the sixth round, Wilson held his fire.

For a moment the gunner stood in place, then his arms dropped and he fell forward, knocked unconscious by the sustained bursts.

Wilson went over the man's body as it sprawled across the steps. He hit the door at the top of the landing and jarred it free of the frame.

The man inside was working frantically at the computer keyboard.

Wilson aimed at the monitor sitting on top of the desk and fired. The monitor evaporated in an explosion of glass and plastic and electrical sparks. "On the ground!" he commanded.

The man dropped out of the swivel chair immediately.

Accessing the T-jack, Wilson said, "Valentine."

"Go."

"I've got the computer system in the office. Get a move on." Peering through the huge plate-glass window overlooking the warehouse area proper, Wilson saw his team had taken control of the field. Mac, Scuderi, Rawley, and January cycled within the building's perimeters without resistance. A few of the players would escape the net, but those were acceptable losses.

The stairway rattled as Valentine jogged up to the office. The young agent glanced around the room and focused on the smoking mess left of the computer monitor. "Did you leave the computer intact?"

Wilson knelt and handcuffed his newest prisoner. "It's okay. I had to take out the monitor to back this guy off."

Valentine seated himself at the desk, rummaged through the equipment pack he'd carried in, and took out his laptop computer. Working with precision, skill, and the small bag of tools he had with him, he spliced his way into the office computer.

Wilson felt some of the tension inside him ease when the monitor screen on Valentine's laptop filled with frames of information, increasing as the cybernetics expert opened window after window in his exploration of the files contained within. "Find me something I can work with."

"If it's there," Valentine replied, "I'll find it." He stared in rapt attention at the laptop as he downloaded the files.

Wilson pulled his prisoner to his feet and headed the man out the door. Two strikes were down out of the possible eight Triumbari had given them. The six that were left would become increasingly harder as DiVarco's people tightened the ranks. But if Valentine could get a picture of what was going on behind the scenes, busting those other operations could be managed with a larger force than just his team. However it turned out, he knew, their maneuvering space was close to running out. If DiVarco didn't take more violent steps soon, Police Commissioner Isaacs would.

The phone in the van rang as Wilson was headed west on Providence Street. He lifted the receiver when he coasted to a stop at a red light. "Wilson."

"Me," Earl Vache said. "How did the warehouse hit go?"

"Fine." Wilson glanced over at the passenger seat where Valentine was working with his laptop, hooked into the telephone system through a designated line set up in the van. Valentine's fingers flew over the keyboard and he was totally absorbed in what he was doing. "All the preps are handcuffed and waiting to be picked up by Isaacs's men."

"I take it Isaacs wasn't too keen on that."

"No."

"What did you net?"

"What we'd expected. Stolen auto parts, hospital supplies, cigarettes, electronic hardware."

"The usual shit any bust of this type will bring in."

"Yeah."

"But no black-market organs?"

"No."

"So you and Omega Blue have made another bust that appears to be unrelated to your investigation into Sebastian DiVarco's jackal network."

"The key word here is *appears*."

"You and I can keep that in mind," Vache said, "but the local law-enforcement people don't have to see it that way. From their viewpoint, you're trespassing into their jurisdiction, something the FBI isn't supposed to do unless they're invited."

The light changed to green and Wilson rolled forward, checking his rearview mirrors to make sure the other two vans were with him. DiVarco had to have people out moving on the streets now. The team's mobility at the moment was both an asset and a handicap because they had no real safe house to retreat to. "How are the warrants coming for Staghorn Publishing?"

The publishing house was also owned by DiVarco business interests. Producing pornographic videos, tapes, books, and magazines, it was another millions-plus a year operation.

"It's not coming," Vache said. "Shoemake's dragging his feet."

"Why?"

"I can't figure whether it's because I keep calling him up every couple of hours with something new, or because he knows how flimsy your reasons for the investigation are. And we both know you're reaching on this one. Also, I've been told that Congressman Cashion has been in touch with the judge."

"Somebody traced the warrants."

"Probably your friend the police commissioner."

"That puts him in bed with Cashion, who we think we can tie to DiVarco. But what's the link between Isaacs and Cashion?"

"DiVarco would have been the logical choice."

Wilson scratched his chin as he considered. "Yeah, but DiVarco's out."

"Only because Triumbari put him there."

"I believe Triumbari."

"Could be the old man doesn't know as much as he thinks he does."

"There's still the Korean angle," Wilson said. "I haven't quite figured out where that fits in. The Mafia is pretty prejudiced when it comes to people they're willing to do business with, and DiVarco doesn't seem the type to go against the grain of his raising."

"Yet he's busting caps on people that have links to his own family."

"That scans, though. That's part of the heritage. You have to wonder what he has to offer the Koreans, and why he's so sure they won't try to take it away from him when the dust settles on this thing." Newkirk's voice trickled into Wilson's mind, telling him to trace the money, reminding him that cash flowed like a river and could be tracked back to all its points of origin. "Back to Staghorn Publishing."

"I'm pushing. If I get anywhere, you'll be the first to know."

"Remind Shoemake about the snuff films rolling out to the people on Staghorn's preferred customers list."

"You don't have anything solid to tie the jackal network to Staghorn."

"I've got DiVarco."

"Maybe. Maybe, you've got DiVarco. Let's not kid ourselves here."

"Remember the homeless slayings five months ago in Portland, Oregon?"

"Yeah."

"Snuff films started circulating through the underground special-interest groups only a few weeks after that. At first the distributors claimed they were only showing unused footage the media had shot. But investigators were able to prove that the footage was shot an hour and more before the bodies were even discovered, and that those tapes had scenes of the killers."

"The video company later claimed they bought the tapes from a citizen who stumbled on the bodies, right?"

"Yeah."

"I remember the case," Vache said.

That case was one of the reasons Wilson had decided to pursue the jackal organizations even more aggressively, in spite of political pressures on the team to stay away from controversial subjects. "The DA's office was trying to get a line on the photographer through the video company and get the tapes squelched as evidence. Instead, the video company gave limited-showing rights—of the killers in action—to one of the television newsmagazines before the judge made a ruling, and moved the film into public domain."

"And even when that film was released, it showed no incriminating evidence that could be used in a court of law."

"It also showed signs of being edited. The scenes

showing some of the killers at work were thought by experts to have been tampered with to cloud the features and ruin them for identification purposes."

"That was never proven," Vache pointed out.

"Close enough. The lawyers just raised the question of whether the tampering had been done by the company or by the photographer. The DA couldn't decide who to go after."

"And your point in bringing this up?"

"Once the tapes were released from Portland, they went international. The video company made a fortune off of them, and it started a new onslaught of snuff films in the private video sector. Staghorn Publishing may have demo tapes of the killings in Miami."

"And the moon may be made of green cheese."

"No," Wilson said. "People have been to the moon. I haven't been to Staghorn Publishing."

"I'll see what I can do."

"That's all I'm asking."

"Keep your nose as clean as you can tonight," Vache warned in a more somber tone. "Besides chatting it up on the phone with Judge Shoemake, rumor has it that Cashion may be jetting up your way by early morning to look into your recent activities."

"By invitation?"

"I haven't confirmed that yet, but at this point I'd say so."

"It would be nice to know who extended the invite," Wilson said. "I'm betting it wasn't DiVarco, and it could be our missing link."

"I'll look into it."

Wilson said thanks and broke the connection. He stopped at the traffic light on Clarendon Street. The John Hancock Tower covered the block on one side of the street. He blew into the T-jack's mike, then let the rest of the team know they would be standing down for an indeterminate period.

"Do we find a hole and pull it in after us?" Mac asked.

"No," Wilson said. "We proceed to the Staghorn stakeout just like we planned. When the warrants come through, I want us to be in position to act on them." He put his foot on the accelerator when the light changed, and the van surged forward. He couldn't help wondering how much time was left before the investigation was labeled off-limits.

"Want to hear what I've got so far?" Valentine asked.

"Sure."

"I need somebody to bounce it off of. I feel like I'm going around in circles inside my own head."

Wilson handled the van easily and periodically checked the rearview mirrors. A feeling of vague unease trickled across the back of his neck as he drove through the dark streets, but he couldn't name what had instigated the reflex.

"The warehouse was shoving eight percent of their profits into a special account in the Cayman Islands," Valentine said. "Just like the bookie operation."

"The same account Hobart was interested in?"

"Yeah. I was able to track it to the point of origin this time."

"And the percentage was the same?"

Valentine nodded. "From what I see here, the money disappeared in the States, was lost in the dummy account books the warehouse was running, then it resurfaced in the Cayman Island accounts. If we hadn't gotten our hands on these files and if they hadn't been as complete as they are, we wouldn't have been able to trace the cash. Once it was there, it showed up as overseas profits in business interests held by JetStar Investments, then was brought back into Boston."

"What's DiVarco's connection?"

"He's on JetStar's signature card."

"Who else is on it?"

"Tonsung Min and Alexander Silverton."

"Who're Silverton and Min?"

Valentine shrugged. "So far, names on a bank account."

Wilson lifted the mobile phone and dialed. Scuderi answered on the second ring. "Quinn's turned up two names. Tonsung Min and Alexander Silverton. Run a background check on them and see what you can get, then get back to me."

Scuderi said that she would.

"Tell me about JetStar Investments," Wilson said.

"Not much to show here. They're an investments company specializing in Boston development. They hit the boards three years ago, showed marginal success for the first two and a half years, then started moving along. No doubt aided by the monies contributed by DiVarco's little empire."

Wilson considered that, turning it over in his head and trying to figure out how it fit. Sebastian DiVarco was hardly the investments type. And if the dirty business the man controlled was turning the profit Wilson suspected, there would be no reason for DiVarco to attempt to branch out into legitimate ventures. The man simply wasn't trained for it, and Wilson didn't believe for a moment that DiVarco would place his fortunes in anyone else's hands.

Unless DiVarco had no choice in the matter.

The thought struck Wilson and he toyed with it, refitting the pieces until a restless, nervous energy filled him. DiVarco didn't have anything on the surface to attract the attention of the Koreans. Changing the focus, he looked at the problem from the Koreans' viewpoint, wondering what they might have had to offer DiVarco, why they would make the offer, and what they might hope to get in exchange. It didn't scan. There was still too much information missing, but he felt they were getting closer to the whole truth.

"What exactly did JetStar invest in?" Wilson asked.

"Electronics firms, assembly and development. Canneries and fisheries. Video and film. Medical and dental instruments. The service economy. High-tech defense weapons manufacturers. Banks, savings and loan associations, and venture-capital organizations." Valentine checked the laptop's monitor. "They also invested heavily in public transportation systems, Logan International Airport, and warehousing along the seaport."

"How much capital is involved?"

"I don't know."

"You're talking about a substantial amount," Wilson said. "Could DiVarco's business have come up with that much?"

"I'll have to dig more to let you know how much of it came from DiVarco," Valentine said. "But I can tell you right now there were other investors in JetStar. A couple of accounts from Zurich poured money into the JetStar bankroll at the first of every month for the last eleven months."

"The same time frame that DiVarco started making his move through Boston Mafia circles."

"Yeah. And as the profits from the various rackets DiVarco gained control over went into JetStar's coffers, the amounts coming in from Zurich went up as well."

"It wasn't all from DiVarco's proceeds?"

"Don't see how it could be. A rough estimate puts DiVarco's interests contributing a third of the operating capital."

"Back up a moment to Hobart, the bank manager." Valentine caressed the keyboard of the laptop. "Okay."

"Hobart was tracing activity going on in that account?"

"Yes."

"So he knew when JetStar invested in a company or corporation?"

"I'd think so. According to his personal files, he made a number of inquiries."

"Without getting caught?"

"I'd assume so," Valentine said.

"Did he have access to that account?"

"No. I can see by his files that he was using an info dump and cutting out the Cayman bank security."

"Illegally?"

Valentine nodded.

"Is stock for JetStar up for sale?"

"No. It's privately owned.

"Okay," Wilson said. "Given that Hobart had knowledge of JetStar's movements in the stock exchange, there was only one way Hobart could have managed to make any kind of profit from the transactions."

"He could buy up the public stock he knew JetStar was trying to accumulate, then sell it later when the prices went up, provided JetStar was going to make a bid for a hostile takeover.''

"Right,'' Wilson said.

Valentine busied himself with the laptop.

Wilson crossed Dartmouth Street and angled down toward Huntington Avenue. The phone rang and he answered it.

"Alexander Silverton,'' Maggie Scuderi began without preamble, "is old money in Boston, and he's very proud of that fact. His ancestors were reputed to have come over on the *Mayflower*. He's very active in political circles.''

"Any ties to Cashion?''

"Silverton headed up the reelection campaign both terms.''

"And probably does some heavy lobbying on the Hill supporting his favorite congressman's views.''

"I think that goes both ways,'' Scuderi said. "Without checking, I'll bet you that Cashion has reflected Silverton's views on every ballot in the House.''

"No bet. How else is Silverton connected in Boston financial affairs?''

"Family businesses are docks and canneries, with a slight resurgence of new growth directed toward the computer industry in the late 1990s. He's very conservative, and has had numerous public arguments with labor organizations regarding concessions made to employees over the last few years.''

"What kind of arguments?''

"Silverton's businesses have been laying off employees because of the decline in the state economy. Lately, he's become increasingly paranoid about appearing in public. A few disgruntled workers attacked him at business functions and at his restaurant, the

Crystal Palace. His approach to foreign investors has made him even less popular with the working class."

"What approach?"

"Silverton has campaigned for years for state and federal regulations to be loosened, allowing less restrictions on foreign investments in the United States. Tonsung Min has been one of the chief investors Silverton has been trying to bring into Boston financial circles. So far, the attempts have netted nothing."

Wilson understood the resistance. Too many people were still afraid of foreign investors, with good reason. America had been founded on ideals of free enterprise and free trade. But the last four decades had been nothing but grim, as foreign investors treated the nation as a fatted calf that had come to fruition, carving off choice pieces and leaving the unwanted carcass behind. "Who does Min represent?"

"Officially," Scuderi said, "a group of Korean businessmen wanting to bring Korean industries into the nation. The Bostonian resistance has centered on the fact that the proposed work force is Korean, not American. Unofficially, Min's connected with a number of the larger crime families in Korea, often acting as a negotiator of sorts for areas of conflicted interests."

"Min doesn't take an active part in casting about for new profits?"

"His fortune's already made," Scuderi said.

"Where is he?"

"In Boston."

"Why?"

"By invitation of Alexander Silverton."

"Who is looking for investors interested in American business."

"Yes."

The pieces fell into place in Wilson's mind as he rearranged the motivations of the three principal players the team had uncovered. He thought he had most of it, but proving it was going to be difficult if not impossible. The Staghorn operation might shed a little more light on the scheme, provided they got the chance to uncover it. Either way, when morning came, Omega Blue would be making its final play to stay alive on more than one front, and he knew it.

CHAPTER 19

"**A**gent Wilson, is it true that you're not only going to be relieved of command of the Omega Blue unit, but that you're going to be arrested on the grounds of repeated aggravated assault as well?"

Sliding out of the van, Slade Wilson put a hand over the camcorder's lens and shoved the cameraman out of his way. It didn't exactly set a precedent for FBI relations with the media, but it did cause the other reporters who were waiting like carrion birds on the steps of the main police station to back off and give him space.

The sunlight streaming down onto the street was harsh and sharp. Wilson was grimly aware of the camcorders and cameras pointed at him as he made his way around the front of the van and started up the steps. It was 8:05 A.M. Although he'd changed clothes, he hadn't shaved or had breakfast. All the sleep he'd gotten had been in intermittent snatches during the night in between the reports Valentine and Scuderi had collected. The planned raid on Staghorn Publishing had never come off. However, Vache had called to let him know Cashion was going to put in an appearance at the police station that morning and wanted Wilson on hand. There'd been no doubt in Vache's mind that the congressman was bringing the ax up with him. Wilson hadn't said anything in his own defense.

MacDonald, January, and Rawley joined him at the steps, falling in behind him as they moved toward the front doors. Scuderi and Valentine were hidden away for the time being as they continued to break through the cybernetic defenses set up by Silverton, Min, and DiVarco.

A dozen uniformed officers formed a flying wedge at the top of the stairs and started backing the media people out of the way, barking orders and brandishing their nightsticks as they came down the stairs.

Wilson and his team stopped halfway up and let the policemen approach them. Without looking up, he knew a number of SWAT sharpshooters had him and his team in their sights.

"Wilson," a burly sergeant called out, "you people are under arrest. Put down your weapons and lie facedown."

"I want to talk to Vache and Isaacs and Cashion," Wilson said quietly.

The media recorded the images as the two lines of men closed in on one another.

"The sarge didn't ask you what you wanted, asshole." The speaker was a young giant in uniform. His short shirtsleeves were rolled up to show off his biceps.

He moved his baton without warning, slamming it toward Wilson's head.

Taking a step back, Wilson hooked his arm inside the young policeman's elbow and broke the force of the blow. The baton slid by without touching him. Grasping his attacker's wrist, Wilson jerked it behind the man's back, then twisted the baton free with his other hand. He swung the baton forcefully between the policeman's legs, hooked the pistol grip handle in front of the guy's crotch, and yanked.

With a shrill bleat of pain, the policeman dropped to the steps and tried to curl up in a fetal position.

Wilson let him, but kept the baton's pistol grip pressed against the policeman's throat.

Instantly guns were drawn on both sides.

Wilson knew the policemen wouldn't fire. There were too many bystanders, innocent and otherwise. Mac had revealed the cut-down Mossberg 590 shotgun under his trench coat, while Rawley had fisted the MAC-11 holstered under his sheepskin jacket, and January showed them the explosive detonator in his hand.

"Jesus Christ," one of the cops said.

"Holy Mary, Mother of God, he's got a bomb."

"I want to see Vache," Wilson repeated.

The sergeant peered at the FBI SAC over the sights of his pistol. "You can't do this, Wilson."

"I already have," Wilson replied. "Isaacs didn't leave me a choice."

"They're going to lock you up and throw away the key."

A momentary image of Kasey at the center filled Wilson's mind and he had to force it away before it distracted him. He had to remain cool and aloof in order to force Isaacs and Cashion to deal with him. "I don't think so."

"You guys aren't going to get away with this," the sergeant said.

Wilson read the sergeant's name tag. "I'm not here to get away with anything, Knox. I'm just trying to set some things straight before they get any worse."

"You're insane." The pistol was wavering in Knox's hands. "You people can't come in police headquarters by force."

Mac spoke in a drawl, soft and deadly and without passion. "You boys given any thought to how you're going to walk back inside that police station without us?"

"Oh, shit," one of the cops said.

The two lines of media defining the combat zone instantly dropped back a few more yards.

"Even if your SWAT snipers get off killing shots," Rawley said, "there's gonna be a hell of a mess on these steps. The man wants to talk. Me, I'd let him talk."

"Tell Isaacs," Wilson said as the young policeman at his feet moaned. "Tell him right now."

Knox spoke rapidly on the walkie-talkie belted at his waist. There was only a brief hesitation before the answer came back, then they were moving slowly toward the front entrance of the building.

Wilson blew on the T-jack's mike. "Maggie."

"Go."

They walked through the entrance to the police headquarters, guns still out and pointed. In the background, other uniformed officers scurried around the desk sergeant's workstation and hustled the morning's collection of lawbreakers to different parts of the building.

"It's show time," Wilson said. His boots sounded loud as they thumped against the floor.

"We're only minutes away," Scuderi replied.

"That's going to be cutting it thin."

"We're in!" Valentine shouted. "Goddamnit, Slade, we're in!"

"Don't break your arm patting yourself on the back, kid," Wilson said. "Stand by to transmit."

"You got it."

Mac was smiling as he tugged at the T-jack's receiver in his ear. "Boy can be a downright exuberant little shit, can't he?"

Wilson nodded. "Not the elevator," he told Knox. It would be too easy to confine them in the cage. "I want you and two other people to accompany us up the stairs."

Knox volunteered two people that didn't look like they felt honored.

As a group, never out of arm's length of the Boston policemen, they started up the stairs with Darnell January in the lead.

Wilson gazed up the flights of stairs and saw armed men waiting above them as more armed men filled in the gap they left as they went up the stairs. "I want a conference room," Wilson told Knox. "Something with a computer, and a modem with sending and receiving capabilities."

"I've got to hand it to you," Knox said as he holstered his weapon. "You've got to be the ballsiest bastard I've ever seen."

"Who dares wins," Rawley said.

"The Special Air Service, right?" Knox asked as they started up another flight of stairs.

Wilson saw the flash in Mac's eyes that said the

man had filed away another possible tidbit concerning Rawley's mysterious past.

"Darth Vader," Rawley said with a crooked grin beneath the mirror shades.

Long minutes later, as perspiration was starting to dapple Knox's round face, they reached the third-floor conference room. Earl Vache was standing in the hallway beside the door, looking tense and confused.

"Slade," Vache said.

"Later," Wilson replied. "We need to talk in private so I can lay this thing out for you." He told Mac and the others to stand guard while he stepped into the conference room with Vache. Knox and two more policemen continued to serve as hostages. The door hissed closed behind them, and Wilson stepped to the room's telephone and computer. Opening a window in the upper right-hand corner of the monitor screen, he accessed a local cable news channel he remembered from the array of vehicles parked in front of police headquarters.

The window cleared at once while he dialed, showing Congressman Lamar Cashion engaged in an animated discussion with reporters. ". . . my promise to arrest FBI Agent Slade Wilson and put the whole Omega Blue department in stasis till we review and decide whether this kind of unit is a viable law-enforcement tool."

"Cashion's not kidding around here," Vache said quietly.

"Neither am I," Wilson said. "It's time some housecleaning was done in this department. And I've finally got a broom." He switched off the volume on the television channel but continued watching the congressman posture and pontificate.

Scuderi answered the phone.

Putting the phone on speaker function, Wilson said, "Download the files as I cover them."

"Affirmative," Scuderi answered in a professional tone.

"Pay attention," Wilson said to Vache, "we're going to have to move fast."

Front and profile pictures of a distinguished-looking man filled the screen.

"Three men," Wilson said in summary as he pointed to the screen. "First up, Alexander Silverton."

"Boston blue blood," Vache said as he unwrapped a stick of gum and slipped it into his mouth.

"You're familiar with him?"

"He funds a lot of the stuff Cashion represents in the House. I've had occasion to check him out."

Wilson nodded, then quickly filled in as much of Silverton's background as he deemed necessary, bringing up the connection to JetStar Investments last. Scuderi and Valentine moved through frame after frame of information, showing how JetStar worked, showing how widespread the buyouts had been. "Across the board," Wilson continued, "this city was quietly going up for sale. Economic hardships, labor layoffs, government funding for several projects like housing and DHS, all those factors were contributing to tighten the cash flow in Boston. Need a loan to expand your business, settle insurance claims, float your company for a few months till the current cash crisis goes away, or to buy new equipment to replace the machinery that's gone beyond anyone's ability to repair? JetStar Investments was there. Only you didn't know it was JetStar because JetStar was twenty-six different investors on paper. Tracing an investment back from stateside was damn near impossible. Valentine and Scuderi tried it. If we hadn't turned up the information in the jackal network, and from the bookie and hijacking operations, we wouldn't have known about it either."

"How much?" Vache asked quietly.

"JetStar Investments owns twenty-one percent of Boston as of this moment." Wilson paused to let that sink in. "And they are continuing to buy. In another year, possibly a year and a half, JetStar will own forty percent of this city."

"Silverton can't do that. Why haven't RICO and the antitrust agencies uncovered this?"

"We weren't exactly looking for it ourselves." Wilson had Scuderi move the monitor on, revealing a picture of Tonsung Min in front of a Korean restaurant in Pyongyang. More stills circulated across the monitor, showing Min with the diplomatic attaché in Washington, D.C., obviously trying to avoid the cameras. "Know him?"

"No."

"Tonsung Min. He's registered in the Korean Embassy under another name."

An ID stat flashed onto the screen, showing Min under the name Dae Li Yun. According to his cover, he was an undersecretary and wouldn't be exposed much to the public.

"I take it," Vache said, "that he's not the undersecretary he's supposed to be."

"Hardly. He's an intermediary used by Korean crime syndicates. Supposed to be retired, and only involves himself in the biggest of big deals for a large percentage. The CIA had a thick file on him. They've used him a few times themselves."

"Does the CIA know Min's inside the United States?"

"If they do, they're not telling. Valentine checked, but he couldn't nail down any paper circulating on Min."

"What's he doing in this?"

Wilson went through JetStar assets again, showing Vache where Min's signature represented a third of the investment capital flowing through the veins and arteries of Boston's financial pump like blood poisoning. "Silverton has been lobbying in favor of foreign investments for years. Whether he or Min put this deal together, Silverton would know who in Boston financial circles would be willing to join with them. Besides investing their liquid assets, Silverton's Boston partners could contribute information about businesses that were foundering, probably even pointed some of those people into the false safety net JetStar Investments was weaving under all those different aliases. Maggie checked through financial reports and movement of stock. During the last year, it's possible that Silverton and some of his partners have maneuvered a number of corporations into vulnerable positions through stock-market machinations. All they had to do was temporarily raise prices on some aspect of the business that was dependent on something they already controlled, then that business suddenly had cash-flow problems."

"And JetStar was only too willing to make them go away."

"On the surface. But when you boil it down, Silverton was selling this city out from under the people who live here."

"Where does DiVarco fit into this?"

The monitor shifted to DiVarco and Wilson

pointed at the screen. "DiVarco's supposed to be the enforcement arm. Every time a country has been invaded, the invading army has struck deals with the criminal element inside that country. The practice dates back to Sun Tzu, five hundred years before Christ."

"Sun Tzu."

"A Chinese military strategist. Forget it." Wilson paused a moment, glanced at the clock, and tried to figure out how long he'd been in the room with Vache. It couldn't have been long. On the television window on the monitor, Cashion was still talking. "When the U.S. joined in World War Two against the Germans, they used the Italian Mafia behind the lines to ferry supplies as well as men. When the reconstruction of Japan began after the war, MacArthur's people released high-ranking Yakuza members from prison in return for promises to keep Japanese politics on the straight and narrow. The CIA used the American Mafia in their bid against Fidel Castro, and they used Vietnamese guerillas in the Vietnam War. Precedents have been set. This isn't a new idea."

"But using it against an American city?"

"Think of it as a beachhead," Wilson suggested.

"What you're describing sounds like war."

"Economically, maybe it is. To the victor go the spoils." Wilson looked into the FBI liaison's eyes. "Someone else can figure out the semantics after the dust settles. Right now, we need to move fast."

"You're planning on taking these guys out of business?"

"If you try to push this thing through channels to RICO and the antitrust guys," Wilson said, "Min and Silverton will be long gone, and maybe they'll be able to close most of this operation up behind them. They may even be able to continue working through JetStar Investments once they're out of the country after changing the computer records we've tumbled to. The Justice Department doesn't carry any weight in the Cayman Islands or in Switzerland."

A knock sounded at the door, then Mac called, "Slade. Isaacs wants to talk to you."

Wilson worked the computer board and tapped into the police headquarters security net. The monitor cleared, then the pixels rearranged themselves into a picture of Isaacs standing in front of the conference-room door while a phalanx of camera-accoutered reporters waited expectantly down the hall. "The commissioner's going for high ratings points in the news services," he said to Vache. He raised his voice so Mac could hear. "Tell him to wait."

"Goddamnit, Wilson," Isaacs roared. "You can't stay in there forever."

"I don't intend to, asshole," Wilson said softly. He accessed the T-jack. "Maggie."

"Go."

"Prepare to send."

"Standing by."

Wilson turned to Vache. "I need a judge who'll issue warrants on the basis of the information I've given you."

"For who?"

"Cashion and Isaacs. They're both on the JetStar payroll."

"You can prove that?"

"Yeah." Wilson accessed the T-jack. "Give it to me."

The screen filled with page after page of bank account statements showing monies received over monthly periods by accounts maintained in Boston and Washington, D.C., from other accounts traceable to Jet-Star Investments. Arranged the way it was, it was easy to follow the paper trail leading to the police commissioner and the congressman.

"Both of them used false identities," Wilson said, "but it'll be easy to verify everything we've documented there. And the evidence against Cashion is even more damning this time because he accepted ownership in JetStar Investments as part of his payoff. It's recorded and in his real name."

"Son of a bitch," Vache said as he approached the phone and dialed. He spoke in a low voice. The modem line blinked as the feed was redirected. When he was done, he hung up the phone and switched on the fax machine. "A congressman and a commissioner. Judge Shoemake was impressed, and wants to make sure the media spells his name right."

"That's your department," Wilson said. "I've got work to do, and we're going to be scrambling. When we clear up this mess here and walk out, Silverton and Min are going to know we're coming. Silverton's addressing a group of visitors in one of the buildings he owns, and I'm betting Min's somewhere in the wings. We put too much pressure on yesterday afternoon and last night for them to ignore."

The fax clattered and spit out a stream of paper.

Wilson ripped the sheets off and checked them. Judge Shoemake's signature was reproduced faithfully at the bottom of the documents.

"Wilson!" Isaacs yelled.

"Let him in, Mac."

The police commissioner walked into the room

and gave Wilson a hard-eyed stare. "I don't know what the fuck you're trying to prove here, you son of a bitch, but it's coming to a screaming halt right now."

In the window opened up on the computer monitor, Congressman Cashion continued citing what he considered to be a number of infractions caused by Omega Blue under Wilson since its inception.

Wilson switched the television channel off.

Three men crowded in behind Isaacs, flanked by the Omega Blue team.

Wilson ignored Isaacs and looked at the young man in a three-piece suit beside him. "You're Harlan Wells, the assistant police commissioner."

Looking undecided about what to do, Wells only nodded.

In his peripheral vision, Wilson saw Vache moving into position to support him. "We know about JetStar Investments," Wilson said to Isaacs.

The color drained from Isaacs's face and he tried to bluster his way through it. "I don't have any idea what you're talking about."

Wilson gave the warrant to Wells, who opened it up and looked at it. "Your lawyer will explain it to you. Just have him go slow."

"This warrant is for your arrest," Wells said, glancing at Isaacs.

"It's some kind of stall," Isaacs said as he reached for the warrant.

Wilson caught the man's hand, ready for the instinctive swing that followed. Keeping hold of Isaacs's clenched fist, he whirled and snapped a side kick to the police commissioner's temple.

Isaacs went down in a heap and stayed there.

The two uniformed cops drew their weapons, uncertain about aiming them because the three FBI agents behind them were still armed, and Vache had reached under his jacket as well.

"You're in charge, Wells," Wilson said levelly. "What are you going to do?"

"Is this warrant legit?" Wells asked. There was a fire in the young man that Wilson liked. Despite being thrust into a situation that he'd probably never envisioned in his whole career, and being seriously undermanned, Wells wasn't giving up his ground because of the odds.

"Yeah," Wilson said. "You can call Judge Shoemake." He pointed at the phone.

Wells's conversation with the federal judge was brief. When he got off, he addressed one of the cops and ordered him to cuff Isaacs. He glanced at Wilson. "The judge suggested I follow your lead till this thing unwinds."

"That sounds like a plan." Wilson reached under his jacket and brought out an envelope with a thick sheaf of papers tucked inside. "I don't know if you're clean or dirty, Wells, but you've got a lot of dirty cops inside this department. Chances are, you know who some of them are. Cut them out of the loop on this. This could be your chance to redeem yourself. Isaacs was as dirty as they come. Even if you've stayed clean, you're going to suffer from guilt by association. By this afternoon, you people are going to be innundated with federal crime task forces. Take my word for it."

Wells glanced at Vache, who nodded. "What do you want me to do?"

"Round up every guy you can find who still deserves to be called a law-enforcement officer and isn't just a thief with a badge pinned to him, and start hitting these targets."

Wells accepted the envelope. "What's in here?"

"Businesses owned by Sebastian DiVarco. You bust these places down, arrest the key personnel, and confiscate both sets of books being kept on the premises. Do whatever it takes to get those records because they're going to be valuable evidence later on."

"And when we have them?"

"Either Agent Vache or myself will be in touch."

"Anything else?"

"You might want to escort me to Congressman Cashion and start spreading the word that I'm hands-off before some would-be hero tries to jump me in the hallway."

Wells nodded and borrowed a walkie-talkie from one of the cops picking Isaacs up from the floor. The police commissioner was still out. "Put him in a holding cell," the assistant police commissioner said. "Mirandize him and book him when he comes to."

"Yes, sir."

Wilson walked out of the conference room and into the hallway. Wells had to jog to keep up with him, ordering the policemen aside and handing out assignments like a drill sergeant. Things started to happen, and Wilson could feel the electricity in the air as the police force galvanized to carry out the orders.

"Where's Cashion?" Wilson asked.

"Fifth floor. There's a press-release room there."

Vache joined them in the elevator while January, Mac, and Rawley scrambled to bring the team's vehicles into action at street level.

"Any advice?" Wilson asked as they got off on the fifth floor.

"Don't hit him," Vache said, "it'll spoil that look on his face. And try not to smile too big when you give him that paper."

The reporters in the big room parted instantly as Wilson made his way through the crowd toward the podium under bright lights. Voices chased him in an undercurrent to Cashion's impassioned speech about a citizen's right to protection under the law, even if it meant protection from the law officers sworn to uphold that law. He heard his name several times but he ignored it, ignored the pop of electric flashes and the spray of electric floods as they washed over him. Power cables writhed like twisting snakes underfoot.

Cashion was dressed in a slate blue three-piece, with his tie loosened a little for effect. He stopped talking when he saw Wilson approaching. He pointed a finger at the FBI man as Wilson stepped behind a camera and came on. "What the hell is that man doing here? Wells! Where the hell is Isaacs? This man is to be placed under arrest! These people have a right to see justice served!"

Wilson came to a stop within arm's reach of the congressman.

There was nowhere for Cashion to flee to, and the man knew it. Perspiration leaked down his face from his eyebrows.

At first the crowd of media reporters and photographers was hypnotized into silence, waiting to see how events would unfold.

Cashion tried to duck away from the flash of steel in Wilson's hand, but the FBI agent's aim was unerring. The handcuff ring snapped around the congressman's wrist with an audible grate.

"You're under arrest," Wilson said. "You have the

right to remain silent. . . ." He continued listing Cashion's rights as he escorted the man from the stage, shrugging his way through reporters impatient to figure out what the latest wrinkle meant.

In the hallway, he turned Cashion over to a group of FBI agents from the Boston office. The congressman was still demanding to know what was going on as he was led away. Reporters filed out into the hallway, some of them obviously torn as to which group to pursue.

The T-jack buzzed for attention. Wilson said, "Go," already en route to the elevator.

"Evidently Silverton was prepared for something like this," Scuderi said. "Quinn and I have been monitoring the JetStar banking accounts located locally this morning to see if anyone had noticed we'd been mucking around in them. So far there'd been no reason to believe we'd been caught. Less than a minute ago, DiVarco's accounts were drained dry."

"DiVarco's?" Wilson stepped into the elevator cage with Vache and Wells, and helped them keep the media people back. Growled curses and complaints were snapped off when the doors slid shut and the cage dropped.

"Yes."

"Did DiVarco do it?"

"We don't think so. Quinn's tracing the cash now, and I just confirmed that the other JetStar accounts under the control of Silverton were also transferred out."

"Trying to cover their tracks," Wilson said.

"It looks that way. Silverton could also be cutting his losses, and cutting DiVarco out of the deal at the same time."

"Does DiVarco know?"

"He has an accountant who watches over things for him. I'd say the chances were pretty good that he does."

"Shit," Vache said in disgust. "We were going to be treading the wire anyway with this much media already at the scene, but if DiVarco goes off half-cocked, this whole thing could still blow up in our faces."

Wilson knew it. To prove everything and make it stick, they needed to take the key players into custody.

"I found the money," Valentine said.

Wilson stepped through the doors on the bottom floor, scattering newspeople out of his way, aware that others were running down the stairs in an effort to get closer. Uniformed patrolmen tried to stem the tide, but their efforts were only aiding the general build-up of chaos. "Where?"

"The Cayman accounts."

"Any chance those accounts can be spirited away before we can freeze them?"

Valentine's smirk was audible in his voice. "Not much. I took the precaution of instilling a computer virus in the banking accounts that would buy us some time. Money can go into those accounts, but Silverton and Min are going to have to be physically present before any of it comes back out or goes anywhere else."

"So if we can stop Silverton inside the States—"

"That money goes no place. As a counter-signature account, Min won't be able to move the money without Silverton."

"Unless Silverton's dead," Vache said.

The thought was a sobering one. Everything seemed just within the team's grasp, yet it hung by a single heartbeat. Wilson pushed the doubts away and sprinted for the van as Rawley pulled it up over the curb and shoved the passenger-side door open. Vache let himself in through the sliding cargo door.

The reporters tried to mob the van but Rawley flipped a switch and electrified the outside, causing them to drop away. As Rawley pulled back onto the street, Wilson saw the reporters fleeing for their vehicles, fighting with each other in their pursuit of an exclusive.

Rawley grinned as he looked into a side mirror and accelerated between lines of parked cars. "Would have been a hell of a parade if they'd gotten to come with us."

The news vehicles surged into motion. Then muffled explosions went off under their hoods and white smoke billowed out, obscuring them from sight. As the cars and vans rolled forward to stops, they effectively blocked the street.

"Only got the first twenty or so vehicles," Rawley said, "but it seems like enough."

"Darnell's idea?" Wilson asked as they made the corner.

Rawley nodded. "Small charges containing a CO_2 payload. The explosive goes off, releasing the carbon dioxide to flood the engine area, which chokes off the oxygen supply to the carburetor and shuts the engine down. Darnell had it rigged for remote control. We covered the vehicles while you were still inside."

"What about those?" Vache asked, pointing out and up.

Wilson looked and saw three news copters hovering just over the tops of the buildings around them.

"I've got a couple LAWs in the back," Rawley said.

"No," Vache replied, then glanced at Wilson as if to confirm whether the man was kidding.

The van skidded around another corner against the light, and the beefed-up suspension struggled to handle the demands. Rawley reached down and flicked on the siren.

"The helos are up there," Wilson said as he took the whirling cherry from the glove compartment and stuck its magnetic base on top of the van. "They'll be able to pinpoint us to anyone able to follow, but they can't get in our way." He reached back over the seat and grabbed an Ithaca model 37 .12-gauge from the racks, then extra magazines for his pistols. He could already see the top of Silverton's building.

"What do you mean my money's gone?" Sebastian DiVarco asked. He paced the floor behind the desk in an office he seldom visited, and looked out over the downtown skyline of the city.

The accountant on the other end of the telephone connection sounded rattled as he tried to explain. "Someone dipped into the accounts and took it only a few minutes ago. I don't know how. You'll have to get someone who knows computers to figure that out."

"I pay you to keep up with my money, mother-fucker," DiVarco screamed.

"I did. I called you as soon as I knew it was missing."

DiVarco took a deep breath and tried to calm down. It wasn't like he hadn't been expecting a double cross. Hell, he was no goddamn babe in the woods here. He'd known from the start that Min and Silverton were only going to use him as long as they needed him. It was just that he'd intended for them to need him long enough to really get full use out of them himself. "Who took my money?"

"I don't know."

"Did you call the bank?"

"Immediately. They said nothing was amiss at their end, and that only withdrawals had cleared through their systems this morning. They're supposed to call me back as soon as they know something."

"Terrific. In the meantime, I'm fucked out of nearly one hundred million dollars. Thank God I wasn't asking you to keep an eye on something important, right?"

The accountant didn't say anything.

DiVarco stopped pacing and pushed the intercom button. "Nancy, get me Angelo." Returning his attention to the phone, he said, "Look, Martin, you'd better figure out where my goddamn money went, and you'd better hope I don't find your hand in the till when I go looking. Because if I do, I'm gonna chop that hand off and fucking feed it to you." He slammed the receiver down.

He gazed across town and saw the building where Silverton conducted business that wasn't settled at the Crystal Palace. According to the guys he had watching Silverton and Min, Silverton was there now, in a meeting with some investment people he represented.

The intercom buzzed.

"Mr. DiVarco?"

"Yeah, Angelo. Get me about thirty of your best boys and make sure they have heavy artillery. Meet me out front."

"Yes, sir."

DiVarco opened the desk drawer and withdrew his

Detonics Scoremaster, checked the action and the magazine, then dropped it into his shoulder holster. He stoked the anger inside him as he crossed the room to the door. He'd worked his ass off to get where he was today, and if Silverton thought he was just going to roll over obediently and play dead because Min was there with his jumped-out hit men in their endo-skels, the bastard had another think coming. DiVarco had killed a lot of friends on his way up. He damn sure wasn't going to let Alexander Silverton stand in his way. Or, he reflected, glancing at the news on the silent television in the corner of his room, the FBI.

CHAPTER 20

"**FBI!**" Slade Wilson announced as he swung around the open door of the building's security office and covered the four men inside with a sweep of the Ithaca shotgun. "Don't move!"

The security men were still shaken, trying to come to grips with everything that was happening. Smoke from the small explosive Darnell January had used to blow up the locking mechanism eddied about in the small room.

"Up against the wall," January ordered. He leaned around the doorway to show them the business end of the MAC-10 he was holding.

"How the hell do we know you're really FBI guys?" one of the security guards asked. He had a brownish coffee stain spreading down his tan shirtfront and an empty cup in his hand.

"If we were the bad guys," January pointed out, "you'd be dead right now."

Wilson tossed his shield into the room. It bounced heavily on the carpet and lay there gleaming.

"Okay," the man said. He raised his hands, briefly exposing the sergeant's chevrons on his shoulders.

"Drop your weapons," Wilson instructed, "then turn and face the wall with your hands on your heads."

"What the hell's this all about?"

"We'll see that you're briefed later." Wilson stepped into the room, recovered his badge, and pocketed it, then glanced across the array of security monitors spread across the main desk. "Quinn."

"Yo." Valentine moved into the room, dropped his CAR-15 beside the desk, and took a seat at the desk. His hands slid comfortably over the keyboard. Pictures on the monitors clicked to different scenes as he initiated a search pattern.

Wilson was grimly aware that time was running out for the team. The media—including the radio stations—were filled with conflicting reports of what had happened at Boston Police Headquarters, but the gist of them maintained that Congressman Cashion had been arrested by a special federal task force. "Where's Alexander Silverton?"

"Twenty-first floor," the sergeant replied. "Is he involved? The man pays our salaries."

Wilson ignored the question and relayed the information to Mac and Rawley. He already knew the main building-security staff was on Silverton's payroll. "Do you know what his agenda is?"

"No. He gives that to his personal security staff on that floor."

Valentine stroked the keyboard and scenes cycled

within the five viewing monitors, sweeping through hallways and rooms on the twenty-first floor. Wilson could tell what floor from the digital readout on the lower right-hand corner of the screens.

"Silverton's got a personal security staff on the twenty-first floor?" Wilson asked.

The sergeant nodded. "Yeah. They go everyplace he does, and make sure that floor is clean. You can't even stop on twenty-one without a special key card for the elevators. Ever since those guys took potshots at Silverton a few years back, security around that floor has been tighter than a fat girl's pantyhose."

"Is this man inside the building?" Wilson flashed a picture of Min toward the security chief.

The sergeant glanced at it, then nodded. "I believe so. This guy's been around for months. He keeps his own bodyguards, real hardass guys that don't take shit off nobody." He looked hard at Wilson. "Is that what this is about? Another hit on Silverton?"

"Thanks for your help, Sergeant," Wilson said, cutting off all other attempts at conversation.

"Slade," Valentine called. "I've found him."

Wilson joined the younger agent at the array of monitors.

Valentine pointed, showing the screen where Silverton stood at a long conference table addressing a dozen listeners, male and female, in business clothes.

"What room?" Wilson asked.

"Twenty-one Q."

"Get me a map if you can."

Valentine nodded and worked the keyboard. A second later the laser printer in the corner hummed and spat out a single sheet laying out the entire floor. Twenty-one Q was marked with a crimson asterisk.

Wilson studied Silverton on the screen and saw Min quietly sitting at the other end of the table. "Can you get an audio pickup on that system?"

"No."

"Maybe you could use some backup," the sergeant suggested.

"Thanks," Wilson replied, "but no thanks. You people are to stay in this room and contact no one except the Boston police officers en route. If you don't, I'll have you up on obstruction of justice charges. Is that clear?"

To a man, they all nodded grimly.

Wilson didn't care. If they were innocent, they needed to stay out of it. Civilian security guards were not prepared for the action he figured could possibly erupt on the twenty-first floor. Min's security people would be equipped with endo-skels, and Silverton's wouldn't hesitate to kill anyone.

He led the way out of the security office, across the immense foyer, and to the bank of elevators. The muzzle of the Ithaca sticking out only inches below the hem of his jacket didn't catch attention. Flashing his badge, he cleared the next cage that opened and ignored the whispered complaints and whining protests of the people who'd been waiting on it.

"I think I can get us onto the twenty-first floor," Valentine said. "Hold that button for me."

Wilson pressed the keypad and scanned the LED readout indicating: PRIVATE, SECURED FLOOR—PLEASE MAKE ANOTHER SELECTION. It reminded him of a soft-drink machine, but the humor of the comparison didn't alleviate the tension in his stomach. He slid the shotgun out into the open, holding it by its pistol-grip stock. The SeekNFire programming already had him wired into the weapon so that it was an extension of his body.

Valentine took a small device about the size of a cigarette pack from his backpack. After sliding a card free of the package and making sure the electronic leads were properly attached, Valentine shoved the card into the magnetic strip slot and punched the small keypad on the device's face.

Wagon wheels rolled across the LED readout, then changed into letters that read: CARD ACCEPTED—NO STOPS ALLOWED. The elevator lurched upward.

Valentine smiled as he put the magnetic lock-pick kit away. "Nothing like homegrown magic."

Wilson dropped a hand on Valentine's shoulder and gave the man a tight grin. "Stay alive, kid, and you're going to make me proud of you yet."

At the fourth floor, the elevator went on the outside of the building, surrounded on three sides by glass.

Wilson felt a moment of vertigo as it seemed like the streets were dropping away from him while he shot up the side of the glass-and-steel canyon. He was conscious of the tension filling the people beside him as they watched the level indicator speed by. Vache seemed detached, chewing his gum methodically. Scuderi was cool and professional as always, her emotions hidden away behind the dark wraparound sunglasses she wore while holding her CAR-15 canted from her waist. January was patting his free hand against his leg to a beat that was heard only inside his head. Leaning against one of the glass walls, Valentine was breathing in through his nose and releasing his breath through his mouth. It was martial arts training, and it was the same thing Wilson was doing to keep the adrenaline up without borrowing into the fatigue factor.

At floor nineteen, Rawley broke in over the T-jack com net. "DiVarco just made the party."

"Where?" Wilson asked.

"Your side of the building."

Wilson peered down and saw a limousine that looked like a child's toy had stopped in front of the office building. There were other cars behind it. At least two dozen men spilled from the open doors and raced for the building. "You've confirmed that?"

"Or I wouldn't have reported it," Rawley said. "The FBI guys we left covering our back door spotted him on his way in and let Mac and me know."

Mac and Rawley were at the other end of the building. They had taken the elevator up to the top floor and were using the fire escape stairs to drop back down. Although they hadn't known for sure what floor Silverton would be on, they'd guessed it would be somewhere near the top. Mac and Rawley were there to try for a squeeze play if Silverton and Min had tipped to the operation too soon and tried to bolt. They were running the outside FBI teams Wilson had borrowed from the Boston office.

"The twenty-first floor," Vache predicted quietly, "is going to be crowded like hell a few minutes from now."

Wilson didn't bother to respond. There was no time. The elevator cage slowed, seemed to hover for a moment, then locked into place. The doors opened with a soft *bong*.

A small room led directly off the elevator, a ten-foot-square cubicle holding an X-ray machine and metal detector that looked sleeker and leaner than the ones in most airports. The walls were stark white, and made the black one-piece uniforms of the three security personnel stationed there look even more forbidding.

Before anyone could move, Wilson swung the shotgun by its grip and caught the first man on the side of the face. After the dull, meaty crunch of impact, the guard slumped to the floor.

The second man managed to get his pistol free of the holster and was thumbing the safety off when Scuderi closed on him and knocked the weapon out of his hands with a roundhouse kick. He threw himself at the woman agent. Meeting the rush head-on, Scuderi wrapped her fists in the guy's one-piece, lifted her knee into his crotch, and executed a sweeping inner-thigh throw. The guard landed on his back and tried to scramble out from under Scuderi. Without pause, Scuderi headbutted the man in the face, then applied a sleeper hold that rendered her opponent unconscious.

January had taken the third man out with a quick series of jabs that culminated with a short right cross.

Peering around the door and finding no one, Wilson moved out into the corridor with Valentine on his heels. The rest of the team spread out behind him.

No one moved in the corridor. The lighting was good, with large window groups at either end of the building. A news copter hovered outside, and Wilson managed a quick glance at the photographer hanging outside the craft in a safety harness.

He turned left, then right again, following the series of hallways he'd marked in his mind from the map Valentine had retrieved. The T-jack crackled in his ear. "Go."

"DiVarco has definitely arrived," Rawley said.

"The crazy bastard has already shot up the main lobby and is on his way up here."

"Silverton's security knows?"

"I don't see how they could miss it."

Room Q was ahead of them, less than twenty yards away. The letter designation on the door was some kind of red stone inlaid in a white pebbled design.

The door was locked when Wilson tried it.

"I got it," Valentine said, slinging his assault rifle and kneeling in front of the lock. A heartbeat later the door swung open at his touch.

Wilson entered at the back of the room, his gaze sweeping the interior.

Alexander Silverton was at the front of the room, at the head of the long, oval conference table. The room's decor was Spartan, arranged and designed not to detract attention from what went on at the table. Overhead, a four-sided monitor assembly showed a list of names and probable stock forecasts regarding returns. Wilson recognized most of them from the information contained in the portfolio Valentine had assembled. Silverton stopped speaking and glanced irritably at Wilson.

"Discussing the latest P & L reports?" Wilson asked. "Have you told these people yet how the money they've been investing through you has gone into an effort to sell this city out from under them? Or that your real partners are a Mafia don who you helped establish in a place of power, and a man representing some of the largest crime families in Korea?"

Silverton glanced at Min, who remained expressionless.

"When were you planning on telling them?" Wilson asked, walking slowly around the table. "After this city was taken over by foreign investors?"

Four of Min's guards were scattered around the room, their hands already reaching under their jackets. A low rumble of consternation rose from the conference table, swelling to a dull roar. Demands were made of Silverton, but the man ignored them.

"This city is already being taken over," Silverton said. "The homeless, the useless, and the godless are a blight on our futures." He swept his glance around the table. "You've all seen it. This city is drowning in its own pathos and sewage. The streets are filling with carrion scavengers waiting to take from us everything we've worked for. They're jealous of us because we're successful, and they wouldn't hesitate a moment about sacrificing us for their own gains. They've already proven that. What I was doing, I was doing to protect us—the deserving few who've made something of ourselves. Our ancestors came to this country and made their fortunes from the things this land had to provide, invested their blood to build for their families. I was not about to see all that go to waste because we've got a passive government in power that refuses to open its eyes to what needs to be done to set things right in this country."

The quiet that followed Silverton's words was almost complete. Nearly all the faces at the table showed combined fear and incredulity.

"Who are you?" one of the people asked.

Wilson showed them his badge and held the combat shotgun canted loosely over one shoulder. "I'm Special Agent Slade Wilson of the FBI." He pointed a finger at Silverton. "And I'm here to arrest that man on federal charges."

Tonsung Min pushed himself out of his seat with the aid of his cane. Immediately two of his men closed on him to form a protective ring. Without looking in Wilson's direction, the Korean crime lord rounded the table, apparently heading for the door at the other end of the room.

"Min," Wilson called softly.

The Korean turned to face the FBI SAC. "I have diplomatic immunity, Agent Wilson. You are aware of that. Your laws hold nothing over me."

"I also know you can't let it end like this," Wilson said. "You're responsible for too much money that has been invested through your connections with Silverton. There's no way the people who trusted you are going to be willing to write that money off as a loss. And you can't recover any of it without Silverton's help."

"You're right, of course," Min said with a shark's mirthless grin. He snapped his fingers.

Immediately the four Korean bodyguards pulled out their weapons and opened fire.

Silverton ducked and reached under the conference table. A split second later, the booming roll of a series of detonations filled the conference room. The wall behind Silverton came apart as smoke billowed out.

Going to ground, Wilson flipped the Ithaca model 37 forward and aimed at the nearest gunman. The shotgun bucked in his hands, following the direction of the SeekNFire programming.

The double-aught charge caught the gunman in the chest and shoved him backward.

Wilson racked the slide and pumped another cartridge into the firing chamber, then touched the trigger again, aiming higher. The pattern whipped across the gunman's face and threw the nearly decapitated body to the carpet.

A combined force of Silverton's security people and more Koreans ran into the room from the entrance at the other end. Some of them worked to hustle Min and Silverton toward the secret door hidden behind the false wall that had come down with the explosions.

Losing sight of Min and Silverton in the smoke, Wilson racked the Ithaca's slide again as he shoved himself to his feet and attempted to pursue. A Korean stepped in front of him and blocked his charge. Unable to bring the shotgun into play, Wilson swung a forearm at the man's face, felt cartilage smash under the force of the blow and felt the warm wetness of blood smear his skin. But the man remained standing and tried to track his pistol on Wilson's head.

Clasping the Korean's gun arm in his free hand, Wilson stopped the pistol's movement but temporarily went deaf as the gunshot split the air by his ear. He was only able to halt the man for a moment, then the power of the endo-skel implanted beneath the man's flesh took over. Wilson felt the gun sight of the pistol rake his flesh as the Korean's hand smashed into his face. He fell backward, his back thudding hard against the floor, concentrating on getting the shotgun up in time. When the Ithaca was in line with his opponent's crotch, he pulled the trigger, and watched the man melt away, staring in agonizing disbelief at the ruin that had happened to his body. Wilson's second round finished the man off.

The last cartridge in the shotgun took out a Silverton gun, then Wilson swung it like a baseball bat to clear the way to the blown-out wall. At least two rounds smacked into his Kevlar-covered back as he gazed down into the escape tunnel.

It was a cylinder that spiraled down at an angle, very similar to the inflatable fire escape slide routes used on most modern buildings. The material was slick and dull yellow.

Before Wilson could throw himself down the open throat of the escape route, flames belched out of the tunnel and singed his hair, burning his face like a light sunburn. The fire swallowed the escape route from the inside, leaving only flaming bits hanging behind.

Wheeling, he drew the Delta Elite, feeling the buzz of the SeekNFire programming as his palm read the information contained on the chipped butt piece. He squeezed the trigger as soon as he recognized an enemy, and made his way to the door. He had to step over corpses of security people on his way.

At the door, a quick glance showed him that Scuderi and the others were still operational. He slammed a fresh cartridge into the 10mm and fired it dry again. Valentine was bleeding profusely from a thigh wound, and January was raking the room with controlled bursts from the Ingram machine pistol, blood seeping from three deep cuts across his forehead. Vache had kicked over the conference table to use as a shield, and was busy pushing a new magazine into his weapon. The surviving Silverton men and Koreans had been driven up against the false wall without any defense.

He called Scuderi's name.

"Go!" she told him. "We can handle this." A round caught her in the upper shoulder and spun her around, but didn't penetrate the Kevlar underneath. Gritting her teeth, she locked onto her target, squeezed the trigger, and put another man down.

Wilson ran, sheathing the Delta Elite after recharging it, then slipping fresh cartridges from his ammo pouches into the Ithaca's loading gate. He pumped the slide to seat the first round, then pushed one more shell in to complete the reload.

Despite the escape tunnel, he knew Min and Silverton couldn't go far. There was no way it could drop them through all twenty floors below and remain inside the building. That left the elevator as the quickest means of leaving the skyscraper.

Unraveling the map inside his head, he continued to run back the way they'd come. He blew on the T-jack's mike to access the frequency. "Rawley."

"Go." Gunshots and screams sounded in the background of the transmission.

"I lost Min and Silverton. They had an escape tunnel in the conference room."

"I've been in contact with the agents covering the stairwells at both ends of the building. They're at the eighteenth floor and they haven't seen anyone but DiVarco. He blew past them a couple minutes ago. They couldn't hold him. The guy brought a big war party with him."

Wilson made the final turn and came within sight of the elevator bank. All three floor-indicator panels were lit up. He punched the up and down buttons, wondering which way he should go if any of the cages ever made it to him. He had no doubt that a mass exodus from the office building had already started. Fire alarms shrilled out into the hallways.

"Slade," Darnell January called.

"Go."

"I dropped through the escape tunnel after the fire died down, used my grappling hook to lower myself."

"Where are you?"

"Nineteenth floor. Oh, shit, I missed them. They just got on the elevator. Damnit!" The sound of autofire echoed along the frequency. "DiVarco's up here too."

"Which elevator?" Wilson asked, pressing himself up against the reinforced glass between the elevators.

"One on the right."

The elevator was just jerking into motion, starting the climb up the side of the building. A helicopter suddenly swelled into view, slowing as it approached the top of the skyscraper.

Stepping back from the reinforced glass, Wilson fired two rounds from the combat shotgun and watched glass fragments explode outward from the frame. It was almost a sure bet that Silverton could bypass the remaining floors to the rooftop. Taking a deep breath, aware of the dizzying panorama of heights falling away below him, he stepped up through the frame and leaned out. He wished he had time to set the small grappling hook he carried in a concealed pocket of the motorcycle jacket, but he didn't. The elevator was only half a floor beneath him and climbing.

His breath locked in his throat as he stepped out and suddenly dropped. The top of the elevator came up hard beneath him, numbing his legs. For a moment he thought he was going to slide off, then he found a handhold and squeezed it tight.

The rooftop was five floors up. The cage docked gently, and Wilson scrambled to his feet, looking out over the helipad in the center of the building.

Out on the middle of the helipad's blue-and-orange bull's-eye, a jet-assisted UH-12 fat-bodied Huey sat waiting. The rotors created a windstorm that rolled over the top of the skyscraper, only partially blocked by the huge HVAC units mounted on top. The dull roar of the idling jets filled the open space. When the cargo door slid to one side, it revealed the door gunner seated in a skeletal chair behind a Browning .50-cal machine gun. Locking into place with mechanical movements, the machine gunner targeted Wilson and opened fire.

Diving from the top of the elevator, Wilson rolled to the side of the nearest HVAC unit and pushed up into a standing position. The booming drumbeat of the .50-cal rounds slamming into the HVAC unit made even the jetcopter's engines inaudible.

Glancing around the unit, Wilson saw two body-guards on either side of Min as they hustled the man toward the helo. Silverton was beside them. Another pair of Koreans came around the side of the elevator bay and closed in on the FBI SAC.

A second elevator had arrived at the helipad station and let three men out. Two of them went down under the door gunner's deadly aim, but Wilson thought the third man escaped injury before dropping out of sight. The quick glimpse of the man had told Wilson that DiVarco had made the rooftop.

The SeekNFire programming thrummed inside Wilson as he whirled around the side of the air-conditioning unit and fired at the approaching Korean bodyguards, racking the slide to chamber another shell, and firing again.

The first man went down with a shrill yell, his legs blown out from under him. Bullets from the second man's weapon chewed holes in the sheet-metal hull of the HVAC unit. Only one of the rounds skidded across Wilson's bulletproof biker jacket.

Ignoring the sudden flare of pain that ignited in his abdomen from the bullet's impact, Wilson met the second man almost head-on, pulling the Ithaca's trigger when the muzzle was only inches from his target's face.

He felt warm blood dapple his skin, but he shoved the corpse out of his way and ran for the jetcopter as Min and Silverton scrambled aboard.

The news chopper hovered only a few yards away, keeping broadside to the escaping jetcopter so the camcorder photographer could film the footage.

Wilson didn't break stride as he closed on the jetcopter. There was no choice. Either he stopped Silverton now, or the man could easily slip out of the country with Min's connections and the proof against the conspiracy to take Boston would vanish with them. And the threat would remain in place, dormant until Silverton and Min got ready to move again.

The two guards who'd helped Min board turned to face Wilson and attempted to draw their weapons. A line of .50-cal rounds chewed up the helipad as the door gunner also tried to target Wilson.

He gave the first guard a forearm shiver that crushed the man's exposed throat and drove him from his feet, then snap-fired a round from the Ithaca that caught the other guard in the face and shoved the corpse backward.

The jetcopter lifted and drifted over the side of the building.

Focusing on the escaping chopper, telling himself in an audible voice that he could make it, Wilson's boot caught the edge of the roof and he leaped from the building. He released the shotgun and it went tumbling away, spinning end over end toward the street twenty-six floors below.

Wilson caught the landing skid of the jetcopter with one hand, but missed with the other. The shock of his bodyweight hitting the end of his arm almost tore his grip loose, but he flailed stubbornly till he could close his other hand on the skid. With the combined rotor wash and movement, it took both hands to hang on. The door gunner's servomotors whined as they tried to make the adjustment to bring Wilson into target acquisition but failed.

The wind blurred Wilson's vision and he had to look twice to make certain that there was another figure hanging onto the other side of the landing skids.

Sebastian DiVarco's grin held a light of insanity as he struggled to pull himself up the other side of the landing gear. His face was bloodied, but it didn't look like the blood was his own. His gun was thrust into his pants at his waist, but he didn't appear able to use it.

Wilson knew he couldn't draw his own.

"You won't make it!" DiVarco yelled. "These bastards couldn't stop me, and you're sure as hell not going to!"

Wilson saved his breath for the climb, straining hard to pull himself up.

A Korean who had been inside the jetcopter stepped down onto the landing skid, then leaned out, trying to get a bead on Wilson.

Instantly, Wilson reached out for the man's boot and yanked. The boot slid off the metal surface and the man came tumbling down, holding himself by one arm. Swinging up, Wilson kicked out as hard as he could. The blow connected with the man's face with enough force to rip the Korean from the landing skid.

The Korean fell backward, away from the jetcopter, screaming and firing his pistol dry.

Wilson reached for the lip of the cargo bay, snared it with his fingers, and worked to haul himself up. He saw the door gunner struggle to push himself out of the computer-assisted rig, then resettle into the seat as if slapped back into place. A single red dot gleamed wetly between his eyes, then leaked crimson.

"That's the best I can do," Rawley called out over the T-jack. "You're on your own. Good luck, amigo."

The cargo area was plush, designed for conversation in the round with small couches hugging the walls. Min sat at the back with a small pistol gripped in his hand atop his cane. Silverton was belted in beside him.

As Min raised the pistol to fire, Wilson triggered the spring-loaded release on the Crain dagger, caught it in his palm, and hurled it across the cargo bay. The sharp blade sunk to the hilt in Min's throat and two wild rounds from the pistol drilled through the panel separating them from the pilot.

Without warning, the jetcopter suddenly bobbled out of control and bucked like a marlin fighting a fisherman's line.

Wilson almost lost his hold, but managed to pull himself into the cargo bay as DiVarco did the same on the other side. DiVarco already had his pistol in his fist and fired in staccato rhythm. One of the rounds tore through Wilson's chest where the Kevlar didn't cover. He knew from the feel that the bullet had passed on through. Three other bullets smashed into the jacket but didn't penetrate.

The H & K VP70Z in Wilson's boot came away in his fist. The SeekNFire programming in his palm scanned the chip and made the proper neural connection as the barrel came up into point-blank range. He fired over DiVarco's pistol, putting 9mm rounds through both of the man's eyes from less than four feet away.

Crimson tears suddenly splashed out onto

DiVarco's face and bled down his cheeks as his body dropped to the floor of the jetcopter.

Breathing raggedly, his arm numb but operational despite the bullet wound, Wilson got to his feet inside the badly vibrating jetcopter. Silverton was struggling to reach the gun Min had dropped, but Wilson slapped it away from him before he could close his fists around it.

Moving forward, having to lurch across the uneven floor, Wilson opened the door to the cockpit. Black smoke billowed out of the chopper's nose, indicating the amount of damage that had been done by Min's bullets as well as DiVarco's. Blood smeared the Plexiglas nose, letting Wilson know the pilot had been wounded as well. The jetcopter had become a flying coffin waiting to be laid to rest.

Abandoning all thoughts of taking over the controls, Wilson glanced out the cargo doors and saw the little Bell news copter hovering less than thirty feet away slightly above them. Looking forward, he saw the jetcopter was on a drifting collision course with one of the skyscrapers surrounding them like concrete stakes.

"We're going to die," Silverton said in a hoarse voice.

"No you're not," Wilson said as he pulled the grappling hook from the pocket inside his jacket and fashioned a slipknot at the end of it. He put a boot into the slipknot like it was a stirrup. "If we get lucky, you're going to stand trial for your crimes and let the people of this city get some sense of justice after what you were trying to do to them." He reached over and yanked the Crain combat knife from Min's throat, slashed the seatbelt holding Silverton, and grabbed the man's belt. "I hope that's a good belt."

The jetcopter started to wobble even worse as Wilson leaned out the cargo bay. It began to list hopelessly to the side. Swinging the weighted grappling hook around his head in a tight arc, Wilson made his cast. The jetcopter lost more altitude with a dying shiver, and for a moment Wilson thought he would run out of cord before the grappling hook reached the news chopper.

Then the hook swung around the little Bell's landing skids. The cord whipped taut, burning Wilson's palm. He leaned forward, falling out of the jetcopter's open bay and holding onto Silverton's belt as the man screamed in wide-eyed terror. The slipknot pulled tight, almost cutting off circulation in the FBI agent's foot as they swung wildly in a wide arc under the news chopper. The strain on his injured arm was incredible, but he forced himself to keep hold of the cord. His other hand was locked solidly around Silverton's belt, aided by the man's arms holding onto the cord as well.

As they swung back and forth, Wilson saw the jetcopter smash to fiery bits against the glass-and-steel surface of a skyscraper. A rolling cloud of orange flames and black smoke crept up the side of the building from the point of impact. Then, like a crippled dragonfly, the chopper twisted over and fell more slowly than he would have thought to the street below.

Looking down, Wilson didn't think anyone had been hurt by the falling debris. The police had arrived now, and had cordoned off the area. Cars were backed up in all directions.

Above them, the camcorder operator was still filming furiously.

Wilson's muscles were trembling from shock and exhaustion as the news chopper wheeled back over the helipad where the rest of the Omega Blue unit and the FBI teams were waiting. Twenty feet above the surface, his hands gave out and he dropped Silverton and lost his hold on the cord.

Silverton fell and was covered instantly by Rawley, Vache, Valentine, and members of the Boston FBI.

Hanging upside down by his roped foot, Wilson clung to consciousness as he was lowered to the helipad. January cradled him and took his weight while Scuderi cut the cord tying him to the news chopper. He struggled to get to his feet but Mac pushed him back and started working on the chest wound.

"Lie down," Mac growled. "You get up and start walking around, you're liable to bleed to death."

Wilson relaxed and felt the deep pain settle into him. "Silverton?"

"He's alive," Scuderi replied standing above him. "We'll take care of it."

"Good," Wilson replied, then let the swirling darkness take him away.

EPILOGUE

"Agent Wilson."

Following the feminine voice through layers of sleep, Wilson opened his eyes and blinked to focus. The room was dark and smelled of hospitals. It was a smell he'd grown accustomed to in the two days following the events in Boston, first in McClean Hospital in Boston, then at Walter Reed in Washington, D.C. DiVarco's bullet had also damaged his clavicle, requiring minor surgery.

He blinked again and made out Dr. Davette Culley looking down at him. The woman was dressed in a simple beige dress that emphasized her slender good looks. Her hair brushed her shoulders.

"I didn't mean to wake you," she said.

"It's okay." Wilson rubbed his face sleepily.

"But I didn't know if you were comfortable like that."

He gazed down, for a moment wondering what she was talking about. Then he realized he had fallen asleep with his shoulders against the wall in a half-supine position. Kasey was spread over him, snoring quietly, her breath soft against his cheek. He smiled easily as he stroked his daughter's hair. "I'll be a little stiff when I get up, but it's worth it."

"I've talked to Dr. Means about his virtual reality therapy," Culley went on. "He's anxious to start working with the two of you."

"I'm glad."

"I'm also going to see if I can smooth things over for you with your ex-wife. Kasey deserves the opportunity. So do you."

"I don't know how much good that will do, but I appreciate it."

"Who knows? Maybe I'll surprise us all."

Wilson nodded. Something else seemed to be on the doctor's mind. He could tell by her body language. He glanced at his watch, saw that it was past nine P.M. and that she was working late, and waited. Kasey's hand trailed across his brushed denim shirt and he could feel her heart beating against his chest.

"Actually," Culley said hesitantly, "I didn't just drop in unannounced because I was worried about your comfort. I've seen you sleep in this room plenty of times before. But I was wondering if you'd like to have dinner and maybe a coffee afterward with me."

Before Wilson could reply, she hurried on.

"I lost a patient today. A little boy almost Kasey's age. I don't want to talk about it, but I don't want to be alone either. With your job and what you've just gone through in Boston, I thought maybe you'd understand. I can't promise good conversation, or even good company, but the restaurant I have in mind has good food and good coffee. I just need to know that there's someone else out there besides me for a little while."

"I think I could use some of that myself," Wilson said. He moved slowly, mindful of his injury and Kasey's comfort. Gently he laid her on her bed, then got to his feet.

"I'll make sure they know at the desk that you'll be coming back after dinner," she said.

"Thanks." He followed her out the door, spared a glance at Kasey, and walked beside her.

"Some days," Culley said in a brittle voice, "it just seems like everything I do is so futile. There's so much I don't know, and so much beyond my control."

"So things seem pretty hopeless."

"I'm sure in your job things sometimes seem pretty much the same."

"Sure." Wilson nodded, thinking over the last few days, realizing they weren't that different from the last few years, with only the promise of more to come. At least there'd be a new head of the House subcommittee soon, now that Cashion was gone, maybe even someone who'd be more understanding of what the world was really like out there on the streets. "Occasionally I even get to feeling like you're feeling now: that everything's hopeless. Then I remind myself that hope isn't something you look for and find, it's something you make and share with the people that matter to you."

"And you believe that?"

"Yeah," Wilson said truthfully as he looked into her eyes. "I really do."

Mel Odom lives with his four children in Moore, Oklahoma, and is the author of a number of books in the action/adventure and science fiction fields. Besides a very full life taking care of his sons and daughter, he enjoys traveling, racquetball, and the lost art of conversation with friends.

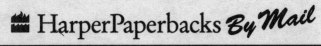